Outlaw's Brat

Outlaw's Brat

The Lady Among the Outlaws

Lee Scofield

SUFFOLK COUNTY LIBRARIES & HERITAGE	
HJ	07/08/2006
F	£17.99

Five Star • Waterville, Maine

Copyright © 2006 by Ruth Scofield Schmidt

All rights reserved.

This novel is a work of fiction. Names, characters, places and incidents are either the product of the author's imagination, or, if real, used fictitiously.

No part of this book may be reproduced or transmitted in any form or by any electronic or mechanical means, including photocopying, recording or by any information storage and retrieval system, without the express written permission of the publisher, except where permitted by law.

First Edition
First Printing: February 2006

Published in 2006 in conjunction with Tekno Books.

Set in 11 pt. Plantin.

Printed in the United States on permanent paper.

Library of Congress Cataloging-in-Publication Data

Scofield, Lee.
    Outlaw's brat : the lady among the outlaws / by Lee Scofield.—1st ed.
      p. cm.
    ISBN 1-59414-454-0 (hc : alk. paper)
    1. Mothers and daughters—Fiction. 2. Outlaws—Fiction. I. Title.
PS3569.C5834O94 2006
    813'.6—dc22   2005028623

Outlaw's Brat

Prologue

". . . outlaw's brat, that's what she is!"

The hard edge to the speaker's voice slowed young Mattie Adams's descent on the stairs, out of sight from the women gathered in the parlor. She'd come from refreshing herself in Nella's pretty bedroom, all pink and white and frilly, and lingered to look.

The quilting bee at the Ryan home had broken up temporarily, so that the women could take noon dinner. But someone still talked in the parlor around the quilting frame.

"Now Sally . . ." a protesting older voice intervened.

Who were they talking about? Should she creep by the parlor on her way to the dining room and leave the whisperers to keep their confidences? Could she pass the arched opening without being seen? Or should she join them?

Undecided, Mattie bit her lip. Mattie was horribly shy with the dozen town and ranching women and girls who'd gathered for the quilting party. Nella Ryan and her mother were hosting for bride-to-be Josie McCarthy, and Cousin Beatrice urged her to come.

At fourteen, skinny and tall and with a newly developed bosom, she was proud of the dark blue dress Cousin Beatrice had stitched for her. Still, Mattie felt awkward and self-conscious. She certainly was different than the other girls. She'd met only a few while living with Cousin Beatrice and her husband James, waiting to hear from her unknown Aunt Elizabeth. She was an outsider.

Cousin Beatrice had insisted she come. And she had

quite enjoyed her morning in spite of her shyness. The quilt, with its pieces of bright cotton, fascinated Mattie's sense of color and design, and although quilting was a new experience for her, she'd picked up the skill quickly. She liked the rhythm of plying her needle while the other women in the circle talked endlessly.

"Will found her in the middle of nowhere all by her lonesome—"

Mattie stilled, her hand going to her chest. Her. They spoke of her!

"Dressed in nothing but rags."

Mattie recognized Sally Smith's voice. Sally was a rancher's daughter, one of Nella's friends. "And my pa says she has probably been roamin' with that outlaw bunch that's been raidin' the countryside. Her own pa rode with the Missouri raiders, you know."

Mattie's heart tightened. Sally had talked to her kindly once or twice during the morning sewing session. Now her words had the sharpness of a needle, reminding Mattie of a needle's purpose.

Jab and thrust, up and down, pull . . .

It wasn't polite to eavesdrop, her mother once said. But Mattie decided she might as well know what the womenfolk of Wayside Station thought of her. As though she couldn't guess.

"And she was days and days on the trail, alone with five men!" Nella's sneering voice said. "Not one of them a relative."

Jab!

"But the McCarthy men are honorable," protested Lucy Walters. "They wouldn't do—"

Pull . . .

"They're men, Lucy! Just 'cause you're stuck on Luke,

don't make him no angel," Sally mocked.

"But Mattie seems nice enough to me," Lucy protested.

Up . . .

"Well, you should've seen her when Will and Luke brought her to the McCarthy ranch. I was there visiting," Nella said. "She was dirty, and her skirt was too short. Like a saloon woman with her legs and ankles showing, and with her hair all wild—"

Definitely a punch.

It was all true. Mattie had spent days in the wilderness, alone, lost, out of food. Running for her life from Nate Dorsey and her stepfather, Larry Potter. Then Will and his men had found her.

". . . And she's probably no better than she should be," Sally finished with condemnation.

"The Cramers are her people, an' the McCarthys seem taken with her," the older voice kindly intervened once more. Mrs. Brown, Mattie thought.

"That's true," said Lucy.

"That's all well and good, but the Cramers had no choice but to take her in because they're kin, and the McCarthys always feed the drifters and help strangers. It's their Christian duty. But the girl is who she is. A dirty outlaw's brat. And, if the truth was known, most likely an outlaw's whore."

"But she's so young," protested Mrs. Brown.

"They start young, Pa says," Sally continued. "And once a whore, always a whore, you know. She might as well go to work in one of them saloons and quit pretending to be a good girl, 'cause no decent man would ever have her, that's for sure."

Sally delivered the judgment with a resounding thrust.

"I agree with Sally," Nella added on a sniff. "I don't

think a decent man would court her."

No decent man. Not Will McCarthy, anyway.

The hidden shame Mattie kept in the deep dark pit of her consciousness slithered forward, smothering her innocent hopes and dreams in slime. She stood like stone, facing the truth. She was an outlaw's brat! Her father had been killed while raiding just after the Great War, and her stepfather ran with the Nate Dorsey gang. And in some eyes, that made her mother a whore. As for herself . . .

Mattie moved soundlessly out the front door and down the steps to the front gate. The property sat in the middle of a new picket fence, the first in town. She felt frozen inside with raw hurt, as isolated as the house inside the fence.

She didn't look back at the Ryan house. Those women didn't like her; they thought she was dirt.

She paused at the pristine white post, yearning to be alone to lick her wounds. Was all society like Sally and the others? Would she always wear the tag of outlaw's brat?

She looked down the street. Only a quarter of a mile to the center of town. To her very core, she longed to run from this house. But then where? She had nowhere else to go and no money, and was grateful that Pa's cousin Beatrice Cramer had taken her in.

Mattie fervently hoped Aunt Elizabeth answered her plea soon. She couldn't impose on Beatrice and James any longer, and now that Ma was gone, Aunt Elizabeth was her nearest relative. Her deepest fear was that her aunt would be of the same opinion as those ladies inside and refuse to have her.

Oh, Ma . . . I wish you were here.

Mattie's heart wailed with terrible guilt and loss. After hearing of Dorsey's plans to take Mattie as soon as she turned fifteen, her mother, Marianne, planned their escape.

She'd lost her life getting Mattie out of that hidden outlaw stronghold that dreadful night nearly two months before.

Mattie had wandered in the mountains for five days till running into Will and his men, out looking for strays.

"This is where you've got to." Cousin Beatrice found her a few moments later. "Aren't you cool without a shawl?"

"No, ma'am, I'm fine." Mattie turned her face away until she could control her features. She did feel a bit chilly, but she hadn't noticed until now. An outlaw's brat was tough and unfeeling, she thought bitterly.

"Come and get something to eat now, child. They'll start quilting again in a little while."

Mattie's feet dragged as though weighted with anvils as she obediently rose and followed her cousin into the house. After she pretended to eat, Mattie dutifully sat at the quilting frame again and bent to the stitching. Her anger and hurt lay silently buried.

"This is really turning out quite beautiful," remarked Mrs. Brown. "How many quilts will this give you, Josie?"

Mattie couldn't look at Josie, Will's sister. Josie must think the worst of her, too. Did Will, even knowing that nothing happened that shouldn't have while she traveled under his protection? Did he think she had no virtue?

Yet she couldn't deny that she and her ma had lived the outlaw life until a few weeks back. Why would Will believe she was as pure as his sister Josie? Or Nella?

He had no reason to believe her virtuous.

"This'll make an even dozen, Mrs. Brown," Josie answered.

"I've only got seven in mine," wailed Lucy.

"You better hurry, Lucy. You wouldn't want to get caught short if the need suddenly arose, would you?" Sally chided.

"Well, Miss Sally Smith, how many do you have? And when are you going to start your wedding ring quilt?" Lucy quipped sharply. According to Cousin Beatrice, it was bad luck to start a wedding ring quilt before an engagement was announced. Everyone waited for such today from Sally; Sally expected a proposal from Nick Fulton.

"I'll start it when I'm good and ready," the pretty blonde sniffed. Petite, she had sharp blue eyes and slender bones. Since no announcement was forthcoming, the women refrained from asking her more questions.

"How about you, Nella?" asked Mrs. Brown.

Nella's heart belonged to Will, Josie had told Mattie. Tall and lean, Josie's older brother represented one of the finest families and spreads around, the M double C. Will, in his mid-twenties, was already a force in the territory. Yes, according to Cousin Beatrice, Will was the catch of Wyoming.

Mattie kept her eyes lowered. She didn't know about that, but Will McCarthy made her heart flutter more than a little, too. Well, she might as well wrap that up and put it away. The handsome cowboy would never choose her.

"Oh, I've a few beaus to my string," Nella, brown haired and plump, answered in a mysterious tone as everyone laughed. "I'll be ready for my even dozen one of these days."

"And what about you, Mattie?" Mrs. Brown asked kindly. Or not, Mattie decided. How could she have a stack of quilts?

Caught off-guard, Mattie slowed her needle before she raised her eyes. How much of the pleasant chatter and easy smiles concealed unkind, even vicious thoughts? Calling forth that lump of ice that had settled inside her, she took her time to gaze around the circle. She allowed her attention to rest on Sally and Nella before she spoke in a steady, even voice.

"Oh, I won't have need for quilts. I'm going to live with my Aunt Elizabeth, soon, in St. Louis. She is wealthy in her own right, you know, and very self-sufficient. She never found it necessary to marry . . . so I suspect I won't either."

Mattie returned her attention to the circular blue and green cloth against which she applied her needle.

Someone dropped a pin on the bare floor.

One

The lumbering stage rolled to a complete stop and the driver called out, "Here we are, folks, Wayside Station, Wyoming. Thirty minutes, and we'll be headin' out."

Twenty-year-old Mattie Adams held her emotions in control with an iron determination. The happy anticipation of seeing Beatrice and James bubbled to the top, of course, since those were the emotions she could talk of with Aunt Elizabeth. On a deeper level was the desperate hope for additional news about her mother. Mattie had believed her to be dead. If she lived, Mattie would find her.

Beyond that was the beating awareness that she would see Will again. For a very long time after moving East, she'd both fought and cherished her childish love for the man who had rescued her from the wilderness. Never mind the townspeople, what they thought. But as the years passed, she packed away her feelings as "impossible" and "heartbreak."

She'd never marry—anyone.

Yet all the way west, Mattie had wondered what Will would be like after nearly six years. He hadn't married; she knew because Cousin Beatrice wrote her long, informational letters.

Every man Mattie'd met in the six years came up short when measured against Will McCarthy. Her St. Louis swains suffered by the comparison, and the New York men she'd met seemed much too civilized. But she doubted that she'd find Will the near-god her girlish heart had once thought him.

Mattie hid a sigh from her Aunt Elizabeth, sitting beside her. It wouldn't do to allow the past to claim any more of her heart and soul than it already did. However she found him, it would be best to approach Will simply as the old friend he'd proven to be when others thought her less than respectable. After all, he'd been friend enough to send word about the possibility of her mother being alive.

"Thank goodness, this is our destination," said Aunt Elizabeth. "I'm sure I have too many bruises to count."

The long trip from St. Louis, first by train, then by coach, had been exhausting. They waited patiently while the heavy door swung open, drawing aside to allow the beefy salesman who had shared the coach to push past them in his haste to leave.

"Oh, there's Bea and James!" Aunt Elizabeth's excitement to see her cousins with whom she'd once been close sparkled. Untangling her skirts, Mattie followed her aunt out of the coach. She reached for James's extended arm and stepped down into Beatrice's waiting embrace.

"Mattie child, I'm just tickled pink to see you." Beatrice pulled back to see Mattie's face. "Just let me look at you."

"Don't appear she's a child no more." James chuckled as he received her kiss on his cheek. "She done growed up."

"Yes, driver, that trunk there, and the other one," Elizabeth directed behind her. "I think we have it all now, James."

"It's a right good thing you only packed fer a couple of months, Elizabeth," James teased. "Else we'd needed a six-team of mules."

"Oh, hush, James," Beatrice admonished.

Slowly, Mattie became aware of a prickle along the back of her neck and, still listening to Beatrice, reached up a hand to brush it away. From the corner of her eye she caught a movement and turned instinctively, only to be caught and held by Will's crystal blue gaze.

Memory had not failed her. Leaning on the wall behind him, he was exactly the same Will. Light hair, shimmering under a black hat. A strong face, high cheekbones. The same heart-shattering blue eyes that had read her very soul when she was so young. Could they, still? His expression told her nothing, yet behind the blue gaze something leapt to life.

Silently, she took in the rest of him. He remained very still while she stared, one lean shoulder against the clapboard wall, his black hat pushed back, framing thick golden hair that gleamed. He stared back at her through dark blond lashes. He'd grown a mustache that looked as silky as his hair. From beneath it, his bottom lip pushed out.

He owned a face full of strength. It all played on her thoughts of him during that brief spring so long ago, spinning her feelings into that of the untutored child she'd once been. She wondered if Will McCarthy was still the catch of the territory.

Dropping her gaze at last, Mattie squared her shoulders and stretched herself to stand taller. There was no need to be in a state of nerves, she told herself. A lady is composed at all times . . . now smile . . .

She mentally repeated the rote she'd learned at Mrs. Bates's Academy for Young Ladies, finding amusement from that memory. She smiled widely as she moved toward Will and his brother Luke, giving them her best society greeting.

"Will and Luke, how do you do?" She held her hand out in a formal extension. "It's so nice to see you again."

Will pushed himself lazily away from the building to

meet her halfway, with Luke a step behind. When he touched her hand, she felt the strength she saw in his face. He was Will McCarthy, a man who exuded an indomitable will, a character of monumental proportions, and Mattie thought there would be few who would dare to go against him.

"Miss Mattie."

The low timbre of his voice rumbled over her like distant thunder, and with all the poise she could muster, she prevented a shiver from becoming obvious. Yes, indeedy, he could still cause her heart to pick up its beat, but she wasn't here to practice flirtation. Carefully, she withdrew her hand and turned to greet Luke.

"Howdy, Miss Mattie." Luke enthusiastically shook her hand. "Whooee, what a fine lady you've become!" He then took both her hands and stepped away, openly assessing her. "And some looker, too. You've sure left the gals in this town in the shade right enough. Yessiree, you'll turn some heads around here."

She followed the sly glance that Luke threw Will, only to catch a glimpse of the older brother's quickly hidden admiration. A wave of warmth flushed her cheeks.

Drat it to pieces! She'd grown quite used to compliments on her looks, and she'd outgrown that childish telltale blushing. Hadn't she? Why then should the admiration of the McCarthy men shake her?

Not both McCarthy men, her honesty compelled her to admit. Will. It was the look in his eyes that spoke to her. Taking a grip on her composure, she relied on formality.

"Thank you, Luke. How kind of you. I hope your mother is well?"

"Ma's just fine, Miss Mattie, and sends her greetings," Luke answered. "She'd be pleased if you and your aunt would come to supper after you get settled."

Mattie wondered if the supper invitation also came from Will, but when she dared glance his way again, his eyes reflected nothing but sunlight.

"We'd be delighted to come, but I'm sure you realize I must first know of my mother . . . that is . . ."

She turned her full attention toward Will. "Has there been any more information? Anything at all?"

"No, Miss Mattie, there hasn't." Will spoke soberly. "And I'm not too sure of the source of what we have."

"The source? Who is this source?"

Will hesitated a moment, not wanting to alarm her. The men who had been a part of her past were dangerous, conscienceless men, and he wasn't sure how much truth she was willing to face. Besides, what he had been told about her mother might very well be lies.

Always cautious, he wasn't ready to admit to that, yet; he hadn't deciphered everything he'd learned about the Dorsey gang and there were still too many questions unanswered.

Luke turned to help James load the luggage into the buckboard; the two other women were in quiet conversation. Will shifted his attention back to Mattie. She waited for an answer, impatience in her eyes.

"The man you know as Maxwell."

"Maxwell?" Mattie stared into the blue eyes that watched her so intently and felt a shiver of apprehension. One of the gang members she'd known, one that caused revulsion to tighten her stomach. She'd had her own run-in with the man, years back.

She put that aside. "Where is he? I want to talk to him myself."

"You can't."

"Why can't I?"

Will shifted from one foot to another. "Take it from me, Mattie, we have all the information the man was able to give."

"Why can't I see him for myself? Isn't he in jail?"

"No."

"Then where is he?"

"Dead. He was hung last week."

Silence.

Mattie stared at Will in appalled silence while the quiet voices of her aunt and cousin suddenly sounded clear in her ears. Sharp disappointment mixed with smoldering irritation abruptly exploded into a full blaze of anger.

"Why did you do it?"

"He was guilty."

"But you allowed him to be hanged before I arrived?"

"The jury decided. I didn't."

"But you could have delayed it."

"No, I couldn't."

"Couldn't you?" The frustration of weeks of waiting stiffened every line of her body as Mattie glared her challenge at him. The McCarthys were a powerful family in the territory, and Will, himself, often took a leading role in guiding the community. A word from him to the right people would have delayed Maxwell's hanging. Why hadn't he done that, knowing she would be here soon?

Will spoke through gritted teeth. "Maxwell was caught red-handed."

"Damned traitor," added James, standing at her shoulder. "Yella-livered skunk. He'd been ridin' for Landon's brand as an honest cowhand, knowin' where our cattle were to be found."

Cousin Beatrice placed an arm around her shoulders. "Mattie, dear, it really wasn't Will's doin' . . . Folks felt betrayed, you see. Will did good just to keep the ranchers from hangin' Maxwell outright."

"Perhaps we could discuss this more privately?" Elizabeth suggested.

Breaking eye contact with Will, Mattie became aware that several townspeople stood close by and were listening. Embarrassment flooded her. She hadn't been here more than five minutes, and already she'd lost her self-command and allowed her temper to rule. And she hadn't remembered to introduce her aunt.

"Aunt Elizabeth, may I present the McCarthy men, Will and Luke." She held her voice even through stiff lips as she acknowledged Will. "My aunt, Miss Elizabeth Adams."

"I'd recognize you anywhere, Mr. McCarthy," Elizabeth said with wry humor as she shook hands. "You look exactly as, er, my relatives described you."

"Let's get on our way, 'steada lollygaggin' around here," said James. "No need puttin' on a show fer ever'body."

"Miss Mattie." Will took her elbow as he helped her into the buckboard. "I have business in town just now, but I'll call on you after supper, if I may. We do have things to discuss."

"Indeed we do," she agreed crisply. "Very well, Mr. McCarthy. I'll expect you then."

James put his team into a spanking pace and they rolled out of town.

Hours later, Mattie was drying the supper dishes in Cousin Beatrice's familiar kitchen when she heard the hoof beats of a single horse arrive outside the opened kitchen door. Although the evening was warm, she placed the coffee pot back on the stove plate. She took off her apron and smoothed her hair, tucking a loose strand back in place.

"Good evenin', Will," Cousin Beatrice announced in a

bright voice. "Right nice weather we're havin', don't you think?"

"Yes, ma'am. Could use some rain, though."

"Sit yourself down, now, an' Mattie'll be right here."

Mattie walked into the parlor with firm resolve to keep her composure, though she'd been fuming since leaving town. She wanted answers to all her questions, not just a few. But she'd learned that a reasonable, modified approach granted her the best response from most people.

"Good evening, Will. No, please be seated," she said, and gestured graciously when he started to stand. She took the straight chair opposite him.

"I hope you've had a chance to rest, Miss Adams?" Will asked Elizabeth politely. His voice held the faintest hint of irony as he turned his full gaze on Mattie. "And you, Miss Mattie."

"Yes, we've rested," Elizabeth answered. "And I'm sure we'll feel even better after a good night's sleep."

"Yes, ma'am."

Mattie flashed Will a lightning glance. His mild acquiescence was a sham and they both knew it. As if a mere rest would soothe her from her irritation with him. But she'd keep her quick temper under control if it killed her.

"Now, then," Mattie said, sweetly smiling. "I'm very grateful to you for sending that cable about my mother, Will. I'd be very much in your debt if you'd tell me all you know about her whereabouts. Everything that Maxwell told you."

Will's strong fingers drummed against the arm of his chair while he contemplated how he should explain what he knew. He certainly didn't want to embarrass Mattie in front of her aunt or the Cramers. Maxwell had said some ugly things concerning her mother, though how much he could believe, he wasn't too sure.

He cleared his throat. "Well, according to Maxwell, your ma didn't die that night you got out of the hideout valley as you thought, Mattie. She was hurt real bad, though, and given up for dead by your step pa. Maxwell said she was hidden and cared for by an old fellow named Jack. Didn't get his last name."

"Linder. Jack Linder." Mattie turned to her aunt. "He knew my father, Aunt Elizabeth, and was loyal to him." Her nerves tightened as memories trickled down; she swallowed hard against them. Her voice dropped to a murmur. "Jack tried to help us get away that night . . ."

As Will's voice spoke softly, she recalled that night. Pitch dark, it had been the night she escaped from the outlaw camp. She and her mother had planned the escape for days, a plan of reality and not only dreams . . .

"Wait until the men are totally absorbed in their game, Mattie." Marianne spoke in whispers, though Larry had already strolled down to the Sanders's cabin for his poker game. "You leave first and find Jack down by the lower corral. Jack will help."

Jack knew the way out of the mountains, Mattie reminded herself, and he wanted to leave here as badly as they did. His loyalties lay with her ma and herself, too. He'd known her dad . . .

"That corral is away from the cabin, where they'll be deep in their play. I doubt they'll hear you. You can saddle the horses without interruption, I hope. But you must be as quiet as you can and be on the alert for the guard. I'll join you as soon as I can."

"Why can't you come now, Ma?" Fourteen-year-old Mattie begged for the third time. Already taller than her petite mother, she brushed her long dark braid to her back. "Why can't you just ignore ol' Larry and get out of here?"

"Because . . . you know Larry. I promised I'd come down and serve liquor for the men. He's counting on it. I'll serve it. But if I make an excuse while you're saddling the horses, then pretend I've forgotten something at the house, he won't question the time I'm gone. He'll merely think I've dawdled, or you've kept me. But if he catches us before we . . ."

Ma's eyes flashed with emotion. Mattie knew what her Ma didn't say. He'd likely beat the daylights out of her, and Mattie, too. The bruising on her mother's cheek had barely faded from when Larry had back-handed her only a couple of days ago.

Marianne couldn't take another beating. "I don't want to take any chances. Now do as I ask."

"All right." Excitement and apprehension filled Mattie all the way from her toes to her eyes, but she didn't like the idea of separation one tiny bit. She and her ma had been a team for a long time. This escape was for her, Mattie. "You promise you won't be far behind?"

"I'll be there . . ."

Mattie slipped out of the cabin and waited a moment for her eyes to adjust. She knew the five cabins in the small village well, having come here when she was six. She'd played all over the road, and the woods nearby.

She listened intensely.

"Go!" her ma hissed through the barely opened door.

Now or never, Mattie thought. They had to escape!

Mattie kept to the shadows as she made her way down to the lower corral. She gave the Sanders's cabin a wide berth, the men's raucous laughter spilling out into the night. The game must be going well.

She knew which horses she wanted; she'd looked them over earlier. But when she came alongside the Dorsey cabin, silent and dark, she spotted a huge bay stallion tied to the porch post.

Dorsey's bay! Saddled, no less! Why? When was Dorsey going to use it? Where was he going in the night?

"Hi, there, Bay? How are you doing?" The horse snuffled, turning his head toward her. She reached out to pet him.

"Mattie . . ." The urgent whisper came from down the way. Jack Linder. Sighing, she dropped her hand.

She turned and, swift as an antelope, leapt down the slope toward him.

"Where's your ma?"

"She's coming any minute. She had to take food in to the game."

"Well, you get that black," he said, pointing to five horses huddled on the far side of the corral. "And the sorrel. I'll go look for your ma."

A few moments later, as she was tightening the saddle on the black, the explosion of a shotgun erupted in the night quiet.

Mattie jerked around. Where was it? She swiftly climbed over the corral rail, racing up the road.

Another burst of gunfire. She saw figures running, and her ma fall. Her heart beating hard, she started forward. From out of nowhere Jack yanked on her arm. "No, Mattie. You've got to get out of here. That's what your ma wanted."

"But Ma . . ."

"I'll take care of her. You just get on that horse."

"How? I don't know the way."

"Down the trail about three miles, then take the left

fork. Straight down, through a meadow." He was speaking so quickly, his speech was garbled. "In the valley, follow the stream. It'll take you to Wayside Station. Now go!"

She'd leapt toward the bay, grabbing the reins and mounting even as the powerful horse moved into a startled turn. The stirrups were too long, and she bent her knees and grabbed the horn to hang on. She took one last, quick look over her shoulder.

A distant glance. Three men gathered about her fallen ma, and she heard shocked murmurs. No one was paying attention to her, and she raked her heels into the bay's side.

She'd gone, plunging away and down the mountainside in sheer panic. A moment later, she heard the faint yell. They must have discovered her absence—or Bay's.

That was a long six years. Mattie sighed, her attention on Will's face now as he told her what had happened after she'd left the camp.

"Well, Maxwell said your ma almost died, and would have, but for old Jack and a Mexican woman. He reckoned that's how you got so clean away. Those sidewinders were looking for tracks of the three of you. Maxwell said your step pa didn't find out about your ma and Jack still being in camp for a couple of days."

"It's a wonder Larry didn't kill her then." Mattie voiced her thought on a whisper.

The rhythm of steadily increasing hoof beats sounded in the quiet room. Mattie scarcely noticed. She leaned forward.

"What happened after they found her, did Maxwell say? I'm sure Larry was furious; he could be deadly. And Nate Dorsey! Nate must've been beside himself after I'd taken his prize horse. Oh, he must have blamed my mother. He had a wild temper."

"I don't know much more, Mattie. They killed old Jack, that I know."

A shaft of grief and guilt shuddered through her. Even though Jack Linder had ridden with the Dorsey gang, he'd been kind to her and Ma, and then paid the price. She should've guessed what they'd do to him.

Thumping boots on the porch preceded a loud knocking by only a moment. James opened the door and three men pushed past him with barely a nod to stand before Will and Mattie. One of them was Sheriff Kimmel; Mattie held unpleasant memories of him from six years prior. He'd tried to browbeat her into telling him all about the outlaw gang then, but at the time, frightened and intimidated, she'd steadily refused to acknowledge anything.

Mattie didn't know the other two men.

"Make yourselves to home, boys," Cousin Beatrice said pointedly at their rudeness, and without her usual warmth.

"Beggin' your pardon, Miz Cramer, ma'am," a red-faced, barrel-chested man stuttered out, glancing at Mattie expectantly. He removed his hat. "We just had ta come. Had ta know. Is she gonna do it?"

Mattie glanced from one man to the other. What was going on here? What did these men want?

Will shot from his chair and faced them with a heavy scowl. James's face went rather sheepish, yet he didn't seem surprised at this visit. Alarm shivered up her back.

"Couldn't you men wait?" Will demanded harshly.

Sheriff Kimmel smiled with false politeness and glanced around the room to share his friendly feelings.

Mattie thought he was about as friendly as a rattler.

"Now Will, perhaps we are a bit precipitous, but you got no need to get all riled up. We're all working to the same purpose, ain't we?" Turning to Beatrice, his voice smoothly confident, he asked, "Can we sit down, ma'am?"

Her hospitality appealed to, Beatrice responded automatically. "Why of course, Sheriff. An' Mr. Landon, Mr. Smith . . . please." The small parlor seldom held so many people, and Beatrice glanced around as though she didn't know where they would all sit.

Mattie had risen along with Will, and now she silently waited as Sheriff Kimmel turned her way, bowed, and gave her a benign smile. A smile she distrusted.

"Please be seated again, Miss Mattie." The sheriff waited until she had done so, and then sat in the chair Will had vacated. His attitude made her feel she was on trial.

"What is this all about?" Mattie threw her question toward Will. She felt stiff with outrage, and the sense of foreboding grew stronger.

Will clamped his teeth tightly, throwing the men a commanding stare. He began quietly. "Miss Mattie, we have some problems that we want your help with."

"My help, Mr. McCarthy?" she spoke in icy tones. "How? What kinds of problems?"

"It's this way. The ranchers are losing more cattle every year to the rustlers. The thieves have become bolder. One band in particular is hitting with regularity."

"What has that to do with me or the fact my mother may still be alive?"

"Mattie, you have to know." He spread his hand wide, appealing to her sense of fair play. "It's the Dorsey gang. The small ranchers and big spreads alike. We're taking more losses than we can afford."

His appeal was genuine. He needed her help.

"We gotta get them varmints cleaned out," Mr. Landon broke in. "We aim ta get that dadgummed Dorsey gang."

"Every last one of 'em. Miss Mattie, ya gotta help us," Mr. Smith added in a you-owe-it-to-us tone.

"Help you?" She stared at one man and then another. Their faces held excited expectation mixed with strong demand and determination. The sheriff held his polite smile as though she were a child he needed to placate, but his eyes roved over her full bosom nonetheless. Mr. Landon, who owned the spread north of town, looked fierce and stood with one hand on the butt of his holstered gun. She couldn't quite capture the knowing look Mr. Smith wore.

Mr. Smith? Recognition dawned. Sally Smith's father. An unpleasant taste filled her mouth, and suddenly she knew what that expression was. Like his daughter, he thought the worst of her, thought her a whore; and although he might scorn what he thought her to be, his expression also held salacious delight.

Mattie swallowed down her distaste and shifted her gaze to Cousin James. He'd known about this too. Although embarrassed, he looked hopeful.

Her gaze returned to Will. His face was set with anger; his eyes, as they met hers, slowly narrowed into attentive waiting. Her own anger and stabbing hurt rose sharply.

Yes, Will waited far more patiently than the others to see what would happen, waited for what her response would be and what she would do. He'd shown more sincerity toward her, too, and had even understood her feelings about her mother. But he was still one of them!

Was that why Will had sent her the telegram? To get her help in tracking down the Dorsey gang? Was any part of the telegram true?

Was her mother still alive?

Two

Mattie felt like a sheep being led to slaughter. Will had used his knowledge of her for his own purpose.

Of all people, he would know that she couldn't bear not knowing whether her mother still lived or not. Or how, where, and under what conditions. Or whether she'd suffered even more at Larry's hands because of her, Mattie's, escape.

Deliberately, Mattie invited the coldness that took hold of her as she buried the knife-thrust hurt to her heart. These men had deliberately played on her emotions and taken her for a fool, hoping to gain their own ends.

Well, well! They needed her help, did they? For what? If they were willing to have dealings with the outlaw's brat, they were pretty desperate.

She lifted her chin in haughty defiance. She hardly needed to ask what kind of help they wanted while certainty grew. They wanted her to tell them how to get back in there, back into the mountain hideout. To give them directions through the canyons and mountains.

That was it!

Her cheeks burned with hot anger. How dare they?

That hard knot in her breast turned to ice. These men, these respectable, law-abiding men, were little better than the rough, lawless vermin she'd known as a child. They wanted her help, almost demanded it, but they couldn't give her any respect or value beyond what was convenient to them at the moment. No doubt they would scarce speak to her at all if she didn't have knowledge they wanted.

They needed her help? Well, they'd have to beg it! She wouldn't make it easy for them. And ask again, for all the asking would be worth. She'd remain silent. And then she'd leave, just pack her bags again and leave tomorrow morning.

Mattie glanced at Elizabeth, who appeared totally baffled by the whole situation. Her poor innocent aunt had no idea what all this was about. Beatrice wouldn't look at her, but Mattie spotted moisture against one cheek.

A bit of the ice melted. Poor Cousin Beatrice. She couldn't help any of this, and was sorry about it. Mattie owed a great deal to Beatrice and James, and she wondered how to soften her coming refusal for their sakes.

But Will . . .

He held her gaze with steady purpose, the planes of his face stretched, his mouth firm. He knew all about this meeting well enough. She felt the mental gap between them widen. Had she ever really thought he held a tenderness for her? Even a little?

"Yes, Miss Mattie . . . we need your help." Will spoke in a low but resolute tone, breaking the expectant quiet.

"We'll plan a raid of our own, if you'll draw up a map for us." Sheriff Kimmel spread his hands wide excitedly, as though to draw her into the group. The heavy smell of liquor on his breath repelled her, but she refused to look away. "We'll gather enough ranchers and town men to make an army, if need be. I'll make deputies of 'em all."

"A map, girl, that's what we want." Spurs clinked as the burly Landon stomped a few steps up and down the small room in agitation. "You give us a map, an' we'll take care of your ma, if she's there."

Smith snickered just under his breath. "Yeah, we'll take

care of 'er. She should like us better'n those polecats."

Behind her, Mattie heard Cousin Beatrice gasp at the insult to her mother. Aunt Elizabeth, now standing, looked every inch a lady while she silently observed the scene with cold eyes. Her aunt had caught the gist of that, finally.

"You fool!" Will exploded at Smith. He half turned her way. "Mattie . . ."

"Here, now! Ya got no call fer that, Smith," James said.

Slowly Mattie rose, keeping her gaze on Will. Although she could see that Smith's words angered him, hope of her cooperation still lingered in his expression. A flood of painful loss shafted through her. How could she have been so mistaken? How could she have believed Will McCarthy different from other men?

Mattie drew on six years of training on how to be a lady, and, her chin held high, faced them.

"Gentlemen—" she allowed heavy sarcasm to lace her voice and a half-smile of contempt to appear at the corner of her mouth. "I fear you have brought me West in vain. Your purpose means nothing to me. I cannot help you."

You slimy toads! She knew her expression reflected her thoughts as her gaze raked over Smith and Landon in scorn. "I will not help you!"

Moving away, she glanced at Beatrice, noting her face full of misery. She was sorry if Cousin Beatrice and Cousin James were hurt, sorrier than she could say, and she hoped to find another way of helping them. But the ice inside of her remained.

"Now please excuse me. My aunt and I are very tired, and we must retire."

"Oh, no ya don't, missy," started Smith.

"Now wait a minute there, girl," Landon protested.

"Hold on there, men," Sheriff Kimmel interrupted,

holding up his hand in conciliatory fashion. Then he turned to Mattie and spoke patronizingly. "Perhaps tomorrow you'll feel better, Miss Adams. We'll talk about it again."

"Good night, gentlemen." She ignored the sheriff's implication, refused to look at Will again, and turning precisely, left the room. She marched through the kitchen and into the small bedroom beyond, and closed the door with a decided snap.

He needed a new mattress; this one was getting old.

Will thrashed about and punched his pillow as he turned over in his lumpy narrow bed. He'd get a new bed altogether when he moved into the new house he had built over the last three years. That would be this summer, damn it, come hell or high water. His house had stood empty long enough!

It was a large house meant for a family and built of stone to stand as a bulwark against the heavy winters. Beyond the creek bend and just out of sight of this one, it was still close enough to be a part of the M double C's daily running. He'd wanted to get married and move into it with a bride.

With Mattie, he now admitted only to himself.

The familiar memories of a Mattie as a child-woman haunted his thoughts as they frequently did, yet tonight they were overlaid with the stunning reality of how she looked now. While he yet could recall how the sharpness of her shoulder bones felt through her dress as they waited for the stage that long-ago June morning, the way she now filled her clothes stunned him.

Lord, he'd waited too long for her to grow up. But he wanted her to find and feel comfortable with her womanhood.

She'd been so young—too young.

Outlaw's Brat

★ ★ ★ ★ ★

He'd first seen her as he rode with his men far from the ranch, looking for cattle. The brakes frequently hid the strays, and they'd rounded up a few. He was whistling, a few yards out from his men, when he heard a youthful shout, then a rifle shot resounding in the air. He pulled his horse to a halt.

Snapping his head around, he saw a figure flat out racing toward him, shouting, "Savages."

What was that?

"Indians . . ."

Startled, he glanced about him. His men milled five hundred yards beyond him, driving the fifteen head of cattle they'd gathered. He thought Reuben was down in the draw after a calf. He saw nothing that would tell him he was in any danger.

Then he heard a high yelp! And another. Behind the racing figure were a half-dozen Indians, dressed for a hunt. They must've come from the reservation, he briefly thought.

"Behind that boulder, that way!" he directed his men with a wave. He saw Reuben appear over the edge of the draw, take in the scene before him, and head toward Will. His three other men laid spurs to their mounts and rode hell for leather toward the boulder.

Will glanced again at the youthful rider. Closer now, he spotted a long dark braid swing over a shoulder.

"Head toward the boulders, ma'am!" he shouted at her above the high, ungodly yelps and a whizzing bullet gone past him. The fact that he'd used a feminine thought pattern didn't occur to him at the moment. He was only intent on protection.

Will arrived at the boulders before her. The other men each swung down from their saddles with guns drawn and took up places from which to return fire. A moment later, the young rider, rifle in hand, came skidding to a stop in the midst of them.

Breathless, she came down from the saddle in one leap into his waiting arms. "I saw them from that bluff. They were waiting for you, hiding. I couldn't let you all walk into a trap."

The sounds of fighting lessened. Fewer gunshots erupted.

"They're leaving," stated Brown.

"Guess they're just a scouting party," answered the dark-skinned rider named Shorty. "Out looking for game."

Will continued to stare at the youngster. She was young, all right. And skinny. And she was scratched up, as though she'd come through a patch of briars.

Yet she rode a magnificent horse. His brief glance at the animal told him this was no ordinary horse.

Who was she? Where had she come from? He knew most of the families in the territory, yet he didn't know this girl.

"I'm Will McCarthy," he'd murmured.

"My name is Mattie," was all she'd said.

His thoughts returned to the present. He hadn't learned who she was, then. She was twenty now, by Beatrice's calculations. He'd kept track of her through her correspondence with James and Beatrice; his own few letters had gone unanswered.

The year after she'd turned eighteen, he'd planned to travel to St. Louis to see her and lay a marriage proposal at her feet, but his pa died that year and his mother needed him. The following year her Aunt Elizabeth took Mattie to Europe. That was good for her education, he'd thought. But he'd prayed his way through that year, hoping against hope that she wouldn't choose to marry a European or an Easterner before he'd had his chance. Last year, he'd plotted with the Cramers to invite her back to Wyoming for a visit, but her aunt always had an excuse not to come. By that time, he dared not leave, with the active rustler gang working the territory.

Well, now Mattie was back. A grown-up beauty who drew men's attention like candy drew ants. To find her mother, if she could. But was that all she'd come for?

Abruptly, Will swung his feet to the floor and sat up. He didn't really believe Marianne Adams could still be alive, but he'd used the rumor to his advantage anyway. Sending that telegram to Mattie had been a selfish thing to do, he admitted, but it gave Mattie hope, and maybe the love he'd secretly carried all these years would have a chance to blossom.

Besides that, he felt the need as strongly as the other ranchers did to clean out the rustlers.

He let a husky sigh escape him. It was late, but he couldn't sleep. The scene at the Cramers' nagged at his guts; it wasn't the memories of six years back that stirred him now, it was the woman he'd dealt with today that he couldn't stop thinking about. Mattie had been almighty upset, and not without reason, he admitted.

Disgusted with himself, he pulled on his clothes and left the house as quietly as he could. No good would come of waking Luke or Ma and get anyone else in an uproar. In the yard, he shoved his feet into his boots before heading for the barn to saddle a horse.

He rode out with steady purpose. That glance full of sharp disappointment and pain that Mattie'd thrown him wrenched at his gut. He'd been wrestling with that moment, that look, since he'd recognized it.

He'd known Mattie would buck that vigilante crowd well enough and he couldn't altogether blame her. They hadn't been kind to her before.

But surely she didn't lump him with them? She couldn't. But she did!

The reality hammered at him. She'd lost faith in him.

A curse left his lips. He felt grim.

Well, there was no denying that he was one of those who wanted to wipe out the Dorsey gang. They had to. He'd be willing to join forces with the devil if he must, to drive them out.

Mattie knew Dorsey, knew where the outlaw camp lay. He questioned, though, why Mattie refused to help them or give them a map to the mountain hideaway. Theirs was a mutual need. They'd need a strong force of men to conquer that nest of snakes and, if the story was true about her ma, she'd need his help. He had to make Mattie see that.

Yet she refused. Why?

Unless . . . oh, God no! The thought terrified him.

She couldn't be planning to go in there herself! She'd be a fool to try such a thing. Her chances of getting her mother out unaided were slim to none, and she'd put herself right into the middle of a god-awful peril.

But she might.

His urgency to talk to Mattie caused him to quicken the pace of his horse. He wasn't sure it could wait until morning. The atmosphere among the ranchers was explosive; she had to understand that none of them could continue to take the losses they'd been taking and hold on to their ranches.

It wasn't only the cattlemen and homesteaders, either. Wayside Station had grown almost as bad as other cattle towns, with gunfights every week. And bank and stage holdups were becoming common in the territory.

Sheriff Kimmel wasn't much help. He drank too much, and Will was weary of the lawman's growing ineffectiveness. Two months ago, he had gone after and been secretly sworn in as a special territorial marshal. It was the only way he knew to keep some kind of lid on things.

The soft clopping of his mount sounded loud in the quiet star-filled night. He dismounted as he drew near the J-B ranch yard and, from the illumination of a three-quarter moon, studied the silent house. Not a glimmer of lamplight glow showed through the windows.

He let out his breath. He'd hoped they might still be up visiting. If he woke Mattie now, the whole household would be up.

He started to turn away when a soft patch of white from the porch caught his notice. He threw the reins of his horse over a low tree branch, and edged forward on foot until that white patch evolved into a nightgowned figure in the rocking chair.

"Mattie." Her name rumbled out of him at a low pitch, but she must have heard it, for her chair stilled and she seemed to look his way.

"Who's there?" Her voice too, was a whisper.

"It's Will."

"What is it? What do you want?" Country people didn't come calling at odd hours of the night unless it was an urgent matter. Mattie watched as his tall figure took shape out of the darkness, holding her alarm in check at the quiet nature of his approach. Even after all these years she was slow to accept any man's attention. Slow to trust . . .

"I have to talk to you." He sat on the edge of the porch a few feet from her and raised a knee. Then he leaned back against the post, his arm resting on his knee.

Mattie yanked her shawl closer about her shoulders and bosom. She was tempted to just leave him sitting and go back into the house; she couldn't think of anything more she had to say to Mr. Will McCarthy. Besides, she wasn't used to receiving gentlemen callers in her nightwear. "Couldn't it wait till morning? Everyone is sleeping."

"You're up, and I'm here."

"But what if I hadn't been?"

His answer came hesitantly. "I saw the daybed set up in the parlor. With your aunt needing the room off the kitchen, it stood to reason it'd be your bed."

"You would have wakened me?"

"Thought of it."

Mattie was silent a moment, trying to settle the churning of her thoughts. Will McCarthy was like a bulldog, never letting something alone until he got his own way, she remembered. If he wanted her attention he'd get it one way or another, she supposed. Will had always been a man in command ever since she'd known him, so she shouldn't expect any preferential treatment merely because she was now grown and a woman of substance. She thought her wishes made little difference to him.

Why? Why did that bother her? Other men, men she'd met in the East, deferred to her, accepting her judgments and decisions with few or no questions. Ralph Martin, for instance, the man who currently courted her, would never compromise her by calmly visiting her in the middle of the night, or demand her to comply with what he wanted.

But Will wasn't soft like those Eastern men.

The moonlight outlined the broadness of his shoulders and gilt-edged the planes of his face, catching the gold of his thick mustache. His cheeks seemed leaner, his mouth harder than she remembered. No, he certainly wasn't soft.

He was the strongest man she'd ever met.

Her tummy dipped with the thoughts. "All right I'll talk with you for a little while. But if this is about drawing those men a map, forget it."

Will couldn't see much of Mattie's shadowed face in the darkness of the porch, but her soft voice eased the feeling of distance the six-year absence had created.

"You want to know about your ma, don't you?"

"You know I do. More than anything! But I'll find out on my own without any assistance from those vultures."

"How?"

"I'll go myself."

Mattie's half-formed thoughts began to knit into certain determination. She'd hire her own posse, men who would follow her orders and not question who she was or look at her askance.

Her bare feet started the rocking chair in motion, which caused her loose hair to lift and flutter. A shaft of moonlight caught the gleam in the long chestnut tresses as she swung forward and back and Will watched in fascination while the ends curled against her thighs. It was lovely, loose. So long she could sit on it, he thought.

Nothing of his yearnings showed in his speech.

"Mattie, you can't be seriously thinking of such a thing," he murmured. "Have you forgotten the dangers, how wild that back country is, the ruthless men in the Dorsey gang?"

"I haven't forgotten any of it, not one iota." Mattie couldn't keep her hands from fisting as old fears and anger bubbled along her veins. Ruthless? Without scruples? She knew exactly what caliber of men that outlaw hideout concealed. Those men were deadly, without conscience. They made her blood boil with fury at what they'd done to her mother . . . and to her.

Yet she wouldn't let old fears defeat her. "You forget, Will. My aunt is wealthy and I have money of my own now, inherited from my grandfather. I can hire protection."

"Hired gunmen?" He grunted in disgust and leaned forward in his need to make her understand. He spoke with urgency. "Men who would kill for money without a second thought? Who would protect you from them, once you were alone? Hired killers would create more hell than you could handle, or me either. Mattie, think!"

"Dammit, Will . . ." She swallowed, sorry to have spoken the curse aloud. She started again. She sat straighter, easing her tired shoulders.

"I've thought about nothing else for weeks. Ever since I received your message that my mother may be alive. How to get into the hideout without a fight, how to get her out if she's there." Her angry voice faltered. "If she's still there . . ."

Mattie stopped, knowing if she said another word at that moment she'd be in tears. She couldn't allow herself that luxury, and had determined long ago never to shed another. Not in front of anyone, anyway. Tears were a weakness she couldn't—wouldn't—afford, and when shared, they put too much power into another's keeping.

She'd become chary with her tender emotions. Locking them tightly away served her better. Yet when she drew a breath, she couldn't hide the catch in it.

And she knew Will had heard it.

Three

When Will heard the catch in Mattie's voice, it was as if all the years of separation melted. She was again the young girl on the edge of womanhood who needed him, and he yearned to soothe her troubled heart.

The rocker stilled as she grew quiet. He saw her throat work as she swallowed her tears.

"Mattie girl . . ."

Using the form of address he had used six years before, Will reached out to comfort her and took one bare, high-arched foot into the warmth of his hand. He couldn't resist the need to touch her, and rubbed the soft inner sole with his thumb. Here in the isolated freedom of the dark porch it seemed perfectly natural to caress one small cold foot.

Natural or not, touching her didn't soothe Will at all. It sent his senses bucking and racing toward the danger of being completely thrown.

He was surprised as all get-out at how fast his responses reared. Surprised that Mattie allowed it, they not being kin, married, or engaged, and when just earlier in the evening she'd been madder at him than a cow defending her baby against a pack of wolves. Heaven help him, she'd thought him the pack leader!

Yet she didn't withdraw and her anger seemed to have dwindled. His hopes renewed, some of his tension eased. Perhaps he could redeem himself in her eyes after all and still get her to see things his way.

"Mattie," he began again, quieter, this time. As he spoke

thoughtfully, he stroked her white ankle, observing how darkly tanned his hands were against it, letting the heady desire fill his belly and below, all the while doing his best to ignore it.

"I know Smith and old Landon are harsh men, selfish and uncaring except for their own needs. But they're not the only ones who're in trouble. The small homesteads as well as big ranches, including the J-B and the M double C, are losing heavily at the hands of those devil cutthroats."

He drew a deep breath, hoping she was unaware of the effect she was having on him, hoping her anger was diverted, and continued. "We've been chasing this gang for years, now, you know. I've had to leave much of my ranching to Luke and Sandy—you remember Sandy, my foreman—while I've been weeks leading a posse of men in pursuit."

Too much. Too soon. He wanted her like wildfire—how could he, when he hadn't seen her for six years? Yet he knew he couldn't rush his chances. He moved restlessly, holding back his need to get up and pace; he stilled himself to remain quietly holding her foot.

"Believe me, the ranchers are in a rage to put an end to the Dorsey bunch. If you took a band of gunmen in there on your own, we'd only follow you. You'd end up fighting both factions. Only God knows what would come of that."

Once more, he leaned back against the post, drawing her foot with him. "Be sensible, Mattie," he coaxed softly. "You could get killed or worse if you choose that course. Is that what your ma wanted for you? Her sacrifice to go for naught?"

"No, of course not, but—"

"Mattie girl, we're going in, one way or another."

She wished to heaven he wouldn't address her in that intimate way. It made it much too difficult to maintain her composure. What little of it she had left.

Mattie remained quiet, both stirred by his impassioned speech and soothed by his low-pitched voice and the warmth of his strong hand against her foot. It was comforting and seducing, and she wished she had nerve enough to push her other foot against him for equal attention. She had to remind herself that Will could no longer be entirely trusted.

"If you'll agree to help us find our way in," he said, his voice dropping even lower, "I promise you, I'll do everything I can to get your ma out safely."

A slight breeze whispered softly against her cheek as Mattie contemplated Will's plea. She wanted to hold onto her earlier wrath, but would that be her best choice? Pushing it aside, she considered her options.

She could do as she threatened and hire her own men to go after her mother. But would she really be any better off? She hated to admit it, but Will's plan was the best.

"When do you want to go?"

"Now that you're here, as speedily as possible. A week's time, at most. Two or three days would be better."

She gave a sigh of concession. "I'll be ready."

Abruptly he sat up, allowing her foot to fall to the porch with a thump. "You? Oh, no, Mattie girl, no! You are not going. That's the purpose in your drawing us a map."

Mattie started rocking again. Calmly. She had the upper hand and she knew it.

"It was a long time ago when I was there, Will. I was a kid then, and I'm not sure I could even draw a map, I was so lost. So it seems to me that the only way you'll get in is if I guide you. And I want your promise that the vigilantes will be under your control."

"You're loco, woman." He stood, planting his feet square on the ground, his toes rubbing against the edge of the porch while he faced her. "Mattie, I'm not taking you. And I can't guarantee anything, much less your safety, from a bunch of wild cowmen."

She rocked harder. "You'll take me, or I'll go with hired gunmen. Besides, I'll have to see the area to remember."

"Be reasonable, Mattie. There'll be a dozen men, at least. You're one woman."

"I can ride and shoot as well as the next man, or have you forgotten?"

How could he forget? The first time he'd seen her, she'd come riding into the midst of him and his men, shooting from the hip with that old rifle she'd sported to warn them of the Indian ambush that lay ahead on their path. He recalled how her black skirt flapped and her waist-length braid bounced as she'd raced the big bay thoroughbred up to them. Mattie had fallen in right beside him as they chased the small band of braves back over the mountain and then turned for home.

Subsequently, he and his four men learned she was on her own; she'd remained mum about where she'd come from, telling them only that she was headed for a ranch, the J-B, near the town of Wayside Station. The J-B ranch and the M double C ran side by side.

Yes, he remembered. Her sad eyes had dominated her face even while her wide mouth held pluck. Yet he recalled her fear, too, and that she'd been half starved. She'd viewed them all with a deep wariness at best.

"That was different then," he said, bringing his thoughts back to the present. "You had no choice but to ride and shoot; it was necessary for survival. You've lived a sheltered life since."

She rocked forward in a sudden hard motion and stood, leaving the rocker to clatter rapidly back and forth on the wooden floor. She faced him almost nose to nose.

"Are you afraid of what people will think, Will?" She spoke softly, yet her tone carried an edge. "That my less-than-lily-white reputation will be further smeared? That an outlaw's brat, one woman riding alone with a bunch of men, can't be virtuous?" She laughed without humor. "Well, let me put your mind at rest. I'll ask Cousin James to go with me. As my nearest male relative and as one with a personal stake in this . . . venture, I'm quite sure he'll be glad to act my chaperon."

Will's mind jumped to the gossip that had followed her all those years before. He'd thought he could protect her from it then. That he hadn't been able to stop it had caused him a great deal of heartache; it was a greater part of why he'd let her go out of his life. Listening now, he gathered the old wounds still had the power to hurt, and Landon and Smith hadn't soothed them any with their sly attitudes. But the idea of taking James as her chaperon would answer that objection, he supposed. No one could or would accuse Mattie of unseemly conduct with James around.

Still agitated, Will wrapped his big hands around her slender shoulders, feeling her warm flesh and bones beneath the cotton nightgown. In truth, he couldn't make up his mind whether to shake her for wanting to go or kiss her silly in his delight that she stood her ground. He wanted to do both.

"You're the stubbornest girl I've ever met, Mattie girl. All right. You ride with us. But you'll obey my orders and abide by my decisions. Agreed?"

She hesitated so long, he was afraid she'd back out. And in spite of all the devilment her presence was likely to cause him, he suddenly didn't want her to.

The smell of her, a mixture of flowers and something Will couldn't identify, filled his nostrils while the inches that separated them seemed as nothing. If he didn't move, he was likely to ruin everything by crushing her to his chest.

"Agreed." The word was a sigh.

"Amen!" A gravelly voice growled behind them from the house. "Now as Mattie's personal chaperon, Will, I say ya go home an' get some sleep an' let us do the same."

Will's head snapped around and he stepped back, his hands dropping. "Yes, sir. Good night, sir."

He lowered his voice to a caressing note. "G'night, Mattie girl."

" 'Night, Will."

He rode home, remembering the feel of one small foot in his palm, the moonlight reflecting the fire from sparkling eyes, and the smell of her.

Lord, he'd wanted to kiss her. And more. He wanted to wrap himself all the way around her.

He hunched his shoulders, stretching the blades, and shifted in his saddle. He needed sleep. But he wouldn't get much tonight.

Mattie felt wide awake the next morning when she heard James rise, in spite of only a few hours of rest. The anxiety over her mother's whereabouts ate at her, along with the eager anticipation for the coming expedition. Also, the scene with Will last night had coiled her nerves as tight as bed springs. When Cousin James suggested that she ride with him to the south section, she consented with all the eagerness of a puppy. She'd missed their early morning rides.

She pulled out the two formal riding habits she'd brought with her, looked at them for five seconds, then immediately put them away again. Neither would do for a morning jaunt around the J-B. Coaxing Cousin Beatrice out of an old pair of James's jeans was easy. Tall as she was, she had to cuff them only once, though she filled out the seat solidly. Maybe a little too much, she wondered? Well, she didn't care a snap if she did. Denims, a white shirtwaist, and her comfortable brown boots were just the ticket for this open country.

At that, she beat James down to the corral.

"Howdy, Long." Mattie greeted James's old cowhand with a smile. He'd been one of her friends six years before.

"Well howdy, Miss Mattie. It sure is a plum pleasure to see you again. Missed your purty smile after you left."

"Why, thank you, Long. I've missed this place, too."

"Brung them horses up from the lower pasture. You a'pickin' one this mornin'?"

"Yes, I reckon I am." She'd ridden a lot of Eastern horses in the last six years, mostly purebreds. Ridden an Eastern saddle, too. She found herself eager to choose a mount from James's rangy mix.

James generally kept an interesting *remuda*. She placed herself on the corral's top rail and curled her toes under the middle one while she watched the half dozen ponies circle. After a moment, she felt the fence tremble under Long's heavy weight.

"There's that there sorrel, he's a good ol' horse, though a bit slow. An' the paint's right frisky, but he likes to nip, if'n ya don't watch 'im," pointed out Long.

The sun's slanting rays made the horses' coats shine. A small mare pranced about, looking for breakfast. "What about the gray mare? She seems full of spirit," asked Mattie.

"Yes, ma'am, she's a right good little horse. Just healin'

from a leg sore, but she's ready to go again, I reckon. You want me to saddle her?"

"Yes, thank you, Long. Cousin James will be ready as soon as breakfast is over."

"Yes, ma'am. I'll bring the horses up d'rectly."

Mattie jumped down from the fence and strolled back to the house. Cool air left over from the night caressed her cheeks and she lifted her face to embrace the morning. With neither skirts nor petticoats to impede her, she lengthened her stride.

She'd been so eager to be up and about this morning, she had left her hair loose. Now it swung and bounced against her back as she went up the path. She felt suddenly free and excited to be back in the West.

"There you are, dear," called Aunt Elizabeth from the porch. "Breakfast is . . ."

Mattie couldn't keep a wide grin from breaking across her face as her aunt's voice trailed away when she got a good look at Mattie's jeans.

". . . just about ready. Oh, dear!" finished her aunt.

"Yes, Aunt Elizabeth?" Mattie placed an arm across her aunt's shoulders as they entered the house. Elizabeth was probably lamenting the loss of all those deportment lessons. "Since I'm shocking everyone anyway, I may as well be comfortable while I'm at it."

"An' sensible in the bargain, I say," approved Cousin Beatrice. "I'd wear 'em myself, if I'd Mattie's figure."

"I think I'll take a trip into town tomorrow and get another pair for the trail," Mattie said as she spied the fried bacon. In spite of her worries, she felt lighthearted. Sitting down, she bowed her head as James mumbled out a quick blessing.

"Good idea," James said, as he picked up the conversation as though he hadn't stopped to talk to God. "An' get a hat, while you're at it. Ya never did get a good hat before, and ya need protection from the summer sun."

Mattie laughed. "Yes, sir, I'll do that." She scooped a bite of egg into her mouth and stuffed a biscuit behind it. "Now are you going to lollygag around here all morning, letting the best part of the day get away from you?" she teased. James hated to dawdle.

"Don't get pert, there, girl." He made a scowl, but Mattie saw his eyes twinkle as he turned to Elizabeth. "Thought you was goin' to teach the child some manners back East there, 'Lisabeth."

Elizabeth smiled. "Yes, indeed, I tried hard. Taught her well. And independence as well, James."

"She didn't need lessons in independence," a masculine voice said from the door.

Will stepped through and removed his hat while he took the mug of coffee that Beatrice automatically shoved into his hand. He stood just behind Mattie's shoulder and leaned against the dry sink. "I'd be willing to bet she was born with that trait."

Mattie, caught with her mouth full, flashed her eyes at him and continued to chew. And chew. It seemed forever before she could swallow, but finally she was able to take a sip of coffee without choking.

She laid her fork down. She couldn't eat one thing more.

"Never hurt anyone to be self-reliant, if they can," she defended herself.

"Good trait for Westerners, right enough," Beatrice added.

"Come by for somethin' special this mornin', Will?" James asked innocently while a grin tugged at his mouth.

Mattie looked over her shoulder. Will's gaze rested on

her in pensive concern. And something else? Her heart gave a small leap. Speculation?

"Yeah, James." He averted his gaze as he spoke. "As a matter of fact, I did. Seems Frank found some unknown tracks down by the bend in the creek, where the briar patch is so thick. You know the spot?" He waited for James to nod. "It'll take a day or two for a posse to form. Men have to arrange things, as I see it. So I thought as long as we're waiting for a posse to be formed, you'd be interested in riding down that way with me."

"Sure would. Mattie and I was headin' down that general direction this mornin' anyways," replied James. His rare, teasing smile gave way to a no-nonsense expression.

"What kind of tracks?" asked Beatrice. Mattie noticed a pinched look around her eyes.

"Well, could be just bear. That old she-bear Frank calls Grandma has been hanging around this spring. Frank and Luke both tried to get their sights on her, but with no luck."

"Let's git." James abruptly stood. He patted Beatrice's arm as he moved away from the table, and Mattie realized it was a gesture of reassurance. She'd noticed their show of affection before, long ago, and had wondered at it. It was so different than what her mother had received from Larry.

Since then, Mattie's experience in observing other couples in an intimate setting had been very limited. She'd never again noted such open fondness between married folk.

The men hurried through the door. Hearing Will's heavy boots thump across the wooden porch brought Mattie back to the present. Shoving back her chair hurriedly, she was afraid the men might leave her behind, and followed them out. On the porch, she saw Long come up from the corral, leading the two saddled horses.

Mattie patted the grey mare and climbed into the saddle, testing the stirrups. Long had guessed well, it seemed.

Her knee bumped against the rifle scabbard, and she reached out to rest a hand against the rifle's stock. She pulled it half out of its sling. The silver plate winked and flashed in the sunlight; a sudden memory brought it into clear focus. The rifle was the same one on the saddle the night she'd stolen Nate Dorsey's big bay thoroughbred and ridden as though escaping hell. Which the outlaw stronghold was, for her. The night her mother . . .

She looked at James. He grunted and jerked his chin toward Will.

"You took care of this rifle?" she asked him.

"Thought you might have need of it again someday." Will's steady regard evoked a memory of another time when he'd given her a gun for protection. She'd been scared out of her wits at finding herself in company with five strange men; Will had given his word she'd come to no harm at their hands and handed her his own handgun to prove his good intentions. From that moment on she'd trusted him. Mostly.

Now she didn't, quite.

"Yes. Many thanks, Will. Too bad . . ."

"Too bad about what, Mattie?" James asked.

"Oh, nothing really. I just think it's a shame to have had Bay stolen back." The big horse she'd grown attached to had disappeared one night about a year after she'd gone East. It had been James's guess, Beatrice told her in a letter, that Nate Dorsey had reclaimed it.

"It was a mighty handsome animal, sure 'nough," James said. He took the lead out of the ranch yard and quickly put the horses to a trot. Mattie soon adjusted to the gray's gait and relaxed with the freedom of riding astride.

The sun warmed the morning as they reached the place on the creek that Will had described. Mattie took a deep breath, appreciating the clean fresh smell of earth and grass and sagebrush. Dropping behind to allow the men to search for the tracks they'd come to find, she walked the grey downslope the other way, idly searching the ground as she went.

The creek bank had several cuts made by the spring backwashes, and she followed one several yards to where it ended. She saw signs of antelope as well as cattle, but they were old. Then she saw a track she wasn't familiar with; she dismounted to look closer. Half buried under another one of cattle, she guessed it might be a bear print.

Mattie carefully circled until she found another print that matched. This one was fresh. Following the direction it indicated, she found another. This one too!

Stooping, she ducked under the vine-like limbs of the thorny brambles that grew profusely along the creek bed, and bent to examine her find. She felt the animal imprint in awe, tracing the way the ground faithfully curved and ridged to show a large beast had walked there.

At one edge underneath that was another, partial print. She studied it a moment. It wasn't an animal print. Moccasin?

Inches away lay a small white paper, like that from a cigarette. It also looked fresh—clean and untouched by weather. The men ought to see it, Mattie decided.

Stooped over, she began to back out of the bushes, but caught her hair in a long thorn-filled briar. She went to her knees and twisted, suffering a sharp thorn scratch along her shoulder. She let out an "ouch" and pulled harder at her entangled hair.

"Mattie?" She heard Will's voice call from down the

creek. She started to answer, but held silent when she heard the grey mare whinny. Peering through the brambles, she glanced at her horse. The mare flicked her ears and sidestepped against the reins.

What made her mount so nervous, she wondered? A snake? Curious, Mattie tried to stand, but was jerked back by her tangled hair.

"Mattie . . ." Will sounded closer, but she couldn't see him. The mare whinnied again and Mattie heard rather than saw her move farther away.

"Here, Will. I'm caught."

"Hush, Mattie girl! Be absolutely still," he commanded in a low, compelling tone.

Beyond sight, Mattie heard a low guttural sound. Her heart began to pound; she'd heard that animal growl once before, never to forget it.

Bear . . .

Four

Will felt his heart beat faster as he spotted what he'd suspected when the mare became skittish. A large brown furry body lumbered up the hill away from them, but then stopped, raised its nose and sniffed. An old she grizzly, Will noted, but still dangerous if cornered. At the moment, the bear seemed to be assessing the situation as it turned to look down at them.

In spite of his mount's nervousness, Will urged him closer to Mattie, partially hidden in the briars. He had to reach her before the bear decided to come their way.

Mattie craned her neck to see what Will was watching, fearful that it was what she hoped it was not. But the bear was unmistakable. Mattie's breath caught and she nearly choked on the pungent smell of the animal. A fine time to notice, she scolded herself. Her chest tightened with apprehension as the bear paused to scratch itself.

"Easy, boy, easy," Will cautioned his horse, Lariat. Dismounting slowly, he held the reins tight. Nothing to startle the bear. He squinted against the morning glare, never taking his gaze from the immobile beast as he reached out to Mattie with his free hand.

"Can you see it from where you're sitting?" he murmured.

"Yes."

"Okay. Keep your eyes on it and tell me if it so much as raises its head." Moving with care, he started to untangle her hair. The long strands felt like silk against his ungloved fingers, and even in the stress of the moment, he noticed how some of the strands took on a red hue in the sun.

"Will!" Mattie's low voice was choked with fear.

His gaze flew back to the bear just as it reared to its hind legs. It emitted a loud roar, walked a few paces, its shaggy fur fluttering, before dropping back to all fours. The bear lumbered their way.

Without waiting another moment, Will yanked Mattie's hair free and jerked her upright. Her "umpf" of pain barely registered in the back of his mind as he pulled her up hard against his body. Lifting her, he threw her into the saddle just as the bear picked up speed.

The loud report of James's rifle rent the air with echoing suddenness. James was too far away, out of range.

Will leaped into his saddle behind Mattie, pulled his rifle from its sling, and twisted himself. Clinging with his knees, leaning beyond Mattie, holding the rifle in one hand, he aimed and fired.

When James's rifle sounded a second time, the bear stopped cold and turned away from them. It started up the hill. Picking up speed as it topped the peak, it disappeared over the horizon.

Mattie held the saddle horn in front of her with trembling hands. So tense was she that her stomach muscles jumped as Will slid his arm around her waist. His chest heaved against her back, his heart thumped in double-quick time. His hand felt large against her rib cage and she felt his heat. Oddly enough, she felt safe.

Will drew her tighter against him and turned Lariat down the slope. He bent his head to speak into her ear. Her fragrance was sweet and enticing, and he held his breath. Then he spoke.

"You're safe now, Mattie girl." Her pulse raced; he felt it

all through her body. His own did, as well, but he thought it had little to do with the excitement of seeing the bear.

Mattie turned her head to answer, her forehead running into Will's smooth hard jaw, and then felt the silkiness of his mustache brush her skin. Her breath clogged her throat. If she lifted her chin just so and turned a few inches . . . if she wanted to, she could place her mouth against his cheek.

She almost did. It shocked her speechless to realize how much he affected her. Still . . . after all this time.

"Hey, Mattie!" James called from a distance.

Her movement halted. Suddenly overcome with shyness and sharp awareness of her own unruly emotions, she couldn't speak. She nodded belatedly in answer to Will's query.

James rode up to meet them, leading the mare. "Mattie girl, you okay? What was ya doin' in them briar bushes anyway? Ya shouldn't wander off like that," he scolded in relief.

"I'm fine, Cousin James." She sat up straighter, hoping to put inches between her and Will. "But you should look at what I found."

She twisted, eager to lead them back to where she'd been, when a thought struck her. "Umm . . . the bear won't return, will it?"

"I doubt it," Will said with a chuckle. "It didn't like the gunfire one bit." He tried to appear nonchalant while she wriggled against him.

"Put me down, Will. I don't know if it means anything, but there's something you should see."

Slowly, Will lowered her to the ground and then dismounted to walk beside her to where she'd been caught in the bushes. James remained in his saddle, but followed, still holding the mare's reins.

"Here," Mattie pointed out the bear print that covered the man's. "And there," she added, directing his attention toward the cigarette paper.

"Hold these, Mattie," James bade her as he dismounted.

She stepped back and accepted the reins of the horses, as Will hunkered down to examine the ground.

"Any of your hands been down this way in the last few days, Will?"

"Only Frank." Will studied the cigarette paper he'd picked up. "And he chews tobacco, but seldom smokes."

"Ain't none of my boys been over this way this week that I know of," James said. "An' none of them'd be fool enough to get tangled up in the briars."

"Well, this isn't what Frank described." Will removed a few strands of Mattie's long brown hair from where they lay across a thorn. Carefully, he wrapped them around one finger and pushed the soft mass into his shirt pocket before he pulled out his work gloves. He tugged his gloves on and then held back the thorny brambles to look closer at the track. "Frank described sheep tracks . . . possibly a small herd, milling about before moving on."

"Ya don't say. Sheep, is it? Reckon we've missed 'em?"

"Nope. We're off target, I think. The spot Frank was speaking of is about a quarter mile upstream." Will straightened and leveled his gaze at James and then it flickered over Mattie in an unspoken question. It meant all day in the saddle, likely.

"I'm just fine," she answered firmly and tilted her chin. "I want to go with you."

"Okay, then, mount up." Will swung into the saddle and observed Mattie as she moved fluidly, gracefully onto her own mount without any of the foal-like awkwardness her young body had at times exhibited six years before.

She sure filled out those jeans better, too. A groan nearly escaped him. Involuntarily, his hands tightened on the reins, causing Lariat to shake his head and prance. Will averted his gaze. He'd have to watch it or he'd be rushing her before she was ready. That was the worst of it—waiting until her feelings were wakened toward him. There was an almighty pull there all right, he was sure of that. He just wasn't sure she was ready to face it yet.

He shifted uneasily in his saddle and set his mind back to the business at hand.

They rode the distance in silence while Will studied the ground. Halting by another bend in the stream where it curved away against the low hill, they dismounted by a small copse of trees. The area looked much like the one they'd left, except without the bramble bushes.

"Now Mattie, you stay in sight," cautioned James.

"Don't worry, Cousin James," Mattie said and laughed. "I plan to keep a sharp eye out for bears and stay within ten feet of you and Will at all times."

Ten feet? Will couldn't keep the wry thought from filling his mind as he watched the teasing sparkle in her dark velvety eyes. Heavens above, he'd like to have her no more than ten inches, always within reach of his arms! At all times! It had been hard for him to let go of her just now.

The last years had taken more of a toll on his emotions than he'd realized, he guessed, if all it took was less than twenty-four hours in her company again for him to be as moony-eyed as a yearling.

He schooled his features to show none of what he felt. Instead he made a suggestion. "It's close to noon. Mattie, why don't you stay right here and make some coffee?"

"Right." She felt agreeable, for the hard saddle had pounded her bottom. She could do with a rest. Six years of

Eastern saddles and sedate park rides had softened her. Besides, the sun was hot and she'd have a bit of shade here.

The men moved off. She gathered firewood and stacked a circle of stones that had been used before, placing her wood carefully within to allow air to draw. Soon the coffee bubbled and the noon sandwiches were unpacked.

When she looked up to call the men, she saw them standing at the edge of the stream in deep conversation, too far away for her to hear what they said. Cousin James gestured toward the farther bank and Will nodded. At her call, they turned.

"Did you find what you were looking for?" she called before they reached her.

"Sure thing. A small herd of sheep trailed through here not more'n a couple of days ago, I'm bettin'," said James.

"Why would Frank say that's strange?" Mattie puzzled.

Will hunched down on his heels and poured himself a cup of coffee.

"Well, sheep in this country ain't uncommon, but I don't know of anyone who would dare graze this side of the creek if they know the territory. This is MCC land, and another half mile is the J-B boundary." He took a swallow of the hot brew and accepted the bread and meat she handed him. "And where the sheep have trampled, it looks like cattle have been driven before."

"Probably some of our stolen cattle," grunted James.

"Are those the only tracks?"

"No. We found a couple of obscure prints that could match the boot print you found."

"Moccasin?"

Will shrugged. "Soft enough, though I couldn't tell. But there're no Indians in this neck of the woods who tend sheep."

"Is that the way the thieves have taken the cattle?" Mattie, shading her eyes with her hand, gazed off into the distance toward the way she'd seen James point. The landscape was filled with low brown hills and blue sky, and the stream disappeared beyond the curve. It was a pretty view.

The men held their silence. Mattie turned to look at them. James bit into his sandwich but Will peered at her with questioning eyes over his coffee cup. Puzzled, she watched as he leisurely lowered the cup to rest against his knee.

"Do you recognize this spot, Mattie?" he asked softly.

She continued to search for the answer to what he was asking her. Giving her long hair a flip over her shoulder, she rose and walked a few yards distant. Slowly she turned in a semicircle, observing the round hills and skyline. Finally, she carefully examined the immediate vicinity, the stream and copse of trees they were in.

"We passed by here six years ago on the last day out, didn't we?" The discovery had been slow, but now she was sure they'd stopped here to rest and make coffee. The place where she'd built the fire took on a familiarity it didn't have five minutes ago.

Will saw recognition dawn and her face sober as she remembered what she'd felt during that time. Lost, scared spitless, and desperate. Some of it crept back into her eyes as she insisted, "It's the place where you made me tell you who I was. Isn't it?"

They'd been traveling for days, searching for lost cattle, when Mattie found them. Will, Luke, Frank, Bob, and Sandy. After they'd fought the skirmish with the hostiles, he'd suggested she stay with them for her own protection. She'd obeyed him out of hunger and fear, but Mattie had refused to give them any information about herself except her first name. When they'd reached this place, he'd made her tell him where she wanted to go and who her people were. She'd been so young and easy to intimidate . . .

Shame reached a tender place in him now at how harsh he must've been with her. Yet from the first, he'd felt the overwhelming need to protect her. That need was still there, yet Mattie was no longer a child.

She hadn't been exactly a child then.

"Um-hum." He stood and walked to stand behind her. Lifting an arm, he pointed over her shoulder to a break in the hills far distant. "We came from that direction. The old Bascomb cabin is about five hours' ride from here."

Mattie recalled it.

The old Bascomb cabin . . .

The old log house stood in a small clearing amidst low pines on the side of a foothill. It hadn't been used for years and was in sad disrepair. The weather was misty, so they made camp and slept inside for protection. The men, closer to home and town, began to talk of their lives; some lived in the bunkhouse, but a couple of ranch hands had wives in town.

The talk made her think of her mother. She thought of her recent escape and the unknown future. If they became separated, Ma told her to reach her cousins, the Cramers, if she could. If her ma couldn't attend to her. Had her mother known she wouldn't make it out?

She was to make her way to a town called Wayside Station that was near where her cousins lived. She had no idea if they would welcome her or not. They'd been her father's people.

From there, she was to contact her father's sister—her Aunt Elizabeth, in St. Louis. She'd be safe there, Ma had assured.

She'd be safe . . . from Larry and Nate Dorsey. Her ma had overheard a conversation where Larry promised Mattie to Nate Dorsey when she was fifteen.

What right did Larry have to make such a promise? She despised Dorsey as she despised Larry.

She'd started to cry, curled into a ball in the far corner of that old cabin, muffling her desperate sobs so that the men wouldn't hear. But she couldn't contain them.

Her back to the room, it was moments before Mattie realized the men had grown silent. She lay huddled and lonely. No longer fearing rape or abuse from these men, she'd simply felt terribly alone when they talked of home and family. She tried harder to muffle the broken, desperate sounds, embarrassed because she could no longer contain her emotions. Any dignity was lost . . .

Then she felt Will's arms enfold her, and his face pressed against her hair. He raised her to a sitting position and she turned her face into his chest. Will held her for long moments while sorrow and fear gripped her heart. Slowly, her sobs quieted. He rocked her softly, until she went to sleep.

She'd loved him from that moment.

That was long ago, she reminded herself. She no longer idealized or feared any man, or depended on one for food and shelter or love. She couldn't allow those old feelings to affect her as she had an hour ago. Will was a tough man, one with a mission, and when his mission ended . . .

She ignored his proximity and asked, "That's the direction the tracks lead?"

"Yep."

"And that's the direction the posse will follow?"

"Yep."

She continued to stare into the distance for long moments as the hot sun beat down on her bare head. She passed a hand over her moist forehead, feeling the beads of sweat dampen her palm.

Could she find her way back? Six years was a long time and she'd been disoriented and grieving, sometimes lost, on her way out of those mountains.

Will remained behind her and she knew he studied her profile.

"Do you have a general map of the area?"

"Yep."

"I think I'd better have a look at it. My memories are jumbled." More than jumbled, they were shot through with old emotion.

"All right. I'll bring the map over tomorrow. We'll go over it together."

"You two gonna lollygag around here or eat your vittles?"

"We're coming, Cousin James." Mattie tossed her relative a forced chuckle and walked back to the campfire to reach for a sandwich. "I'm not one to waste Cousin Beatrice's good food."

"Will, are ya gonna report this to Sheriff Kimmel? I ain't heard of any new settlers, but he might know of some. Homesteaders that're runnin' sheep, that is."

"Reckon he might, though I think we'd know if there were any new settlers so close to our boundary lines," Will answered. He finished his coffee and stood, frowning in concentration.

"I'm thinking maybe we ought to leave for the mountains sooner than planned. The more I think about it, this is a pretty odd circumstance. Did you notice that the cattle count seems thin down this way?"

"Yeah, I did at that." James rose swiftly. "D'you think?"

"Yep. I think those damned rustlers have taken more of my herd, and the sheep have been used to cover the trail."

"I say we ride back to home over my ground," said James as he kicked dirt over the fire. His face took on angry color. "I have a sizeable herd grazin' that section beyond where the creek splits off. Think we'll go check on 'em."

They broke camp, kicking dirt on the fire. Mattie swung into her saddle as quickly as the men and they pushed the horses into a hard trot.

"Gol' dang those thievin' skunks!" fumed James nearly an hour later. He craned his neck while they rode. It was obvious that his herd, also, was thin. He stood in his stirrups, straining to see beyond the horizon. "No sign of Jones and Gomez. They're supposed ta be guardin' down this way."

They came upon the remote camp where the cowhands had stayed. There was no sign of anyone, only the remains of what appeared to be a hasty break-up and retreat.

"Double damn it! Looks like they got most of my cattle."

James and Will dismounted to look around.

Mattie walked her horse toward the creek. The ground was trampled and churned and a broken rope lay twisted against a bush.

"James, come look at this," Will called.

Will hunched down, examining the ground. "Spent rifle casings and blood. Probably your men put up a fight."

"But where are they?"

"Looks like they trailed out of here going east. If the raid came before dawn, they could've got away."

"Let's find 'em," said James.

They rode in circles until they picked up the trail of two horses, going slow, heading toward the J-B headquarters.

Mattie was tiring. Her muscles felt tight and her body

wanted to slump. She really had grown soft, she mused, which didn't please her one bit. Determined not to slow the men down, she said nothing.

An hour later, they found the two men hidden in a draw that slashed across the land. Both were badly wounded; Jones was unconscious while Gomez mumbled, half delirious.

James pulled his water canteen off his saddle and, lifting Gomez gently, held it to his lips. "Easy, man. Take it slow."

Will examined Jones. His blue eyes flashed with fury as he looked up at her and James. A hard knot formed at his jaw line as he spoke through his teeth. "We can't take them in on horseback, it would finish Jones for sure."

James looked up from where he tended Gomez. "Mattie girl, can you get back to the house by yourself?"

"Sure."

"Okay, then ride fast, an' send back help with a wagon," he directed. "Take—"

"Huh-uh," interrupted Will. "You'd better go yourself, James."

James glanced a question at Will. Will flickered a lightning quick glance her way and then returned it to James. For some reason they didn't want her to go alone.

"I can go," she protested.

"Not this time," commanded Will without looking her way.

Whoa, now. She wasn't a child! Yet she didn't argue. James mounted and rode out at a fast gallop.

As Will shifted Jones toward the shade, Mattie realized how hot it was. Kneeling next to Gomez, she pulled off her neckerchief, wet it from her canteen, and moistened his lips. She leaned back a moment and studied the ugly shoulder wound. It was matted and crusted over where his shirt stuck to it. Carefully, she dribbled water onto the injury, and gently pulled the fabric away. He groaned and muttered in Spanish.

"*Por favor, senor,* lie still." With what little Spanish she remembered, she tried to reassure him. "Only a little while and we will make you comfortable." She cleaned the wound, gritting her teeth against causing him more pain.

"I didn't know you knew Spanish." Will spoke in surprised speculation. He'd finished his ministrations to Jones and observed her.

Finally, she leaned away. Gomez seemed to rest easier.

"Only a little, and half are swear words." She glanced up and, taking in his expression of slight disbelief, shrugged and continued. "There were Mexicans in the Dorsey gang from time to time. And the boys . . ."

"Boys?"

"Yes. Miguel and Juan, Rosa's sons. We often went foraging or hunting together."

"Did they teach you how to use a gun?"

A strange tightness lay in Will's voice and she looked across the two prone men to where he sat on his heels. He studied her with curious eyes, his mouth stretched.

Mattie had never talked freely of the men and her years in the outlaw stronghold. Shamed, she'd kept her knowledge and childhood experiences tightly locked away in the furthermost corners of her mind. Yet now, she spoke freely, uncaring of what others might think.

Especially Will.

"No, as a matter of fact, I taught them how to hunt," she answered in a bland tone. Why should it bother him?

"You taught them?"

"Yes, when we could swipe enough bullets and Ma

would let me go. Sometimes we had to make do with slingshots."

"Ah . . . these were children." His mouth relaxed into a half-smile.

"Um-hum." She shifted her position to sit fully on the ground beside Gomez, taking in what little shade she could from the earth wall of the draw. She'd felt the sun's burn all afternoon.

"How much longer will it take for Cousin James to get back with help?" she asked. It already seemed like hours since he'd left them. She glanced over at Jones. He lay absolutely still. Was he alive?

Will studied the sun a moment and then glanced out over the draw that sheltered them. Heat waves danced in the sun. "A couple of hours, anyway. Maybe three."

He rose abruptly and went to his saddle, pulling off his rolled blanket. With quick, sure movements, he constructed a covering tent that gave a small square of shade to the wounded men.

"Mattie, move in under the shade," he commanded. "You've already gotten too much sun. You won't be much good to us, sunburned. Blazes, girl, don't you have a hat?"

"I plan to buy one, but I . . . Well, we didn't intend to be out the entire day, did we?"

She flashed her eyes up at him where he stood tall above her. His thoughts were impossible to read. She dropped her gaze down his body, past his strong shoulders and slim waist to his muscled thighs and calves. He was harder, tougher than in the old days. Not much of the tender man she'd once known showed through. She wondered what had changed him.

His eyes suddenly filled with raw male interest, and Mattie held her breath. She'd been courted from here to

Sunday and back by New York society men, and the cream of the European crop, as well as the St. Louis local boys. She'd flirted with a few, and delighted in their frustration when she eventually turned a cold shoulder. But Will was too much of the elemental male to offer a mere flirtation, she knew; he wouldn't know how to play that game and then laugh it off.

His serious stare set Mattie's heart thudding. Nervously, she smoothed down her long hair. Yet she wasn't really frightened. Should she be?

Will watched the feminine action; it made his hands tingle with the desire to do the same. He wanted to run both hands through her hair and cup her cheeks against his palms. Her full soft mouth invited his kiss.

Their isolation hit him full force and desire rose within him so strongly it was like a punch in the gut. He wanted her without reservation, without waiting—he'd already waited for six years. It would be so easy to sweep her up and carry her down the draw.

So easy . . .

Five

Gomez stirred and muttered, snapping Will's whirling thoughts back to attention. Slowly he became aware of the soft trust he saw in Mattie's eyes, though something in her gaze told him she felt his pull. His breath felt harsh as he sucked air into his lungs and fought his need for her. He'd nearly lost his iron control.

Wrenching his gaze away, he turned and paced a few steps, his long fingers curling into fists. This wouldn't do; it was too soon. He didn't want to ruin his chances with her. Always, the time wasn't right, nor was the place. But one day . . .

Yes, one day. But he must wait until things were right, until they were reacquainted, until she wanted him as desperately as he did her.

He walked back to her while the silence of the heated afternoon weighed heavily. What was it she'd just said? He didn't remember and risked a fleeting glance at her. She was braiding the long strands of hair into a loose bun.

"You need a hat. You have to be prepared for anything, Mattie girl, so make sure you have all your gear by the time we leave for the back country." He couldn't control the growl he knew sounded in his voice.

"I do know something about traveling in the wilderness, Mr. McCarthy," she said rather stiffly.

He was right, though. She should have worn something on her head, even if it had been one of Cousin Beatrice's sunbonnets. But she wouldn't allow Will to rule her every move; he was bossy enough already, and they had time before they left. "I'll be completely outfitted by the time you're ready. You'll have no worry about that."

He gave a grunt and restlessly strode up the gully a few yards as though to keep his distance.

Mattie shifted her seat to sit under the edge of the blanket-tent, getting as much shade as she could. The hot sun beat down, and she took out her water bottle. She dripped water into Gomez's mouth.

"*Gracias,*" murmured Gomez.

Jones didn't speak; she thought him unconscious. Pulling her shirt free, she blotted the end with water and placed it against his lips.

The two wounded men needed most of the shade. Another hour, and the sun would cast a longer shadow. She and Will would have enough shade from the earth bank.

"I think I'll even take a small tent." She gazed across the land around them and tried to fill the void of silence. They needed something neutral on which to focus their attention. "As the only woman in the posse, I'll need it."

She'd have the best and newest gear she could buy, by gum, including a good hat. And her own horse. The grey mare was nice, but Mattie wasn't sure the horse was up to the grueling trip that was before them. She sighed. "I wish I still had that bay thoroughbred I came out of the mountains with."

Not knowing his name, she'd simply called him "Bay."

Will paced back to stand before her, his spurs clinking like bells in the still afternoon air. He seemed grateful for the idle talk.

"You miss that big bay?"

"Yes, oddly. I loved that horse. He was my only companion for days, you know. I depended on him. It nearly broke my heart when Cousin Beatrice wrote to tell me that he'd disappeared."

"Well, I have a horse you might like as much as that bay. I'll bring him around tomorrow so you can get used to him."

"Why, thank you, Will. I'll look him over."

The long hours dragged on and Mattie dozed. Finally, faintly, she heard a wagon approaching and she stood up eagerly to see Cousin James coming with the buckboard and two men.

"Thank God," muttered Will.

"Yes, God be praised," she agreed.

"Mattie, I'm so glad to see you again." Josie, looking very pretty and happy, walked out from behind the counter at the mercantile store to give Mattie a welcome hug. "My, my! You look just lovely in that red dress—and your hat. Is this the latest fashion? I'm just green with envy."

"Good morning, Josie." Mattie gave her a wide smile in return. "Or should I address you as Mrs. Henly?"

Will's sister looked scarcely a day older than the last time Mattie had seen her, and her words tumbled out of her mouth just as fast. "Oh, no. Just Josie." She giggled and lowered her voice. "Only the old biddies call me Mrs. Henly."

"Am I one of the old biddies?" Beatrice spoke up from behind Mattie.

"Oh, dear me, no ma'am!" Josie's voice took on an exaggeratedly scandalized tone while her hand flew up to rest on her cheek. "Old biddy, indeed!"

"Well, the 'old' part is right, sure enough," said Beatrice, laughing.

"Please, Beatrice. If you're old, then I am too, for we're

the same age," said Elizabeth.

Mattie drew her aunt forward and made introductions.

"An' how are you feeling these days, Josie?" Beatrice's glance traveled over Josie's plump figure.

"Oh, I'm just fine, Mrs. Cramer, just fine," she answered and patted her slightly rounded middle, obviously pregnant. "And in spite of the old biddies in the town pestering me for working, so's this little one. I'm thinking it's a boy."

She turned again to Mattie and chuckled. "I already have a little girl, you know. Her name is Beth. Some of the women in Wayside Station think it's shameful I'm still working in the store while I'm in a family way, you see." She sighed with a mournful look. "But I'll have to retire from the store at the end of this month, sure enough."

A door slammed from somewhere in the rear, and a moment later Josie's husband Bart walked into the store and stacked a heavy box against one wall.

"Howdy, Miz Cramer, Miss Adams. Ma'am." He nodded to all three in turn. "Heard there was more trouble out your way, Miz Cramer. Sure sorry to hear it." He shook his head in sympathy. Bad luck for the ranchers meant bad luck for the town's businesses. "How is old Jones an' Gomez?"

"Jones died before he got home to the ranch, Bart," replied Beatrice. Worry and sorrow etched her face with added lines. "James is making burial arrangements this morning. Jones didn't have any kin." She paused a second to allow the information to sink in. "But Gomez will make it okay, though he'll be laid up for a spell."

"That's bad news, ma'am. Leaves you short some hands, don't it?"

"Sure enough. James is hoping to do some hiring while

he's in town this morning," she informed him. "Trouble is, it's hard getting somebody quick, what with him going off with the posse in a few days an' all."

"I might have somebody for you, Miz Cramer. A couple a fellas rode in a few days ago, looking for work. They spoke nice and looked clean."

"Where could they be found, Bart?"

"Over to the Lucky Clover, I 'spect. They said they'd hang round till after Saturday if somebody was hiring."

Beatrice turned to Mattie and Elizabeth. "Reckon I'd best go find James and help get this matter settled while you're getting your gear, Mattie dear. This expedition is snowballing faster'n I can run with it."

"I'll go with you, Beatrice," said Elizabeth.

The two women left.

Mattie turned back to the serious business of buying trail gear. Josie helped Mattie sort through denim jeans and work shirts. She chatted of town gossip, to which Mattie made little comment. But Mattie's mind chugged away like a locomotive when Josie started describing Nella's wedding two years before to a banker from Denver.

"Cousin Beatrice mentioned Nella's marriage in one of her letters." Still shy at times, Mattie dropped her eyes while her lips stumbled over the secret fear that had plagued her when she'd heard the news. "I thought at the time . . . well, I remember Nella hoped that Will . . ."

"Oh, pooh! Will never gave Nella a second look," said Josie. "Nella was just dreaming."

"But I thought Will was building a house?"

"So he has, and it's all but finished now. But my brother will choose his own bride when he's of a mind."

"I think I'll get these chaps, too. I'm determined to be completely prepared," Mattie said to change the subject.

"We may be gone for a couple of weeks."

"Yes, so I hear. Will was by early this morning," Josie informed her. "He said y'all would be leaving tomorrow, instead of waiting another two days. What with Luke needing to stay at the ranch with Ma, an' all, he sure is hoping Sandy will get back from his business down Colorado way before you leave. Meanwhile, what about a riding hat?"

Undecided, Mattie was trying on a black one with a flat crown for the second time when a young woman entered the store. She was dressed in a flashy low-cut dress of yellow silk that matched the brassy yellow of her hair. A heavy fragrance of lilacs floated around her like a cloud.

Josie moved to the counter and addressed the woman politely. "Good morning, Miss Coralee. What can I help you with today?"

Mattie turned back to the hats. The black one was attractive, but its crown wasn't quite deep enough to allow her to push all her hair under. She picked up a tan one and pushed her fist against the crown, attempting to give it more shape. It was almost too large, but she decided it would do.

"Uh-oh!" muttered Josie under her breath. "We're in for it now."

Mattie looked at Josie's face and then let her gaze follow in the direction of Josie's. Sally Smith had just entered the store.

Sally visibly stiffened when she caught sight of Coralee, and a blaze of red spotted each of her cheeks. But she halted abruptly when she spied Mattie; her cheeks grew even brighter.

A rich warm contralto purred out of Coralee as she spoke through a half-smile. "Why, if it isn't the town's leading young matron, Mrs. Fulton."

Mattie watched in growing interest while Sally's mouth formed a pinched line. Mrs. Fulton? Then Sally had married Nick Fulton, after all, Mattie mused. What was making her angry now? She looked as though she'd eaten an unripe persimmon.

"Good morning, Sally," Josie spoke up in a bright voice and waved her hand toward the back where the dress goods were on display. "Would you like to see that new lace trim that arrived from New York?"

Sally stood like a post and silently darted her gaze between Coralee and Mattie.

"There's quite a lovely pattern that I've never stocked before," Josie coaxed.

Coralee's smile broadened in defiance and she relaxed back against the counter in a negligent manner, propping one elbow on top while her eyes challenged Sally. The woman looked as though she planned to stay all day.

"We've a beautiful piece of blue silk that would make a ravishing . . . uh . . . that is, a stunning Sunday dress," said Josie sounding a bit desperate. "Back here . . ."

Josie's voice hung suspended in the cold silence.

Finally Sally lifted her nose in the air and spoke, her voice sounding like an ice pond had cracked. "No thank you, Josie. I see that you are busy. I'll return when you've finished serving the whores." She spun on her heel and marched out, nearly colliding with Sheriff Kimmel.

Coralee laughed openly and, turning to Mattie, gave a shrug. "Sorry 'bout that, honey. Didn't mean you to get tarred with my brush."

Mattie shook her head. "It might be the other way around. Mrs. Fulton threw that label at me long ago."

Coralee nodded. "She does have a sour mouth on her, don't she? Good day, ma'am."

"Good day." Mattie watched in fascination while Coralee's high bustle swished as she passed the sheriff and out the door. He returned Coralee's smile with a leer of his own.

"Oh, Mattie, I'm so sorry," wailed Josie. "I wouldn't have had that happen for a million years, if I could prevent it. That Sally's just a spiteful, jealous snot."

"Don't worry about it, Josie." Mattie went back to the clothing choices. "She'll think what she wants, anyway, and I really don't care anymore." It hurt too much to care. That surprised her that she still did. "All is not well in the Fulton household, I take it?"

"No. Unfortunately, Nick Fulton isn't very discreet in his, um . . . dallying."

Mattie picked up the tan hat, chose two bright red bandannas, and laid them on top of the supplies she'd already piled on the counter while she thought about Sally. Obviously, Sally was dreadfully unhappy. That should have afforded her some satisfaction for all the grief Sally had once caused her, Mattie thought.

Somehow, it didn't.

Sheriff Kimmel's voice interrupted her musings. "Miss Adams, nice to see you this morning," he said as he smiled and doffed his hat. "I understand you've consented to guide us to Dorsey's hideaway after all. Most sensible, my dear, most sensible."

"Yes, for reasons of my own, Sheriff, I've agreed."

Sheriff Kimmel's patronizing attitude grated up her spine like a rusty old saw. She didn't like the sheriff and, pretending she wanted to finish her purchasing, turned back to Josie, who was totaling the bill.

Bart came forward to offer his services. "What do you need today, Sheriff? More ammunition, I'd guess?"

He dug into the drawer where he stored the boxes of bullets. "Bad business out the J-B way, ain't it? A killing an' another man down." He shook his head to express his disbelief of the trouble. "An' Will is hot about losing more of his herd, too. The posse's coming together none too soon, I say."

"Bad business, sure enough," replied the sheriff. "Too many good men are being hurt. We're goin' after them this time, though. We're goin' right into that devil's den itself."

"Yeah, heard all about it from Will an' Luke early this morning," Bart said. "Half the men in the territory are ready to follow Will—an' you, of course—to hell and back if need be. Wherever they have to go. Will promised he'd find a way to get back in there an' wipe those thieves out, an' now he has."

"You're right about that, Bart," Sheriff Kimmel agreed. "Will's been my right arm these last two years or so. I wouldn't have half the help I need to do the job without Will's leadership and determination."

Mattie listened to the conversation while she counted out money. Will had promised he'd find a way, and now he had? Tingles of anger started in her toes and spread up and out along her body like a spider hurrying to spin a binding web before another moment had passed.

Yes indeed, Will had kept his promise to all the good people of Wayside Station, all right. He'd found a way. And she was it!

Again, she questioned the purity of Will's purpose in sending for her. Did he really think there was a possibility that her mother could still be alive? Or was it only a lie? Was his need of her help so great that he'd lie outright?

Only time would tell.

Six

Will was determined to get his own way, all right, exactly like other men. Only he was a little more subtle these days in going after what he wanted.

Mattie felt disgruntled and annoyed as she hurried out of the store with a mumbled goodbye to Josie. More than that, deeply disappointed. She was truly caught in a spider's web.

Taking control of her emotions, she scolded herself for being angry all over again. The situation was the same, and she'd agreed to help Will for her own purposes, hadn't she? She'd have to remember her bargain with Will was a two-sided promise and ignore the fact that she was being used by the ranchers. And in all honesty, those ranchers included Cousin Beatrice and James.

Beatrice and James . . . They'd been kind and loving when she was in great need. She'd never let them down now. And for Beatrice's sake, she'd put a bright face on it, but as for the rest of the town, she didn't care a fig.

The wooden sidewalk gave way to an earth path in front of a saloon and Mattie hurried past its closed doors. Locating her aunt and cousin across the street, she moved to the edge of the path and waited for the passing traffic to subside. Beyond where her aunt and cousin stood talking with another woman, Mattie saw Will and Luke exiting the bank. She stared at them, unheeding of the passing bustle.

The McCarthy men were tall; their heads easily showed above the rest of the crowd. They both walked with long strides, with the assurance of who they were—cattlemen, kings of the range. They strode with purpose, intent on business, on completing whatever had brought them to town. She watched a townsman tip his hat to them. Indeed, they were men to be reckoned with and highly respected.

Her focus narrowed on Will. His hat was pulled forward and his face looked sober and thoughtful, even resolute. All at once, he turned and looked at her across the distance that separated them. He abruptly changed his course toward her, closing the space in no time at all.

Purpose and determination!

Will embodied those qualities. Yes, she had to admit, her agreement with Will was a reasonable bargain, and she'd have his help in locating her mother. If it were possible. He would keep his promise to her and was quite capable of completing his own goal of wiping out the outlaws, as well. Because he was a man who would always get what he wanted. After all, hadn't he easily charmed her around to his plans?

And she'd let him, she suddenly thought. She'd better remember that!

Mattie stood rooted while Will approached, remembering the warm touch of his hand on her bare foot, and the seductive brush of his mustache against her cheek when he'd held her close after the bear fright. Even the memory shot desire through her. To feel his touch again.

She hated herself for wanting to repeat that feeling. Will was so attractive, she felt his pull like a magnet. It would be very easy to allow him anything he wanted. And like other men, he probably wanted everything he could get from her, body and soul.

Yes, so easy. Too easy.

Mattie drew a breath up from her toes. Never! Never in

a million years. *I won't be caught in the same trap my mother was . . .*

After Mattie's father died, her mother had given her all because of a man's persuasive ways. As soon as a woman gave in, a man too often changed, treating her like a rag doll, as property, to give away or stomp on as his pleasure dictated. Men wanted total control and exacted any kind of punishment to get it.

Well, it wouldn't happen to her! She wouldn't end up like her mother!

Will stopped squarely in front of her. Puzzled by the strange, wide-eyed expression she wore, he examined her face for a clue to what she was thinking. Slowly, the dark brown of her eyes deepened with pain. Something affected her deeply, he gathered, for she stared into his eyes as if to search his soul.

All at once, she took a deep breath and her eyes shuttered. She greeted him most casually. "Good morning, Will. I see you're in town making preparations for the expedition."

"Uh-huh." He'd give a half dozen cows to know what she'd just been thinking. Because, however civil her tone, she spoke as though she were addressing the mayor, and with pebbles in her mouth to boot.

"I've just completed my purchases from Josie. I'm equipped and prepared to leave at the appointed time," she continued brightly.

"Fine."

"It appears we'll have good weather."

"Yep."

"Well, I really must go. Nice chatting with you."

Mattie turned and put up a dainty, deep red umbrella the likes of which he'd never seen. She strolled across the street to join her aunt and cousin. Will stood where she'd left him and stared after her tall hour-glass figure, observing the bustle of her wine-red dress sway provocatively.

What in heaven's name had gotten into her head now? She responded to him as though he were a mere acquaintance.

When he'd spotted her across the street a moment ago, he'd headed straight for her like a homing pigeon, the gladness to see her muddling his brain. It seemed he couldn't stay away from her. Then this?

Truth was, he didn't want to stay away from her and had no intentions at all of doing so. Yesterday, he'd thought they'd closed some gaps between them, but just now she'd talked to him like a stranger, polite as a ten-year-old bent on impressing the preacher. Like a canyon separated them. He'd half a mind to go after her and find out what she was thinking—but then he'd have to deal with her female relatives, and there was still too much to do. He'd let it go, for now.

Will stalked toward the sheriff's office, trying to put Mattie out of his mind. He had to take care of business before pleasure, even when he wanted to turn his back on the whole thing and simply spend the day in her company. Always one to attend to duty first, he found it unsettling to find her taking up every waking moment. If he'd admit it, every dream, too.

Well, he'd had yesterday. Sort of. His enjoyment of her company was spoiled by the grim business of the rustlers hitting them once more. It was a dirty business. He saw no reasonable way of courting her until it was done.

He forced his mind to this current tricky concern. He wanted to know how many men were in town today, and who'd signed with the posse. Vigilantes, really, and he didn't relish dealing with all the uncertain personalities he'd be facing. Too many men wanted to be a part of it simply for sport. But after racking his brain for years, he simply hadn't found another way of taking care of the lawlessness in the territory, short of bringing in the army. No one wanted an occupation of any degree.

He needed Sandy, his right arm. He relied on Sandy to back him, to be his second pair of eyes. There wasn't a man in the bunch besides Sandy and Luke in which Will had much faith to keep a cool head. And Luke had to stay behind to guard the ranch.

There was the sheriff, of course. But Sheriff Kimmel had allowed himself to go soft, what with the easy town living, too much whiskey, and too many loose women. Will wasn't certain if the man was merely getting slow or losing his nerve, but Tom Kimmel had steadily deteriorated, and Will couldn't be sure of him or his ability anymore.

When they'd chased after the rustlers last spring, which resulted in Maxwell's capture, Will had tried to take one other man alive. But through the sheriff's carelessness, the man was killed. Strung up. He'd barely saved Maxwell for trial.

Also, the sheriff had been lax two years ago in admonishing those hotheads who'd been so quick to string up the thieves they'd caught.

Something else tugged at the back of Will's mind. Tom'd become indolent and slow to react even when a complaint was made against the increasing violence in the town. Sentiment was growing against him. Too bad, too, because he'd been a good lawman once.

Will had talked the matter over with Judge Titus when he was in town to try the rustlers. Judge Titus and Sheriff Kimmel were old friends. The judge was dismayed to see his friend in such condition, but his only answer was to give Will authority with his backing, should Will need it.

Reaching the jailhouse, Will nodded in greeting to the loungers hanging around, and pushed open the heavy door to the sheriff's office. Tom wasn't there. Will turned away in disgust and glanced up and down the street.

"Howdy, Will," Caleb Walters spoke from his position against the hitching post. "Is it true you found sheep tracks running across your lower range?"

"Sure did, Caleb."

"Is there a new homesteader down that way?"

"Don't know, but we aim to find out."

"How soon're we leavin'?" came from a grizzled old man Will knew only as Skeeter. "I cain't see so good as I uster, but my shotgun's still handy."

"How long ya reckon we'll be gone, Will?" queried Dave Hamlin.

"Could be as long as two weeks, maybe," Will answered. "Anybody know where the sheriff is?"

"Said he'd be here 'bout noon," said Smith, joining the crowd with his usual pal, Landon. "Said any man goin' should outfit his self an' be ready to leave on his say-so."

Luke arrived with Bram Lightfoot a step behind. "Will, Bram wants in on this, too."

Will studied Bram closely for a moment. He was part Cheyenne and stood with dark intense eyes while Will made up his mind. They'd hired him to train horses. Bram said little and was somewhat of a loner, but Will knew nothing against him. And he was top-notch with the horses.

"Okay, Bram, you're in. We'll leave at sunup from the MCC's bottom pasture," Will nodded his acceptance and turned to Luke. "Have you seen Sheriff Kimmel?"

Luke made a clicking sound through his teeth and

jerked his chin back the way he'd come. "Saw him a few moments ago, talking to that girl from the Silver Dollar Saloon."

Will exhaled in distaste. Almost noon, with a lot of organization needed, and the sheriff couldn't tear himself away to attend to it. Well, no need to upset the men with his own dissatisfaction; he'd have enough trouble keeping them in line as it was.

Lord, he hated this business.

"Reckon the sheriff's gettin' some lovin' to fortify hisself for the long trek?" laughed Smith.

"He'll need more'n a woman," Landon said. "It's a bottle of the Silver Dollar's best whiskey that helps a man through the dark night."

"Yeah, a bottle'd warm my weary bones right nice, too. Mebbe the sheriff's got the right idea," said Smith.

"No drinking!" Will nearly exploded. "There'll be no drinking in this posse."

The teasing and laughter dwindled and then ceased while all eyes turned to Will. He read real shock in the old man's eyes and not much less in Smith's and the others. They weren't used to these kinds of demands. The personal freedoms of a man were seldom questioned out here in the West.

"We've got to keep clear heads here, men." Will met their gazes one by one. "Clear heads, steady aim, and the ability to follow orders. If we want to put a stop to these rustlers and thieves, then we have to work together. Whiskey isn't going to do anything but cause trouble. You know it as well as I."

"But what about the sheriff?" came a voice from the growing crowd of men.

"Did I hear someone refer to me, gentlemen?" Sheriff

Kimmel elbowed his way through the men to stand beside Will. "What seems to be the trouble, Will?"

"Aw, Will here is insistin' we ain't goin' to take no whiskey on this here expedition, Sheriff," Skeeter grumbled. "Now whoever heered o' suchlike goin's on?"

Low mumbles of agreement came from several of the men.

"Well, now, Will . . ." Sheriff Kimmel started with a benign smile while he rocked back on his heels; he waved a hand loosely, expelling a great wave of foul breath. "It's going to be a long trek. Looks to me like we might need something to help us along the trail."

Will controlled his anger with great difficulty, his teeth clenched. The sheriff was drunk.

Someone in the back of the crowd snickered. A dozen men stood around them. Luke stepped closer, near his shoulder. James walked up to stand on the outer edge.

Will hid his sigh. It might as well be now.

"Sheriff, it appears that we have some serious talking to do. If I'm leading the posse . . ." he paused to allow his words to sink in, for he knew the men were aware there would be no real possibility of them going without him, "then my orders stand. No liquor! I want every man sober to the eyeballs and clear-headed enough so that when I say jump, you can do it."

"Now see here, Will," Landon started his protest.

"I thought Sheriff Kimmel was runnin' this show," persisted Smith.

"So I am, gentlemen, so I am." Tom Kimmel held up placating hands.

"Not quite!" Will's voice held the power that the men on his ranch had heard since he was a boy. "I'm sorry, Sheriff, but your authority doesn't reach beyond this town."

He'd hoped it wouldn't happen this way, had hoped he could spare Sheriff Kimmel—but now he'd no choice. Slowly, he reached into his front pocket and pulled out the badge he'd kept secret for two months. "Judge Titus swore me in as a District Marshal last April when he came here to try Maxwell. He instructed me to take charge of this expedition, if it ever came about."

The crowd caught its collective breath and was quiet for all of five seconds while Will riveted his gaze to Sheriff Kimmel's. The slightly bleary eyes stared back at him in foggy confusion while his face grew pale and then red.

"You! How come we didn't know?" Landon jumped in, his bluster growing loud.

"Aw, you're lyin'," Smith said.

Luke took a menacing step forward. "Watch what you're saying, Smith."

"He's not lyin'," James said from the back of the crowd. "I was there an' saw it."

"An' you're thick as butter with the McCarthys, Cramer. You'd back them up on anything," Smith snarled. "An' over that outlaw girl, too."

Without warning, Will erupted in rage. He threw his fist into Smith's jaw and watched him fall with great satisfaction. He pulled himself up short, barely breathing, and struggled to regain his self control while Landon helped Smith to his feet. He watched as Smith fingered his jaw, and stared at him with bitterness. He'd made an enemy there.

Luke stood in cocked readiness beside him, while the cluster of people waited to see what would happen next.

Caleb Walters, his face resolute, addressed Tom Kimmel. "He's telling it true, Sheriff. I saw it, too."

Sheriff Kimmel scrutinized Will's face for a long moment and then motioned him through the door to the office. "You, too, Walters and Cramer," he instructed and raised his voice. "The rest of you people go on about your business. We'll let you know who's to lead the expedition in due time."

Smith, still holding his hand over his jaw, threw Will a murderous look. "That was a mistake you'll regret, McCarthy."

"My mistake is in not having done that long ago, Smith," Will said through his teeth. "But my authority stands. If you ride with the posse, you'll follow my orders."

Will turned his back and walked into the sheriff's office.

A long whiskey-laden breath escaped the sheriff when he sat down heavily in his chair behind a cluttered desk. Will hooked his thumbs on his belt and stood leaning a shoulder against the wall just inside the door, watching Tom's pale face blotch up with emotion. James sat in a straight chair, while Walters and Luke stood and waited.

"Okay, Will, let's have it. What's been going on behind my back?"

"Not behind your back, Tom," James said. "We tried to get ya to listen a number of times this past year. We told ya things hadta get better. Ya been slippin', Sheriff."

"You talked to Judge Titus?"

"Yep, we did. He told us we'd have to vote you out," Walters stated bluntly. "But we can't do that till next fall. So Will, here, agreed to be temporary marshal."

"You have a signature to show me, I presume?" the sheriff said to Will.

Without comment, Will pulled the folded piece of paper from his shirt pocket, laid it on the desk in front of the sheriff, and waited. The sheriff read it through and looked up.

"Okay, Will, it's your show. But you'll have your hands full with Smith and Landon."

"I know, Tom. I'm sorry it had to come like it did. I don't want your job, you know."

"I'm sorry too, gentlemen." The sheriff rose and faced the men. "Well, I'm still sheriff until next fall, so I'll do what I can to help." He offered his hand and Will solemnly reached out and shook it.

Will allowed the tenseness to leave his body. At least Tom wasn't his enemy. Yet.

Sunset was sending its long rays over the horizon when James came to the ranch house door, calling for Mattie. "Visitors comin', Mattie. An' your presence is called for down at the corral."

"Who is it, Cousin James?"

Avoiding her question, he turned away, saying, "Come on along now, girl. Time's a wasting."

"What is it, Mattie?" queried Beatrice.

"I don't know, but I'm going to find out."

Cousin Beatrice peered out of the open front door and suddenly said, "Oh, yes! Come on, Elizabeth, let's walk down to the corral with Mattie."

She was obviously trying to keep a smile from forming, but with little success.

"What's going on, anyway?" Mattie was suspicious.

Cousin Beatrice linked her arm in Mattie's. "We'll find out, won't we?"

Several men were milling around the corral area and Mattie saw Will's tall form standing in their midst, talking to Cousin James and old Long. Commotion from the corral itself caught her attention and she shifted her gaze to see what was causing it. Chasing around the perimeter of the fence was a reddish-brown young stallion with black mane and tail.

Mattie halted abruptly. It couldn't be Bay!

Dropping Beatrice's arm, she started running, coming to a stop when she gripped the rails of the corral. She stared, open-mouthed. The animal looked very like Bay, but she knew he wasn't. He was too young.

"Oh, my stars!" she used one of Cousin Beatrice's expressions. "He's beautiful." Eagerly, she turned, only to realize all eyes and smiles were on her.

"He looks just like my Bay, but . . . where did he come from?"

"Well, let's just say your Bay is a granddaddy," said James. "He got right int'rested in the mares before he disappeared."

"Oh!" She watched the spirited three-year-old wheel and race in the other direction. "Is this his only offspring?"

A couple of the cowhands laughed, and she turned to see several of them avert their faces in mirth.

"Uh, no, as a matter of fact, this here's one of several," said James and glanced at Will.

Mattie's gaze flew to Will's face. He wore a soft, indulgent expression.

"Bay visited my best mares for a few days, Mattie." His mouth twitched into a smile, his eyes sparkled with it. "He sired three offspring. This is the son from the pick of the bunch."

"He's absolutely beautiful . . . just like Bay."

"He's yours."

"Mine?"

"Yep. I used Bay as a stud, with James's consent. One of

his progeny should be yours. Is it a fair deal?"

"Oh, yes. My, yes! Especially since I stole him in the first place."

"Yes!"

Mattie sprang away from the rail and, dancing up to Will, placed her hands against each side of his face and pulled him down to place a quick kiss on his cheek. Laughter spilled out of her as she whirled to do the same with Cousin James.

"Well, I've been training him, do I get thanked too?" spoke a dark-eyed stranger.

Mattie gave him a curious stare.

"I fed Bay while he was here . . . to keep his strength up, ya know," called a brown-headed cowboy. Mattie thought she recognized him from long ago, but she couldn't think of his name.

"Now lookee here, boys. I done my share," stated old Long.

"I thank all of you most kindly." Mattie laughed at them, a little nervous with returning shyness. She stepped back into safety, placing herself between her cousins and aunt. She could feel her cheeks redden in embarrassment and she twisted her hands behind her back. What had possessed her to kiss Will? And in front of all these people? Especially after deciding this very morning to distance their friendship.

She bit the inside of her lower lip and hoped she hadn't given Will the wrong idea. Freely given affection toward men was out of character for her, but for a moment there, she'd lost all self-consciousness over her happiness with the horse. Bay had been her only companion during a very dark time in her life and now she owned almost a replica of him.

Peeking at Will, she saw the remnants of a smile and

breathed deeply in relief. He hadn't taken her action for anything other than intended, she thought.

"Meanwhile, I thought you might also use the Appaloosa." He moved over to the horses hitched near the stable and led the animal forward. "He has stamina and will carry you long and hard," Will said, and then indicated the dark-eyed cowboy. "I've had Bram, here, put him through his paces."

There he went again, talking her into what he wanted her to do. But that was ungrateful, she chastised herself. She needed a good, dependable mount for the long trip, and it was only sensible that she listen to Will.

The horse was tall and well-formed, and Mattie instantly knew she wanted to ride him. She stepped forward and placed a hand on his nose. He snuffled in response and her heart was immediately won. Now what could she do, but accept as graciously as possible?

"What's his name?"

"Why don't you name him?" Will said.

"All right. I'll have to think about it some. Thank you, I'd be pleased to ride him," Mattie said. "I suppose young Bay will have to remain here with Cousin Beatrice for awhile."

Will nodded in satisfaction, and a moment later the men moved away to inspect the other horses and mules that had been chosen to make the trek.

Cousin Beatrice moved to stand beside her, patting the Appaloosa horse in admiration. "What're you goin' to name this one, Mattie?"

"Sensible." The name popped out of her mouth.

"Sensible?"

"Um," she affirmed in a soft murmur. "I have to be sensible about so many things, you see, and practical . . . and I need to be aware . . ."

She stopped, not ready to share her mixed feelings about accepting the horse from Will, or that she felt overwhelmed by her total reaction to everything he said and did. She tossed her head and raised her eyes to meet those of Cousin Beatrice. "Well, you see I'm glad to have a good mount, and I'm being very sensible in allowing Will to choose one for me."

Cousin Beatrice chuckled in understanding as Aunt Elizabeth joined them. "Sensible will serve you well, I'm thinkin'."

Seven

More than thirty men milled around the predawn breakfast fires in the MCC ranch's south pasture when Mattie and James rode up to join them. Mattie reined in Sensible and sat at the circle's fringe, listening to the joking and excited calling back and forth. Watching their faces in the flickering campfire light, she knew the joking covered the real agitation they were feeling. They were impatient to leave and deadly in their intended purpose. They wanted to exact revenge.

"Morning, Miss Mattie." Luke appeared at her side as she dismounted. He was a handsome young man, not much older than herself. "You and James breakfasted yet?"

"Had coffee," said James. "Knew it'd take time to organize this bunch and figured we'd eat with y'all."

"Come on over to the chuck wagon, then. Ma's there helping Bob with the cooking."

Mattie greeted Mrs. McCarthy.

"Why, Mattie, it's so nice to see you, my dear. Though not in these circumstances, I'm sure. Did you have a nice trip from St. Louis?"

"How are you, Mrs. McCarthy?" Mattie accepted a plate of eggs, steak, and biscuits. "Yes, it was pleasant. While we're gone, you'll have to go and visit with my Aunt Elizabeth, Mrs. McCarthy. And Cousin Beatrice, of course."

The older woman turned to pour coffee. "Yes, I'll do that."

James moved off to talk to a crony and Mattie leaned

back against the chuck wagon's big wheel. She wasn't sure she could eat with the knots in her stomach turning cartwheels.

Sipping the dark, strong coffee instead, she watched the scene before her. Most of the men were strangers to her, though some were familiar from six years before. Heavily armed, they exuded menace. But how many of these men would return?

Mattie shuddered. In the name of righteousness, these men didn't intend to leave any of the outlaws alive if they could help it; it would be a total shootout to the last man, or a hanging. In turn, the gang at the hideout was desperate, with little care for life, even sometimes laughing at death. They'd fight to their last breath. They'd never accept surrender, given a choice.

The thought of the fight ahead made her nerves play jumping jacks.

A moment later Will strode into the center of the group. He stood leaning mostly on one leg, his lean body apparently relaxed while his hand rested on the butt of his gun.

"All right, you men, listen up." Will's voice boomed out above the clatter of tin plates and stomping horses. The noise level quieted and all eyes turned in his direction.

"Now, we're going to divide up into three outfits to travel different routes until we get into the mountains. Gotta remain quiet, if we can. The noise, racket, and such from a large party traveling into the mountains will draw too much attention. If any word of our coming has reached the Dorsey gang, we'll have a better-than-even chance for one of the outfits of making it past an ambush or whatever."

He paused for that to sink in.

"We'll rendezvous tonight. Sheriff Kimmel, Caleb Walters, and I will head up the outfits, so choose your men.

You'll report to and take orders from the boss of your outfit, unless I countermand. You all know by now I have the signed authority given me by Judge Titus." He stared hard at Landon and Smith, who stared back. Landon's face was stony, while Smith's held open hostility.

"Each outfit is responsible for their own supplies and pack animals. There's extra bacon, beans, flour, and coffee on the chuck wagon if anybody's short of rations. And one more thing. The only liquor on this expedition will be for medicinal purposes. Understood?" He paused, waiting until he received affirmative nods, however grudgingly given. "Okay. We'll leave in half an hour, so finish eating and double-check your gear."

Mattie watched Will turn to Sheriff Kimmel and Caleb Walters. The three men huddled for a few moments and then broke, each going separate ways. Will turned to the chuck wagon and, spying her, strode to where she stood.

"Eat hearty, Mattie. We've a long day before us." He leaned past her, his arm brushing her shoulder, for a biscuit from the wagon tail.

She glanced at her untouched steak. "I'm not very hungry."

"Eat it anyway. You'll need the energy."

She pursed her lips to show her irritation, yet obeyed his order. She sat down and shoved a tiny square of pink steak into her mouth. If Will was going to monitor her every move, even to what she ate, maybe she'd choose to ride in Sheriff Kimmel's outfit. At least with that crowd she'd be totally ignored, and she already knew of their hostility, which might be better for her. She'd avoid Will's overprotection and be allowed to take care of herself.

"You'll ride in my outfit, Mattie, behind me and in front of James," Will said in the next breath. Good Lord, was he reading her mind now?

She twisted to look into his face. He stared at the crowd, his gaze shifting from group to group as he took careful observation of the men. Did he miss anything? Anything at all?

"And am I to tie my reins to your horse's tail?" she threw at him.

Will dropped his gaze to study her. The tan hat she wore framed her face, complementing her dark eyes and brows. Only the edges of her hair showed beneath the hat, causing the striking planes of her face to stand out sharply. The bright red bandana around her neck added color to her creamy cheeks.

For a moment, he forgot to breathe. She'd grown into even more of a beauty than he'd expected. Her loveliness hit him like a stone beneath his ribs every time he looked at her. It was harder to appear uninterested with each new encounter and, as much as he treasured his memories of her young self, this mature Mattie affected him in ways that hadn't a thing to do with softness or brotherly protection.

He let nothing of his emotions show and spoke in softly covered steel. "You'll do what's necessary for safeguarding, Miss Mattie. As I will. Agreed?"

Mattie sighed. They were just beginning this journey and she had to face the fact she'd given him her promise to cooperate. "Okay, Will. What else?"

"Frank and Bram will follow with the Whittington brothers, Nick Fulton, Jake Haskell, Sully, and old Skeeter." He stopped to gulp his coffee. "Bob'll be our supply man and cook. He'll take charge of your pack mule."

Mattie didn't know all the men he named, but the mention of old Bob eased her anxiety a bit. She remembered Bob's dark face from six years before. She felt comfortable with Bob, and Frank too. They'd never failed in offering her kindness. She'd have Cousin James as well.

"How far will we travel today?" she asked.

"We'll camp at the old Bascomb place tonight, so you'll have the cabin for shelter."

"Thank you."

"Wish I was going with you, brother Will." Luke clapped Will on the shoulder and the two men shook hands. "But I'll take good care of Ma."

"Much obliged, Luke. I'm counting on that."

Mrs. McCarthy joined them. "God be with you, son. And don't you worry about anything here, you just take care of yourself and Mattie."

"Yes, Ma." He leaned down to kiss her cheek.

"Mattie, I sure hope you get along, and all." Mrs. McCarthy patted Mattie's arm. "Take care of yourself, my dear. I pray you find your mother. I'll pray for you all to come home safely."

"Thank you, Mrs. McCarthy." Mattie blinked away the moisture that threatened, touched by the sincerity in Mrs. McCarthy's bright blue eyes. Not everyone from the territory evoked unpleasant memories, she mused.

The men rapidly moved out in the gray light and James rode up, leading her mount. Mattie swung into the saddle and heeled Sensible, moving to follow Will as the sun's first rays touched the horizon.

They rode at a steady pace until the sun was straight above them. Will called a halt then, and allowed the party to rest for a quick half-hour. Mattie walked away from the lounging men to find privacy behind a clump of bushes. Remembering how closely Will had guarded her six years before, she wondered if he'd follow, but didn't look to see.

"Bless you, Cousin Beatrice," Mattie muttered to herself as she pulled her heavy Levis back into place. She hadn't had time to boil the stiff garment into softness, and the new denims would've chafed her tender skin unmercifully, except that she wore a pair of Beatrice's old ankle length muslin pantaloons as a lining. Mattie chuckled at the tiny pink ribbons hidden beneath the heavy pants—yet they served a most needed service.

Walking back to the resting men, she noted Will leaning against a tree on the outer edge of the circle. He may not have followed her, she mused, but he knew exactly where she'd been. Things hadn't changed that much.

They kept their even pace throughout the afternoon and reached the Bascomb cabin without incident. They were the second party to arrive; Caleb's group appeared fully entrenched around the area.

Will dismounted and, flipping his reins to Bob, strode over to look in the cabin. Several men lay about on their gear. One man tended a pot over the fireplace.

"Okay, men, after you eat, clear out. Miss Mattie will have the cabin for the night."

"Aw, shucks, Will. Why do we hafta clear out? Ain't no objection fer the little gal to share the place," jollied Joe Wilson, a man with a heavy, unshaven face.

"Plenty o'room here," agreed another.

"Out!" roared Will.

"Awr right, awr right. No need ter get riled," Joe grumbled. Cupping his hand around his mouth, he leaned toward his buddy and mock-whispered, "Thought she was a free woman, ya know? He acts like he owns 'er."

Will moved in two swift strides and stood over the man. "For the purposes of this trip, Joe, I do! And I don't want any of you men near her. Got that?"

"Sure, Will." The man half rose. "We was only funnin'."

"You keep that kind of funnin' away from Miss Adams,

do you hear?" Will forced his body to relax. "Now, move out."

Will turned to watch the men depart and saw Mattie standing in the doorway, her eyes large as Kansas sunflowers. Blazes—she'd heard it all, probably. She spun away and disappeared from sight.

He stalked to the door and leaped through.

"Will," called Caleb. "I need . . ."

"Not now, Caleb."

"I think you'd better."

Will stopped abruptly. Where was she? She'd vanished around the corner of the cabin. He'd have to let her go for now and talk to her later. "What is it?"

"This way." Caleb led him to the stand of trees where the horses had been picketed. Bob and Frank were unpacking supplies. Caleb threw them a questioning glance.

"These are my men. You can say what you have to say," Will assured him.

"Look at this." Caleb reached behind a tree and brought out a water bag. It was a large one used to carry extra water for cooking. It was empty, and Caleb pushed a finger against a small rip in the bottom and then held it up for Will to inspect.

It had been slashed.

"You know how this happened?" Will asked.

"No."

Will thought for a moment. "You have another?"

"Yep. But this'll cut down on what we can carry."

"Okay. Caution your men to fill their canteens to the top at the spring. And keep your eyes open."

"Sure thing, Will."

He stomped back to the center of activity. Now he had an enemy in the posse. Besides Smith and Landon, that was. Would either of them do such a thing? Smith resented him, even possibly hated him, but he was hot for revenge against the outlaws and Will doubted he'd do anything to jeopardize that. Besides, Smith was riding with the sheriff's bunch, and they hadn't come in yet.

Will glanced around the camp. He smelled bacon at Bob's supper fire. Frank still tended the horses. The other men stirred about, talking and settling themselves in for the night. James was in the midst of a group of men, engrossed in conversation. Mattie was nowhere in sight.

Removing his hat, he wiped the moisture from his forehead against his sleeve and then clamped the hat back in place. She'd probably be at that little bend where the spring spilt out of the rocks behind the cabin. He remembered he'd found her there once before, on the morning after she'd cried herself to sleep in his arms. Lord, she'd still been half a child, then, but he'd never forgotten how right she felt or ceased to want her since.

Long strides carried him to the spot, but she wasn't there. A small boot print led him to the trickling stream, and he saw where she'd mounted again, and crossed. A small outcropping of trees and brush filled the far slope, all in full early summer leaf, making an effective screen. Carefully sweeping his gaze from side to side, he searched, but he saw nothing out of place.

Stepping across the stream, he started up the slope, following the prints to where they ran out of sight around the curve of the hill.

He'd just about decided to go back for his horse when a small rabbit suddenly jumped and ran for the underbrush. What had startled the animal? He heard the blowing of a horse and then around the curve Mattie came into view. She spotted him. Unsmiling, she directed her horse toward him.

Outlaw's Brat

"Where in blazes have you been?" Will burst out.

She came on, not answering.

Anger at her deliberate defiance of his orders to remain in sight of him or James bubbled over. "You know well enough you're not to go off on your own like that."

She halted her mount a yard from where he stood. The outline of her face was diffused against the background of her hat, but her whole body was etched against the failing light. He couldn't read her thoughts in the opaque brown eyes, but the set of her mouth caused her chin to thrust forward, reminding him of her old gesture of resistance.

Her voice was stony when she answered. "I'll do as I please."

"No, you won't. You'll do as *I* please."

"Contrary to what you'd like others to believe, Mr. McCarthy, you don't own me!"

Will gritted his teeth. He knew it! That small skirmish with Joe had caused more repercussions that a stick of dynamite. It outraged him. But rather than wanting to soothe her, his overwhelming need at the moment was for her to see reason. His reason.

"Well, Miss Adams, contrary to what you'd like to believe," he mocked, using her own words, "I remain boss of this expedition, this is my outfit, and since you're a part of it, that makes you mine too!"

"Oh no! No, sir, you are quite wrong! I don't, and will never belong to any man!"

"Never?" How could she say never when there had been this unspoken bond between them for six years? "Never?"

He moved with the speed of a striking rattler. One long step and he was close beside her, one hand clamping the pommel of her saddle, the other around her thigh.

His voice lowered to a menacing growl. "Never say never, Mattie."

The heat generated from his hand on her thigh seeped into Mattie's stomach and spread. Her heart thumped wildly as she recognized an unknown danger in Will. Unmitigated desire leaped from the eyes that had deepened to sapphire, and his mouth went hard beneath the smooth mustache.

Mattie's breath caught in her throat as his hands suddenly circled her waist, pulling her from the saddle. Her feet hit the ground and she jerked backward, slamming into Sensible. The horse snorted, skittishly sidestepping, and Mattie took another backward step.

She reached up to push her hat back into place, but Will's hands brushed hers aside. He jerked her hat away, letting it tumble unheeded to the ground. Her long dark plait swung free. Sliding his hands along her jaw line to cup the back of her head, Will brought her face close to his. With barely a hesitation, he touched his lips to hers with sure, firm pressure.

Fire sparks lit her insides. The sensation reached her mouth, giving her an instant, unwanted, all-consuming hunger. Mattie's mind fought and denied it in spite of her body's reaction. Will had everything in life; he couldn't have her too. She wouldn't give in . . .

She valiantly battled the desire to press against him, the raging need to open her lips. The battle was going against her, she felt herself slipping over the edge of control.

It pleased her beyond reason.

It frightened her beyond thought.

His mouth lifted. Confusion swirled into clouds, obscuring her mind of all but the seductive appeal of the moment. Passion reigned in the deep sapphire blue windows of his soul, demanding, yearning, questioning. She let her lashes drop to fan out over her cheeks.

With iron restraint, Will reluctantly allowed an inch to separate their lips. He'd scared her. His precious Mattie. He hadn't intended to; dear God, no, he wanted to love her beyond anything in life.

Yet he couldn't deny what he saw in her eyes. He wanted to assault the confusion there, to kiss her again to remove any barrier between them.

He felt her frightened trembling along his body, and her short, shallow breathing against his chest. He had to let her go, yet even through layers of clothing, the warmth of her rounded breasts pressing against him agitated his tenuous control. He sucked in a ragged gulp of air.

Why was she so afraid of him?

Thudding hooves in the distance intruded on his consciousness and he heard his name called. Had that voice called before? Awareness of their surroundings returned with the abruptness of being splashed with ice water. Dropping his arms, he swung away and took a few steps to the edge of the trees, looking toward camp. A single rider had come in.

"Mattie . . ." he turned his head to look over his shoulder. But she'd remounted and was already moving out of the trees, kicking her horse into a trot.

He wished he'd kissed her again, and again wished he hadn't kissed her at all. How could he promise her protection from other men when he knew his own need was a bigger threat to her?

Stomping across the rippling stream, he took a moment to splash his face with cold water, then continued back to the center of camp, coming up behind a group of men. At the center of the hubbub stood the new arrival. It was Sandy.

"My God, man, am I glad to see you." Will eagerly reached out to shake hands with his long-trusted friend. "When did you get back to the ranch?"

"Not long after you'd left, Will." Sandy shook hands just as vigorously. "I only took time out to eat, talk to Luke, and change horses. Looks like I almost missed the big shindig."

"You ain't missed a lot, yet," said James. " 'Cept a run-in with Smith an' that crowd."

"Yeah, Luke told me all about it. So you had to pull out your papers, huh? Well, I suspected it'd come to it."

"Frank, take care of Sandy's horse," Will called, and drew Sandy away. Jerking his chin toward James, the three men hunkered down beside Bob's cooking fire, set apart from the others. "What kept you, anyway? I expected you days ago!"

"Ran into some trouble down by the border, but it didn't keep me longer than necessary. Sweet sister, Will, I been ridin' all night, now all day. Ain't ya goin' to feed a man?"

" 'Bout to dish up," Bob said. "Reckon' you can have firsts."

"Did ya see anything of the sheriff's outfit?" queried James. "They shoulda been here by now."

"Nary a sign," Sandy replied.

Will waited until Bob began dishing up, then glanced about for Mattie. He spied her brushing her mount beyond the other horses. He watched the top of her head bob as she briskly stroked the horse's flanks. Satisfied with her whereabouts, he left her alone. Heaven alone knew how he'd work off his own frustrations.

Eight

The next day, Mattie followed a narrow animal track alongside the river, which led her up and around a curve from camp. While below, the river spread out along low accessible banks, here, the river narrowed, the current ran swifter, and the banks steepened. Scrambling over stones and rough ground, she continued on the slender path. A perfect spot to bathe, that was what she searched for, and then she spotted it.

As the current rushed and then slowed, the water had formed a tiny, beautiful bay, with only a few feet of rocky beach. Behind it, the bank rose steeply, forming a protective cliff. Above, the high ground leveled out again, but eventually sloped gently back down to meet the river.

Mattie quickly scouted the area, but the place was quiet and serene. She didn't hesitate another moment to shed her clothes. She'd grown used to being clean, and two days of hard riding was reason enough to find a spot to bathe. She'd dutifully told Will where she was going. He'd nodded, and said to be careful.

Entering the river to her thighs, she lay down to submerge her body and leaned back to completely soak her head. Mattie sighed with contentment. The water was bliss. Ice cold and silky, it soothed her as it lapped her skin. It would be lovely to spend an hour here, but the icy temperatures brought reality. Besides, the sun was setting and supper would be ready. Reaching for her soap, she began to lather her hair.

Moments later, she rinsed off and left the water. Her long chestnut hair lay in wet tangles to her hips. After a quick rubdown, she wrapped her towel about her head, turban style. She'd dry it later by the fire.

Mattie stepped into her clean pair of pantaloons from Cousin Beatrice and chuckled. This pair had blue ribbons and an edging of lace around the legs. Still amused, she bent over and reached for the camisole top from her bundle, and a clean shirt. She slipped the camisole over her head and pulled it down.

Reverberation followed a sudden ringing sound almost instantly, bouncing around the hills. Mattie jerked to stand straight, cotton shirt dangling from her fingers.

A rifle shot. And close!

Mattie spun on her heel to search the banks above her. Glinting sunlight from a rifle barrel twinkled and danced against the dark kneeling figure whose silhouette stood out against the late afternoon sky.

That gun was aimed at her!

Shock kept her motionless for an instant and then she sprinted away. In rapid succession, a second and third explosion of sound rent the air. Something hit her arm.

She knelt against the steep bank next to a boulder, trying to make herself small. She was only partially hidden, and a fourth shot ricocheted against the stone in front of her. Splinters of rock flew against her bare arms and face.

Who was firing at her and why? How far from camp was she? Surely Cousin James, on guard for her a bit out of sight, would hear the shots and come to her rescue. But how quickly? In time?

The reverberating sounds died away and quiet reigned. Slow seconds crawled by while rough stone scraped against her skin and poked with hard edges through the thin muslin of the pantaloons and camisole.

Her arm bled and she clapped her hand on the wound to stop it. Shivering, she noticed the blood seeping through her fingers. Oh, she had to do something!

Off came her camisole, and she quickly rolled it into a pad. Then she slipped her arms through the shirt, buttoning it two quick buttons before another bullet whizzed by her again.

The air grew silent once more.

She could just kick herself for becoming such an Easterner! It seemed she'd forgotten all rules of survival and now carelessness had left her helpless. Her rifle leaned against a far rock, close to where her dirty clothes lay some yards from her hiding place. She couldn't reach it without exposing herself to view.

The silence continued. Was he still there? She listened in tense stillness.

Edging out, Mattie twisted to look up. The rifle spurted again, instantly followed by another, more distant gun. She jerked back, noting the jab of splintered rock. She scarcely felt it. Neither did she feel the blood trickling down her arm. Moments passed while Mattie waited, scarcely breathing, not daring to move.

The eerie quiet broke when a sudden cascade of tumbling stone and earth rained down nearby. Her heart leapt to her throat. Someone was scrambling down the bank.

Mattie turned to face the attacker. Automatically she dropped the towel, while her other hand clutched a jagged stone.

Dirty black boots hit the level ground and a bent figure raised to stand tall, then turned toward her.

"Will!" Her whisper wrenched from her throat. "Thank God, it's you!"

"Mattie?" His voice sounded as jagged as her stone. "My God, Mattie, you're hurt." He leaped to her side. "How bad? Darlin', how bad?" His voice held anguish and he slid an arm around her shoulders to hold her close.

"I don't know . . ." Was she going into shock? Everything swam, and Will had just called her darling. Or had she imagined it?

"Let me see." He tugged at the shirt.

Mattie instinctively held it tightly closed. Why hadn't she buttoned it tighter? Blood oozed along her arm, soaking the sleeve, and she noticed it was all over the towel. Her knees went weak, and her head felt light.

"Will . . ." She could barely form his name.

Taking one look at her white face, Will scooped her up and carried her to the edge of the river, close to where her heaped clothing lay. He sat her down carefully, and went down on his haunches beside her. Grabbing the closest thing at hand, he wet it and peeled the shirt from her arm. He took one look at the bloody camisole, and peeled that away too. He began washing the blood away, exposing a deep gash where the bullet had plowed through her flesh. All the while, Mattie gripped the towel to cover her bosom, unaware she was pushing her breasts to rounded globes above the covering.

"Where's James?" she whispered.

"Trying to find the varmint."

Will worked swiftly to bind the arm with her neckerchief. He finished the task and leaned back on his heels. She was paler than he'd ever seen her, but her eyes were losing their dazed expression. Dampness from her hair made her shoulders gleam like rich satin. Reaching out, he allowed himself only to brush a damp strand of hair from her cheek. She began to tremble in reaction.

"Who was it, Mattie? Did you get a good look at him?"

"No, his b-back was to the sun so his f-face was in shadow." She turned her back to him, buttoning the shirt awkwardly. The helplessness she'd felt overwhelmed her. She'd faced that level of helplessness once before, when her mother had been absent from their cabin. She'd been subject to Larry's whims.

Mattie shivered. She'd left the hideout soon after—as soon as her ma and she could plan. Then Ma . . . Her ma had given her life for Mattie. Frightened and alone, she'd been terrified. But who would threaten her now?

"I c-couldn't g-get to my rifle," she stuttered out.

For a moment, layers of education and years of Eastern polish peeled away as the helplessness of her situation seared Mattie's mind. She shuddered hard with the realization that someone wanted to kill her.

Will gently pulled her, unresisting, into his lap. She nestled into him, resting her cheek against his shoulder, and drew sustenance from his strength.

"Mattie girl, don't." He rocked her tightly against himself and wrapped his arms around her for comfort. Shifting her slightly so he could see her face, he again brushed a lock of hair from her cheek. His hand slid under the long damp hair and stroked her back. The clean scent of the soap she'd used drifted from her skin. Bending his head, he kissed the bridge of her nose, and then her forehead.

Another shiver coursed through her and once more he placed his lips against her skin. His need to comfort was quickly changing to another kind of need. "You'll be all right now, Mattie girl. I'll never be that far from you again," he murmured, giving her a fervent vow as he moved from her cheek to her mouth with quick, gentle little pressures. "Never."

Mattie accepted the kisses without returning them, but she stopped shivering and moved even closer into his heat. His strong hands felt wonderfully warm and she nuzzled her face against his neck. This was Will, her trusted childhood hero. Her protector. The Will her foolish young heart had yearned for. He made her feel coddled and precious and safe, and she wanted more.

Yet he was a man who kissed her with hot passion, a man's demanding kiss.

His lips grew bolder. She made a low sound of protest as she pushed gently away, even while wanting to give him what his mouth sought.

Pounding hooves thudded hard against the earth above them, the sound magnified in the evening stillness, and Mattie's mind jerked back to reality. She sat up in panic, still clutching the towel.

"Oh, Will. They're coming. Please . . . my clothes." She scrambled away from him and reached out for the scattered items with her one good arm.

"This one?" Will held up her blue jeans.

"Yes, yes. Give them to me."

The hoof beats . . . Closer!

"Close your eyes, Will!" Mattie squealed, frantic. She didn't take time to see if he followed her demand, fumbling and pushing her legs through and yanking the front closed.

"Keep your back turned," she admonished. She tried to listen to the oncoming men. They were almost there, and her fingers kept missing the blasted buttonholes.

"Here, stand still." Will stood inches in front of her, his fingers calmly pulling the buttons through. "Now your boots," he instructed.

She sat again while Will found her socks. Just when

she'd gotten her toes into one, she heard Sandy.

"What goes on there! We heard shots," he yelled down to them from above.

"Yeah, Sandy, we've had some trouble," Will shouted back. James stepped forward from behind Sandy, shrugging slightly. "Bring my horse down here. You'll have to come down the slope up yonder."

Waiting for the men to bring Will's horse, Mattie finished dressing and gathered her dirty clothes. She'd never been almost naked in front of a man . . .

At least not like today. She never let herself dwell on the terror she'd faced as a child, nor the pain.

Odd. She hadn't minded her near nudity until Sandy and the other men had come. Why was that? And she'd liked Will's closeness, the warmth and comfort, especially his stroking hand. Remembering it made her skin tingle with pleasure. She wished Cousin James hadn't come quite so soon. Did that make her a hussy?

What had Will thought? Did he think she was? Shame rose up like bile. She hadn't hurried to dress until she'd had to, and she'd allowed him to stroke her back. In fact, she'd sat in his lap dressed in very little clothing. He probably did think she was a slut, as the townspeople thought her. Willing to give away her favors.

Oh, how had she allowed it to happen? Will wasn't her hero. He was a man like all the rest.

Tears of exhaustion and overwrought emotions prickled against the backs of her eyes. What did it matter, anyway? She'd just have to guard herself better.

Will took her uninjured arm to help her over the rocky path, and they walked to where it widened enough to allow for the horses. Mattie looked hopefully toward James and Sandy where they waited. She could ride back to camp.

Thank goodness, the others remained on top of the low cliff. The pain from her arm throbbed, and she wasn't sure she could face many questions.

"What's up?" Sandy asked when he handed Will the reins.

"Mattie girl, you okay?" asked James.

"No, she's not okay." Deep anger hardened Will's voice. "Someone shot at her from the bank while she was bathing. She took a crease in the arm."

"Shot? The devil you say . . ." James's voice crackled with shock. "Who would do such a thing?"

"I don't know. I couldn't get close enough to see, and I was trying to scare him off at the same time I was scrambling to reach Mattie." Will threw a furious glance at James. "Why did you let her go so far without an escort?"

"Well, I never thought . . ." stumbled James. "I tried to get to the shooter, but—"

"That's enough!" Mattie grated out. "I came up this far because I wanted to be alone. It's not anyone's fault but mine."

Will nearly cursed himself out loud. Her face was paper white and her eyes looked like huge brown pansies. They had plenty of time to discuss the real problems of the matter later. The danger she'd just encountered had made him crazy with fear for her safety.

"Come." Will struggled to soften his command. He lifted her to his saddle and mounted behind her.

This was getting to be a habit, Mattie thought, when his arm slid around her middle. Riding double! Maybe Will ought to breed a horse for this purpose. A horse that's long in the back. But then it would sag in the middle. The thought almost made her giggle. She felt lightheaded.

Hold on now, Mattie! Don't get silly. Everything is crazy

right now . . . I don't want to do anything foolish . . .

She peered through the twilight where pinpoints of campfire lights shone invitingly. Were they at camp already? The distance had seemed long in walking, but short in riding. She drooped with tiredness as she slid from Will's arms and turned away.

Mattie found her tent pitched on a slight plateau, apart from the main body of men. Without waiting for the deluge of questions to fall, she crawled in, lay on top of her bedroll, and fell asleep.

Sometime later, she felt someone remove her boots and cover her. Long hours into the night, she woke thirsty and stumbled out, looking for water.

"Mattie?" Will was by her side in seconds. The low embers of the distant fire looked bright in the dark. She turned, gazing at the sleeping men, making dark lumps against the night. The cool air caused goose flesh to rise on her arms.

"I'm thirsty. Where's the water?"

"Sit here, and I'll get you some." He settled her on a large log by the nearest fire, where she mindlessly watched the smoldering coals until he placed a cup of water in her hand. She drank it without pausing for breath.

"Are you hungry?" His voice was low, intimate.

"Yes, I guess so." She glanced about her at the sleeping figures near her, hoping she hadn't wakened them.

Will dipped from a pot over the coals, placed a cold biscuit on the edge of the plate, and handed it to her. Flavored with bacon and pepper, the beans were doubly hot. She nibbled at the cold bread and laid it back on the plate. She couldn't seem to swallow much.

"Is your arm bothering you?"

"A little. More stiff than pain, I think."

"Mattie, about today . . ."

"I'm all right now, Will." To prove it, she took another bite of food.

"I've been thinking. Maybe you shouldn't go on."

"Not go on?" Her spoon clattered against the tin plate. Her eyes flew open. She was wide awake now.

Near them, a sleeping man rolled over and another half rose on his elbow. When he saw who it was who had waked him, he lay back again.

She lowered her voice. "Will, I've got to continue. I have to find my mother. And you know the campaign will fail without me. It would be the purest luck if you were to find your way alone."

Will rose and paced around the fire. Spitfire! She was right, but placing her in danger from their own camp hadn't been part of her bargain. Or his. Close questioning of the men had revealed no ready answers. That the attacker came from their own camp was doubtful in every mind but his. Yet he didn't know who to narrow his suspicions on. Most of the men had seemed honestly outraged over the incident. Even the men he distrusted.

But he wouldn't allow such a thing to happen again! Earlier in the evening, Will had assigned Bram to keep a close watch on Nick Fulton.

He had no evidence to suspect Nick, except for a recent occasion in which Nick had been seen in the company of a suspected member of the Dorsey gang. And he'd seemed to have a lot of money at the Lucky Chance gambling tables. Since they'd started, Nick had kept low, quiet and casually friendly, but Will was through taking any chances.

Sandy kept tabs on the goings-on of Caleb Walters's men. They seemed to be all right, not one suspicious act among them. That left Tom Kimmel's group. Maybe it would be a good idea to have Bob become more friendly with their cook.

Will's hands curved into fists when he thought of the danger he was putting Mattie in. But they had to go on. Cleaning the territory of trash, making it safe for all of them, meant safety for her, as well. And they'd all work harder at protecting her. Even now, James slept next to her tent wall, vowing, like himself, never to let her out of sight again. He'd raised his head when Mattie exited her tent.

Will reached for the coffee pot. Filling two cups, he handed Mattie one. He placed one booted foot on the log beside her, then leaned toward her as he spoke urgently. "Mattie, I know you need your moments of privacy, but promise me you'll never go off alone again?"

Mattie put her plate down and sipped at the coffee. They'd been having a tug of war over this issue ever since they'd met when she was fourteen. Yet he'd always cared for her . . .

She recalled a particular incident when she'd first met Will and his men.

She hadn't eaten for two days, and she thought her stomach had hit her backbone. After the Indian clash, they'd traveled a bit and made camp alongside the river.

She'd sat apart on a rock, watching quietly. Her gaze was everywhere, her mouth watering. She hid her trembling hands under her legs until the food was ready.

When Will placed meat and bread into her hands, she scarcely contained her eagerness. He turned to get another plate, and she quickly shoveled food into her mouth. She'd never tasted anything so good. Her cheeks were full of biscuits and meat when he turned to look at her. She raised her chin and chewed even while the embarrassed heat rose in her cheeks.

Afterward, while all the others were preoccupied, she sneaked away in the dark into the bushes. After she relieved herself, she walked slowly back up the hill thinking of sleep, only to find Will waiting at the point of her disappearance.

"What are you doing there?" she questioned, her breath caught in her throat. Distrust showed in her outthrust chin.

"I wanted to be within earshot if you needed . . . ah, help."

"I don't need any help, thank you. Don't follow me again!"

"As long as you are under my care, I'll take steps to see that you are protected."

"I'm not under your care. I'm under my own care."

"Well, until we get back to civilization, I'm in charge."

"Not of me, you're not."

"Do you want to go your own way then? Which way is town? Where are you headed?"

"Never you mind. I'll—I'll just—" She bit her lip, confused. Where was town? What direction? And what town was he speaking of?

"You might just be thankful I'm watching your back." He spoke mildly, even a bit teasingly.

She was thankful, but painfully shy. Mattie could never tell him. She had never doubted his protectiveness. She'd never met anyone who wanted to protect her before. She didn't understand quite what he was saying. Yet instinctively, she did.

And now at last, Will had been proven right. Today, she'd been in real danger.

"All right, Will, you win. I'll remain within shouting distance of either you or Cousin James at all times."

"Good." He let out a long, gusty breath. "Good. But I haven't won everything yet, Mattie girl." His voice dropped to a low rumble and his mouth took on a determined line. "But I want to. In time."

Mattie sat silently, holding herself very still. Did Will mean routing the outlaws or winning her complete surrender?

The warmth in his eyes deepened and the air between them hung heavy and expectant. Will hadn't meant only winning this battle with the outlaws. Suddenly, she was sure his intention was to win with her, to exact her unconditional surrender. To possess her totally.

To possess? Like her mother had been possessed by a man?

The thought reverberated around her mind, bouncing off old memories like a child's ball. Possession—her childhood terror! Years of her childhood had been hell.

Fear trembled along her spine. Old, deliberately forgotten fear. She tried to push it away, to make it disappear. But the trust and ease she'd felt with Will that afternoon seeped away like hissing steam into thin air. Disappearing steam . . . gone.

Gone too, was the mellowing need for his stroking hand.

A bright red coal flared and sputtered, then dropped away from the burning log, making a soft sighing sound in the quiet.

Mattie carefully lowered her cup to the ground and stood, her gaze on the earth. Will eased away a few inches, but remained within touching distance. She glanced at him, trying hard to read his innermost thoughts. No tenderness shone through.

Will was a good man by anyone's standards, and she'd

loved him with all of her being, once, but . . . No.

She inhaled deeply, once, twice, and let her breath out.

No. She wouldn't allow any man to take complete possession of any part of her. Men, even good men, often promised anything, everything, to obtain a woman, but then . . . .

"Mattie?" Will said.

Mattie pushed past him and almost ran to her tent.

Will gathered himself to stand, and watched Mattie's retreat with longing and frustration. Had he made a tactical error? He yearned to soothe her fears as he had this afternoon, to erase the childhood he knew still haunted her. He wanted to replace all her troubles with his love. How could he when he couldn't breach her barriers?

Dismay filled him. Would she ever be ready to accept him? Ever be ready to love? Yesterday's rush of passion had turned to tenderness today when she'd allowed him to hold her close. She'd even responded a little. Now this.

Pacing around the fire again, he couldn't hold back his groan of agitation. How could he teach her that love was a mutual giving, of caring, and not just taking or using? He had so much love, so much tenderness to give her, he was aching with the fullness of it.

Exhaustion seeped along his bones and he returned to bed. He had to hold on to hope. She would be his! It was merely a matter of patience.

The rain rolled in with the morning. Mattie poked her head out of her tent flap, and her face was instantly wet. She ducked back in to put on her rain slicker.

"Mattie," Will called, "we need to change that bandage before we leave this morning."

Oh, bother! She bit her lip. She couldn't stand out in the rain with a bare arm and shoulder while he changed her bandage, but she hesitated about inviting him into her tent.

Oh, bother . . . She tried to decide what to do.

"Mattie?"

"Yes, I hear you. All right, wait just a minute." Pulling her arm out of the shirtsleeve, she buttoned the front around her chest. It showed too much of the rounded curves, and she pulled it up higher. But the button wasn't placed right for such a situation and the opening was too loose. It kept falling lower.

"Mattie, I'm coming in."

"No, wait!" She looked up as he pushed through, hunched over, and sat down almost on top of her. She frowned. "You should've waited."

He ignored her protest and turned around to pull a pan of steaming water through the flap.

"It'll just take a little while, Mattie."

"Fine," she snapped, turning her head away from him. She obeyed silently when he told her to lift and lower her arm.

Will stole regular glances at her averted face. If the wound hurt, or the water stung, she gave no sign. Careful not to speculate on what was under the drooping shirtfront, he grimly determined not to start something he couldn't finish. Not right now, at any rate.

He snipped the strip of cotton he had used and tied the ends. "There, that's done."

"Thank you."

"Mattie, if you'd like to rest, we can hold over here for a day or so until the rain lets up."

Her head whipped around and she sat up straight. "Not on your life."

"It's going to be mighty wet and slow going. Are you sure?"

"Absolutely." Her chin tilted in the old way.

"Okay." He stooped to exit. "We strike camp in one hour."

"I'll be ready."

A few minutes later, she sat on her heels around a sputtering cook fire like the others, trying to keep her food dry while she ate. James asked questions about the shooting while Sandy and Bram listened. She told the incident as concisely as she could, except for the fact of her near nudity, and Will's kisses.

"Mattie, I'm right sorry I wasn't more attentive when ya needed me." James's rough old voice sounded shamed. "I guess I just got caught up in all the excitement an' didn't remember I'm here for yer protection just as much as gettin' those outlaws."

"Oh, Cousin James, you couldn't have known something like that would happen," she reassured, patting his hand. "I should've been more alert, too, but I was careless."

"Too bad you didn't see him better, Miss Mattie," commented Sandy. "Didn't anything seem different, about his clothes, or gun?"

"I only saw him for an instant, Sandy, and then ran for cover. The sun was at his back." She shook her head, watching rainfall from her dripping hat. "I'll think about it today."

The first party of men moved out, and Sandy got up to leave. "Glad you're all right, Miss Mattie."

"Thank you kindly, Sandy."

Sheriff Kimmel sat down on the log near her, and she repeated her story. Knowing they were leaving soon, she wasn't surprised when his questions were brief. He made little comment and thanked her politely when he left.

The long day was miserable and wet, climbing into the

mountains most of the way. That night's camp was huddled together, for there was no good ground to accommodate so large a party. It was too much to put up the tent in the rain, so Mattie slept between Will and James under a hastily rigged tarpaulin.

The next morning started out no better. Mattie was wet to the skin in spite of the slicker as she took the lead with Will. She searched for recognizable guideposts as they rode. The area was fleshed out with full summer, and she frequently turned squinting eyes to the rear, trying to capture how it would have looked six years before, when she was going the opposite direction in that changing time between winter and spring.

Toward noon, the sky slowly cleared and the sun shone once more. When they came upon a stream within a small meadow, they made an early camp. Everyone seemed eager to spread their wet bedding and clothes to dry. Mattie gladly shed her slicker.

After the other two outfits straggled in, Will agreed to send out a couple of hunting parties. They could use fresh meat, and this would be the last chance to get it. From here on, they needed to be doubly alert to their whereabouts, especially their noise, and the possibility of running into some of the outlaw band.

Mattie gazed a long time at the range in front of them. Six years before she'd been a desperate youngster riding for her life from that mountain stronghold. The closer they drew, the more she fought the old fear.

It raised all her hackles. She swallowed hard. She didn't want to enter there . . . except for her mother.

Nine

How close were they? Another two days? One? Even Mattie didn't know for sure, Will thought. If she could remember exactly, then they wouldn't waste time. But six years was a long time and memories slipped away.

Will approached Mattie directly after the hunters left. "How're you feeling, Mattie?"

"Fine." Mattie glanced at him curiously. Whenever he used that conciliatory tone of voice, he wanted something. She pursed her lips.

"You feel like a ride?"

"Where to?"

"See the top of that ridge? There's still hours of daylight left. Thought we might see quite a distance from there. Get the lay of the land. You might recognize your route more clearly."

"That's true." She glanced at him in speculation. "All right, let's go."

Mattie wasn't at all surprised when she found Sensible and Lariat already saddled, but she made no comment. She hung her still-damp hat on the pommel and mounted.

They left the meadow, traveling north. They climbed at angles around trees and boulders, avoiding a washout. Switching directions, they climbed higher. Finally, they dismounted to advance the last few feet on foot.

"Oh, my! What a view!" Mattie panted. The last few yards had been very steep.

"Hmm," he agreed. "You can see quite a distance."

Breezes buffeted them with sweet, clear air. Loose strands of Mattie's hair blew about her face and she brushed them from her eyes. At her back, Will's hands came down on her shoulders, and her heart picked up speed when she felt the warmth of his tall body.

"Look around, Mattie," he said, pivoting her slowly to view the valleys, mountain peaks, and canyons. "What looks familiar? Can you tell where you came from six years ago?"

Mattie studied the area closely. Certain formations took on remembered feelings and emotions.

"I can't be certain, Will, but I think I came down that canyon through that opening yonder." She pointed to a barely discernable opening far up a long, narrow canyon. "It took me a time to get out at this end."

Turning, she searched for the pass she knew to be there, hidden somewhere below where they stood. "I'd almost given up and was going to retrace my way when I found the passage."

Yes, she'd almost given up. She'd run out of food and debated about finding game. But her fear of a rifle shot being heard by some of Dorsey's bunch had kept the rifle in its scabbard. She'd no luck with fishing, either, and left the river in disgust.

"How long was that before you found us?"

"About three days, as I recollect." Three days of hunger and growing desperation. She'd feared she might die where no one would ever find her.

"Where did you come out?"

Mattie gazed down on the opposite side of the mountain they'd just ascended. "I can't see it from here, but it has to be below us, on this side of the mountain."

Will glanced at the sun. They still had some daylight left.

"Okay, let's see if you can find it."

Descending was faster than coming up, but the loose rock against the slippery rain-soaked earth was cause for concern. Will held her hand while they stumbled, slid, and ran down the slope. When they reached the horses, she was quick to withdraw from his hold.

Mattie scraped the mud from her boots against a large rock. Will did the same. They mounted, and Mattie took the lead. Stopping twice to get her bearings, Mattie continued descending for some way before beginning a zigzag pattern around the curve of the mountain.

Abruptly, the foliage ended, and so did the easy slope. In front of her, the mountain plunged away in a long drop into a small canyon.

"Whoa, hold on, Sensible." Mattie stopped, grateful for a jutting pine that called her attention to the sheer drop. Hesitantly, she eased her horse into an angled direction, carefully guiding him past the dangerous curve and down once more. Her nerves tightened. The ground beneath them didn't look safe.

Some yards later, an animal trail, narrow and treacherous, cut into the mountainside. It disappeared around a curve below them. It hadn't been used for a long while. Reining in, Mattie twisted in her saddle to look at Will.

"I don't know, Will. This looks like little more than an animal track, and it's pretty muddy. Shall we go on?"

"Are you sure you came this way?"

"Almost sure. I've never been on this particular trail, but I seem to remember starting down a blind canyon like this one. It looks familiar from this direction, anyway. And the pass I eventually found was beyond this canyon. I think we're above there now."

"Can you see the pass?"

"No. But it has to be there. Farther down, perhaps, around this mountainside."

Will studied the area in front of them. True, it was muddy, but it looked solid enough. He wanted to be sure it was the right way or eliminate it. "Okay, lead on."

Mattie squeezed Sensible with her knees, giving him the signal to move forward. Mud slid under his hooves. The horse swung his head nervously and sidestepped.

"C'mon, boy. It'll be all right if we're careful."

Sensible gingerly started down the trail. It wasn't long before he stubbornly halted altogether.

Stones and mud covered the area, erasing any signs of the trail. Looking up, Mattie saw where the wet earth had broken away. The slide was recent, for some of the mud looked glistening smooth and shiny in the afternoon sun, while other parts of the earth looked gouged and ragged.

Will surveyed the scene. There was no way around it. The mountain dropped in a continuous line on the other side, all the way to the canyon floor.

"All right, Mattie. We'll have to go back the way we came."

Mattie heard his disappointment, but said nothing. They had no choice but to turn back.

Will paused to give one last look before he cautiously backed his horse a few steps. "Hold it right where you are a minute," he instructed. "This'll be a bit tricky."

Will dismounted, and carefully backed Lariat, guiding him until he'd reached a slight widening on the trail. Letting out a breath of relief, he turned his horse.

A rumbling rolled around the mountain above them, causing Lariat to pull against the reins and prance. Will looked up to see if the rain had sneaked back in, but there were no clouds in the sky.

A muffled explosion of earth and rocks burst above him just as he turned back in Mattie's direction. Just as she screamed.

"Will! It's sliding again!"

"Quick, Mattie." Letting go of Lariat, he raced, slipping and sliding, toward her. "Dismount!"

Rocks and mud slithered toward them in a roar of noise. Sensible rolled his eyes wildly and fought the reins. Mattie clung to her saddle, afraid to try dismounting, afraid of being thrown. Her horse danced to face outward toward the drop, and Mattie prayed his footing would hold.

Boulders bounced within feet of them. Will clamped onto Sensible's reins and jerked the horse around. A wall of mud loomed close by, roaring down the mountainside, sending flying mud all over them. Will slid to his knees. Instantly, he was up again, pulling Mattie from the saddle, clutching her hard against his body. His boots slid from under him once more and he fell again, taking Mattie with him.

The horse half-reared frantically, and his hooves plunged down only inches from Will's hip and thigh. Will held onto both Mattie and the reins with a ferocious grip.

Mattie felt the rough edge of stone against her shoulder. Reaching out, she clutched solid rock and held fast while she pulled herself up to stand. Will climbed to his feet beside her.

The roar of the slide ruled out any talk. Will started up the mountain trail again, grasping Mattie's arm in a brutal grip with one hand, and the reins of the snorting, jerking horse in the other.

Finding a rocky outcrop, Mattie clung for support as they struggled up the trail. Each step was torture as they slithered their way back to the place where Will had turned his mount only moments before.

Lariat was some yards up the path, standing with his head down. His reins had caught on a jutting boulder.

The noise of the rockslide slowly receded. Mattie didn't watch, didn't want to see if the mud flow had stopped. Continuing upward was all she could manage. They eased past the hazardous break; she felt the force of Will's breath gush against her ear.

Will tightened Sensible's reins to give him more direction, coaxing him to move up. More earth slid away as they edged toward higher ground. At last Mattie glanced down at the mudslide. She put her mouth next to Will's ear. "Look over your shoulder."

It looked starkly different. Boulder-strewn, the old trail completely obliterated, the area was widely covered in mud. Any hope of using that way into the canyon passage was blotted out.

"Looks like we're set to go in the long way," she murmured.

"Reckon so. But as least it'll be safer." He turned his attention to her. "How're you doing, Mattie girl?"

"I'll make it."

"Good."

They reached his mount, and he transferred Sensible's reins to Mattie. Lariat stood with his head bent low to the ground, snorting and blowing uneasily.

"It's okay now, fella," Will soothed, as he worked a long moment to free the reins. "Easy now."

As Will turned him, Lariat favored his left front hoof. Will let a curse roll. He stooped to examine his horse.

"What's the matter?"

"Lariat's lame."

"Oh, no!"

"Yep, 'fraid so," he acknowledged her dismay. "Looks like we walk all the way home."

"We can ride double on Sensible."

"But Lariat still has to go slow."

Will started up again, leading the limping Lariat. It was somewhat easier going now, but slower than before. Reaching the place where they had entered the trail, they discovered another path branching down the other side toward the meadow where the others were camped. Will stopped. They hadn't seen it before. Looking as slick and muddy as the rest of the mountainside, the trail seemed to grow wider as it descended.

"What do you think, Mattie? Do you know where this one leads? Does it look familiar?"

"No. Not at all," she replied, shaking her head. "When I arrived where the camp is now, I'd come through a much lower pass. This is bound to lead into it, though."

"Yeah." He looked at the lowering sun. They'd been out longer than he'd expected, and now it would take them twice as long to get back. He didn't dare trust an unknown trail.

"We'd better go back down the mountain the way we came up," he declared.

"Will, it'll be dark soon."

"So we move as fast as we can," he snapped.

Mattie was silent. Will was rarely in a bad mood. Only when things were beyond his control, she'd noticed, and then he often turned a situation around so he was in control again. But this time, he couldn't do much to change things. Lariat was limping badly. They'd have to go very carefully.

Mattie moved away from the trail as the mountainside flattened out. She paused to take stock of the area. Below, the ground was rougher and steeper than she remembered coming up. Glancing over her shoulder, she observed Will and Lariat's slow progress. She waited for them to catch up.

"Will, do you think we can cut around to the other side of the mountain from here? You know, without retracing exactly the way we came?"

"Hmm . . . yeah, we should be able to. We'll eventually see the campfires to guide us in."

Campfires! Mattie glanced at the fading light. It would be dark soon. They would have to move faster than this to get down the mountain far enough even to see the campfires. And they had twisted and turned frequently; finding the exact way out to the camp in the dark would be nearly impossible. Especially with a lame horse.

She stole a peek over her shoulder to assess their progress. Will's eyes were downcast to watch his footing. Taking her opportunity, Mattie assessed the situation. His figure was bedraggled, his left side covered with mud from shoulder down. His jeans sported a wide tear at the knee where he'd fallen. And he was limping, too—almost as bad as Lariat.

"Will!"

His gaze flew to her face at her demand for attention, the expression alert, ready for whatever she might need. Mattie held her breath. His face looked drawn, the skin around his eyes stretched. He was in pain.

"Why didn't you say you'd been hurt when you fell?"

He looked surprised. "We hardly had time, did we?"

"But you can't walk all the way down the mountain like that."

"There's no choice."

"You can ride Sensible and I'll lead Lariat."

"No."

"Why ever not?"

"Because I'm not taking any more chances of poor footing. I've got to see first hand where we're going."

"That's the real problem, isn't it? It'll be full dark within the hour, and we'll be stumbling around, not sure of where we are."

"You think so little of my wilderness skills, Mattie girl?"

"Will, for Pete's sake, even Sensible is more sensible than to try get down this mountain at night. Now, think about it."

"I'm usually the one asking that of you," he said with some humor.

Irritation at his logic made her want to scream. He would pick now to make jokes. It would take them hours to get back to camp, even in daylight, and if Will further injured his knee, they would be in even more difficulty.

"Well, it looks like this time I'm the one that's sensible," Mattie snapped. "You stay put and rest that leg while I look for a place to spend the night."

"Yes, ma'am."

She glanced at his face, suspicious of his sudden meekness. It wasn't like him to allow anyone but himself to make decisions. Thinking, she licked her bottom lip. He must be in more pain than she knew. Maybe he had really hurt himself. He hadn't hit his head, had he?

Leaving Sensible with Will, she began searching the area. The temperature was dropping quickly, and at this elevation it would be colder than a block of ice in January by the time she got a fire going. Too bad she couldn't find one of the caves to shelter them. She worried she wouldn't find dry wood.

Will limped to a smooth boulder and sat down. His pain was a reality, but laughter bubbled over it to rumble up his chest, erupting against his hand-covered mouth. Mattie delighted him. He'd only seen the saucy side of her personality a few times, and never this bossy.

He'd known for the last half-hour they weren't going to make it back to camp tonight. But if he'd suggested it, she would've balked worse than a Missouri pack mule. Letting her make camp for a change suddenly appealed to his sense of humor. That she was capable of doing it, in spite of her recent years of soft living, he was certain.

Lariat nudged his shoulder. "Relax, ol' buddy," Will patted and soothed. "We're in good hands, and by this time tomorrow, Bram will take care of you."

Mattie came back some moments later. "Okay, let's go. It's a few minutes' walk, but a good location."

She moved quickly to where he sat, and slid her shoulder under his arm as he stood.

"Mattie, I'm not helpless." He was having a hard time keeping his amusement under control. He leaned heavily, then allowed his hand to slide against her upper arm. Instantly, he realized his mistake when he heard her gasp. He'd squeezed her sore arm.

"Sorry 'bout that, honey," he murmured, instantly sobered.

"It's all right," she said. "Can you mount my horse?"

"Mmm, I think I can manage that."

"Come on, then."

She held the reins tight while he pulled himself into the saddle on his injured leg. Sharp pain jagged through it like a punishment, and a grunt of surprised protest erupted. Blast, it smarted!

Mattie threw him one assessing look and took the reins, walking Sensible with Lariat tied to the back of the saddle. The place she'd chosen was almost as good as a cave; three huge boulders formed a horseshoe-shaped nook that would shelter them from most of the night wind. She'd found a small bundle of twigs under the largest rock, evidence of the place's prior use.

They'd have to make do on the water in their canteens, though. In spite of all the rain these last days, she couldn't find fresh water close by and dared not take the time to search for any before the light ran out.

"Good choice, Mattie," he grunted out as he dismounted.

"Sit right here while I get the fire going." She moved quickly about her task, pulling a tin of matches from his saddlebag. Then she carefully coaxed the fire into full flame.

Will stretched out his leg, leaned back against a stone, and watched every graceful move. Her hat tumbled down her back held by the cord against her long throat. The fire, flaming bright in the twilight, shed its glow against the cream of her skin. A tangled lock of hair was plastered against one cheek by mud smears, and another dirty line ran across her forehead. His gaze followed the caked mud down her body, marks of where she'd fallen with him.

She was beautiful.

Mattie sat back on her heels, watching the welcome blaze. She flickered a glance toward Will. He seemed awfully quiet and cooperative. Maybe he had hit his head. Glancing into his face again, she announced, "I'll get the horses settled and be right back."

"Fine."

She worked swiftly, doing all she could for the horses. Hauling the heavy saddles one at a time, she placed them against the boulder closest to the fire. Moments later, she dug into her saddlebags for the few supplies she knew to be there. A packet of coffee, a little jerky, and her rain slicker.

Too bad she didn't have a blanket, but all her bedding was back with the pack mules.

"Hand me my bags there, Mattie. I'll take care of supper." He scooted to sit closer to the fire. "Why don't you rustle up more firewood? We'll need plenty."

"All right." She glanced at his torn jeans. Was that blood oozing through the smeared mud? "Don't do anything more on that knee till we've cleaned it."

"Yes, ma'am."

Again, she gave him a hard suspicious stare. Will was altogether too complaisant. It worried her and she hurried off to search for enough dry wood to keep them going through the night. She made several trips, finding a few dry sticks under some brush. Each time she dropped another load, she watched him. But he seemed calmly involved with the task of making a meal.

Will's mind was elsewhere. Spending the night alone with Mattie, however necessary, was going to tax his restraint. He almost welcomed the pain from his knee, counting on it to keep his thoughts and desires under control.

Their delay in getting back to camp was another worry. Oh, he knew James and his men would be out looking for them at first light tomorrow, so that wasn't the problem. They'd find each other. But the thought of a bunch of men sitting around, waiting, with little to do, bothered him. With tempers short and geared up for trouble, men often found the trouble among themselves. And even though he'd banned whiskey except for medicinal purposes, Will knew enough to expect some would be making the rounds during his absence.

He only hoped the sheriff wouldn't indulge too much. Whether Tom was up to keeping the explosive situation in hand, only time would tell. He hadn't proved ready to do the job this past year.

Will restlessly stood and limped about the fire a few paces. Mattie'd been gone a long time this trip. He peered into the dimming light. The breeze whispered around him, but he heard nothing more. Maybe he'd better just see where she'd got to.

Taking his rifle from its perch against the boulder, he started off in the direction she'd taken.

Ten

Mattie stepped in front of him with all the noise of a cat. "Ho! Where do you think you're going?"

He leaned his weight on his good leg. "To find you."

"Well, here I am." She moved past him with her heavy load, letting it roll out of her arms to the ground with satisfaction. She'd found a cache of dry wood in a hollow log, probably hidden there by one of the outlaws or an Indian. It would be more than enough, but she couldn't help but be concerned that they might be treading on someone's territory.

"Stars above, Mattie, you were gone too long." Will felt irritation rub up his back. "Don't do that again."

Mattie turned to appraise his scowl. This was more like him; she felt more comfortable. "Sit down now, Will, and pull off your boot. It's my turn to play nurse."

Will complied, and watched while she pulled a feminine garment from her pocket. It looked familiar. A scrap of beribboned muslin, swiftly torn in two, immediately was put to use.

"Too bad we don't have a coffee pot to heat our water in," she murmured, examining the swollen knee. They'd never get his pant leg rolled above it. She'd have to minister her first aid through the tear. Gingerly, Mattie pressed around the joint. Nothing felt unduly out of place, but she wasn't sure what to look for in any case. Pouring water directly from the canteen onto the wound, Mattie bathed the gash.

"Yeah, too bad," he said through his teeth. "But I'd rather have it for coffee, if I had the hot water. But there's a little whiskey in my saddlebags you can use for disinfectant."

Mattie found the bottle and noted it had only about two inches of liquid in it. "Not much here."

She poured a little over the cut, ignoring Will's hiss of pain. Using the remainder of the camisole for a pad, she bound it in place with her neckerchief.

"No, not much. I normally use it only for medicinal purposes. But right now might be a good time to start. Just as well to drink the rest of it now to ward off the chill, since we haven't any coffee."

She threw him a questioning glance. "All right, if you want it. Go ahead."

"You first."

"Uh, no. I don't like the stuff."

"Might need the warmth."

She reached for a piece of the jerky Will'd laid out for supper and started to chew. "Maybe later."

Will shrugged. Sure enough, they might need the whiskey more later. He pushed his hat to the back of his head and reached for his own jerky. Outside of a couple of cold biscuits, this was all they had between them.

"Going to be cold tonight."

"Mmm," she acknowledged as she chewed. It was indeed. Looking around at their nook, she said, "I've enough wood to build another fire. At least for part of the night." She sipped from the remaining water in the canteen and passed it to Will.

"My blanket will help. We'll share it."

"A blanket? I didn't see a blanket when I unsaddled your things."

"It was rolled in my slicker."

"Marvelous." She swallowed the last of her food and threw him a nervous glance. "You go ahead and curl up, then."

"It will do for both of us," he insisted firmly.

"Uh, no thanks, Will. I can get by between the fires." She couldn't share a blanket with him. She just couldn't.

"Mattie . . ."

She got up to start the other fire. "Besides, I have my jacket and rain slicker. I'll make out just fine."

"Mattie!"

Startled, she jumped. "What?"

"We both need to stay warm. Dawn will come soon enough. Now I order you to come over here so that we can get some sleep. That's the end of the discussion. Understand?" It wouldn't be all there was to it, but he couldn't add to her fears by letting her see how much she tempted him.

Mattie let out her shaky breath. "Yes, sir, I certainly understand. You're in command. Well, I won't—"

"What of your promise? Survival isn't a matter for childishness, Mattie. We have a job to do, both of us, but we have to get through a tough night to go on with it."

"All right, all right. In a minute."

Yet she lingered to build the fire and made the job last as long as she could. When the blaze was crackling merrily, she reluctantly moved back to the main one and picked up another piece of jerky. She put it to her mouth and ran her tongue along the salty meat, and put it down again.

"I think I'll go after more firewood," she said a moment later and started to rise.

"No, we have all we need." He clamped her arm tightly and pulled her to sit down beside him. "You're staying right here where I can see you."

"But—"

Will sighed deeply, a sound of near defeat. "Mattie girl, don't." He took her hand, gently squeezing it. "Don't run away."

Startled, she looked into his eyes with a frown. "I'm not running away."

"But you want to. You do, all the time." He searched her eyes for her thoughts. "Why? And when will you stop wanting to?" He reached up to remove her hat, laying it beside them.

"Are you so afraid of me?" He bent and laid a light kiss on the corner of her mouth, tremulous beneath his. "Of this?" He let his voice drop to a low, sensuous throb and pressed his lips to hers again.

Will slid his other arm around her waist and drew her tightly against him. "Or this?"

His mouth took hers with an all-out assertion of tender need. He let her feel it in full force, pressing and probing until her lips parted to receive the complete impact of his.

Mattie, trembling in reaction, didn't know how to answer his questions. She lay in his arms and allowed the kiss to go on and on, not protesting until she could no longer breathe, overwhelmed with the suffocation of sensations. Pleasure and fear battled for supremacy. She never dreamed any man's mouth could be so sweet or give so much pleasure.

But it led to other things, other invasions. Her body felt as though her skin had shrunk to draw her into a ball. She couldn't let go or let him have what he wanted.

She pulled away, turning her face away to pant for breath. She felt the soft brush of his mustache against her eyelid and raised her face slightly, gently bumping her nose against his.

"Oh, Mattie girl," he groaned, pulling hard for his own breath. "Sweetheart, please . . ."

She felt lost in his beseeching murmurs.

He sought her mouth again while his arms gathered her ever closer. He lowered her to the ground. He lay hard against her, pillowing her head in the crook of his arm. He lifted his head momentarily, pushing his interfering hat away to tumble on the ground behind her.

Mattie barely registered the momentary absence, for Will lowered his mouth to hers again, filling her with the most consuming need she'd ever felt. Of what and for what, her mind continued to grapple with and deny, while her body responded with a passion beyond her wildest imaginations. The blood sang along her veins to the very tips of her fingers and toes, making her aware of her entire self all at once.

Slowly, her arms crept around his neck. She clasped him tightly and fervently returned his kiss, opening her mouth to him. He took more, and it felt as if she would die of hunger.

Streaks of lightning flashed through her like a running wall of flame. She wanted to give him everything. Every bit of herself. And she wanted everything he had to give her.

Yet she couldn't live through such a flame and come out undamaged. Her own depth of feeling shocked her. How could she be so ready to give him everything? Give herself into his possession?

Possession . . .

Everything she had fought against.

Like a dunking of cold mountain water, dawning recognition of her own passion washed over her. The coldness grabbed her while her mind cried out. If she was so eager to give away her virtue, her life would become what people thought it was now.

Her need to withdraw suddenly rose in a frenzy. She tried to cry out against his passion, but Will didn't hear her gurgled protest.

She tried to pull away, but her back was hard against the ground. She made a child's whimpering sound low in her throat, and pushed hard against his shoulders. He didn't respond immediately and images of another time, another place, when a man refused to recognize her denial caused her mindless panic. She hit out, beating at him, and caught the edge of his head with the heel of her hand. Jerking her face to the side, she gasped for breath and choked on unreasoning, mindless fear.

"Mattie, sweetheart, what is it? Have I hurt you?" Will raised himself to look down at her averted face.

Tears streamed down her cheeks, and Will felt her stomach clutch with sobs beneath him. Rolling away, he sat up. "What is it, Mattie girl?"

She wouldn't look at him or answer, and he groaned aloud. He'd frightened her again, and while she hadn't actually run away, he thought her mind and emotions had. "Oh, Lord, darlin', I'm sorry."

Gently, he tugged her into his lap and cradled her. She didn't exactly come willingly, but she didn't fight him, either. Her body was as taut as fresh-strung wire. He had to get her back.

"Mattie girl, there's nothing to be afraid of. I'd rather be hung by my toes than do you any harm. I love you so." He stroked her arm with the lightest of touches. "We were doing so good there for a minute. Can you tell me what frightened you?"

His hold on her was gentle and undemanding, which had the effect of calming Mattie's need to retreat. Slowly the tears subsided and she nestled against him, seeking comfort. Mattie didn't completely understand, herself. "I don't know."

"Were you afraid of me?"

"Yes . . ."

Well, at least he had an honest answer.

"Sweetheart, I've wanted you, waited for you for so long. It feels like forever." He held his breath a moment to see if she reacted, bending to see her face. Her silky hair lay against his jaw, and he risked a gentle kiss on her temple.

"I yearn to have you for my wife, Mattie. Do you understand?"

He was met with a long pause, then, "Yes."

"Look at me." He tipped her chin up and stared into the drenched brown eyes. At least she didn't avoid his gaze. He took courage.

Her lashes were tangled with tears, and he placed his lips against her lids, tasting the residue of salt. "Is this what you're so afraid of, Mattie? Being my wife? The marriage bed?"

Mute, she nodded.

Will stared into her face a long moment, then sucked in a deep breath to ask her the question that had plagued him from the first time they met. He'd rather walk through fire than ask it, but they needed to, had to, clear up the fear she felt.

"Mattie, I need to know. Were you ever . . . raped, or . . . or harmed in that way?"

She gasped. Never had anyone asked that question so directly. She averted her gaze and moved out of his embrace.

"Oh, no, Will. My mother protected me really well, considering the circumstances. But that's why I escaped the hideout, you know, because Nate Dorsey tried to, and . . . and . . . Ma heard Larry bargaining with Nate over me. You remember, I told you and Cousin Beatrice all about that . . ."

Relief flooded him. "Yes, I remember, but . . . well, you . . ."

He stopped abruptly, the horrible, awful dread refilling him. He didn't know how he knew, but he knew she was lying. "Mattie . . ."

Mattie drew away and rose, piling wood on the two fires. She didn't look at him. She knew he watched her, knew he wanted answers. Walking around to sit on the opposite side of the fire, she kept her eyes on the flames as she poked the burning logs with a stick. She hurt so much inside, she thought she wouldn't feel it if she put her hand in the fire's midst.

"I'll . . . try to explain, if I can." Her throat felt as if she'd swallowed a handful of rocks. She nervously licked her lips. "Maybe we should drink the whiskey," she commented.

"Sure, Mattie girl. But you're stalling."

Mattie hunched a shoulder and stole a glance at him. He silently held up the bottle. If she wanted it, she'd have to go after it. She sighed and remained where she was.

Dropping the stick, she pulled her knees to her chin and wrapped her arms tightly around them.

"I think you should forget about me, Will. I can't . . . can't love . . . any man."

"You can't? Why would you say such a thing, Mattie? You love me," Will told her calmly.

She lifted her gaze to look at him. Did she? Why did he say that when she didn't really know? She'd thought so, once. What was love, anyway?

He regarded her with his own steady love reaching out to her across the fire. It clutched at her heart as nothing else in the world. But she couldn't tell him the truth or shame him with soiled goods. For the first time in her life she felt a return protectiveness.

She lightened her tone. "But Will . . . I'm probably as bad as people think me."

"Why do you say that?"

"Because, just now, I felt a total lust for you and I hardly think that's what you want in a proper wife."

He nearly choked on laughter. "Oh?"

"Yes. Mrs. Francis, my teacher at that St. Louis girl's academy, said real ladies—good women, that is—don't feel . . . those feelings. So, you see, I suppose I'm a slut at heart, just as most of Wayside Station believes me to be, or I wouldn't have allowed you to kiss me as you did."

"That's hogwash, Mattie. Real women do feel desire."

Mattie couldn't hold on to her light banter. "Well, I've seen lust before, and I don't like it. It's ugly. Men become brutal with it and it makes women weak. That's what got my ma into trouble, she once told me. I guess she let herself be carried away with it, and that's why she and my pa ran away from their families. And Rosa, the Mexican woman I told you about, regularly was beaten by her man. And Ma . . ."

Mattie hung her head. Swirling images, memories deeply buried of nights she lay listening to sounds she'd dreaded from her mother's room—of slapping and hitting, of her mother crying. Her mother had warned her never to interfere. Never. Even now Mattie could hear the dreadful fear and caution in her ma's voice. Never. And she hadn't, but that shamed her now.

"Was your ma ever hit, Mattie?" Will's voice, soft as it was, still demanded to know. She idly wondered if her thoughts showed.

She nodded, biting her lips to keep the tears at bay. "Larry was mean and hateful and hit her often when he was drunk. And before that, at the hotels and gambling halls where Ma worked, she would sometimes come home bruised and bleeding. She wasn't a whore!"

Mattie's voice rose, caught on a sob, then dropped to a near-whisper. "She wasn't a whore, Will. Just a lady gambler and hostess, trying to make a living. I scarcely remember my father. But when he was killed . . . why, then she married Larry and we thought things would get better. But they didn't."

"And you think that is all due to lust?"

"Yes, indeed, lust. And men, wanting it. Once when I was a little girl, I was hiding around the corner in the hotel where we were staying. I saw a man and woman pause beside a door, and the man got nasty with woman because she didn't want to let him into her room. He ripped her top down and pinched her . . . her . . . When she started to cry, he hit her. Right there in the hall."

She paused a long moment. "Later, when I asked Ma about them, she said they were married, and nothing could be done about it."

Will got up and limped around the fire to sit beside her. She hadn't been able to tell him of her own experience yet. Perhaps she never would . . . Rape was an unspeakable violence beyond most women's ability to cope, his own mother once had told him.

Gently taking her hand, he turned it palm up, placing a kiss against it. "You think lust is only in bad or weak people, Mattie, and destructive. But that's not exactly so.

Being married isn't always terrible for a woman. Look at James and Beatrice. Many good, honest, married people share lust, only with them it's mixed up with love and cherishing. Did your ma ever say she regretted loving your pa?"

Will watched her give a faint shake of the head before continuing. "Did your pa love your ma?"

"I suppose . . ."

"Ah-huh. Well, my folks loved each other a heap. They were real affectionate with each other and I bet my ma enjoyed my pa's lovin' in bed, too. I swear, my pa never hit her once. True love, Mattie, has many sides to it, including passion. God created it to procreate, but I'm thinking he meant it as a gift to married folk as well. He only said it was wrong when folks aren't married. It doesn't have to be ugly. On the contrary, when it's right, it's beautiful."

She turned to look at him, watching his face with wide eyes.

"Mattie, what you were feeling a bit ago—you don't need to be ashamed or fearful of it. It's just as natural as any other part of life."

Dark lashes dropped to hide what she was thinking.

"Let's let it go, for now. Just never mind. Now, my darling Mattie girl, we are going to bed."

"Oh, but . . ." she started, her panic rising again.

"Hold on there, don't spill the milk by kicking over the pail. I meant to merely sleep." Taking her hand again, he held her gaze. "Mattie, I do want to hold you . . . but I'll settle for just that, for now, I promise. All right?"

Mattie slowly nodded. "All right."

The blanket, with the rain slickers on top, was warm, and Mattie lay stiffly curled against him with her head on his shoulder. After a time, when Will made no further attempt to caress her, she relaxed. A feeling of safety and shelter enveloped her.

Long after she fell asleep, Will pondered and raged against the kind of childhood hurts and invasion with which she struggled. She had knowingly and unknowingly revealed more of what he had only guessed at—the abuse and hardship. And the rape, although she mustn't realize that he'd cottoned onto her lie. It might do more damage and widen the gap between them. He only prayed that she'd one day be able to tell him openly, so that they could dispel the attached fear and shame.

God, he hated what had been done to her. *Lord, I've got to fight her fears . . .*

When had she suffered that, and who had done it? Yet he knew, instinctively. Larry, her step pa, was the likely swine. No wonder she was fearful of men and their passions.

"One day, Mattie, I'll show you real loving, and you won't be afraid of it," he whispered into her hair. "You do love me, I know it. And that's what will pull us through this damnable knothole."

Mattie and Will, riding double on Sensible and leading Lariat, were halfway down the mountain the next morning when they ran into James, Sandy, and Bram.

"More trouble?" queried Sandy with a cocked eyebrow.

"Not the manmade kind, this time," Will replied.

"You two look like ya been rollin' 'round in a mud bath," James observed, looking them over critically. "What happened?"

Bram had already dismounted to examine Lariat's leg. Will joined him.

"We almost did, Cousin James," Mattie explained. "We

ran into a mudslide, and nearly got swept over a drop. Lariat came up lame and Will injured his knee."

"Well what in tarnation next?" said James. He rode up closer to Mattie, lowering his voice for her ear alone. "Uh, you, uh, all right, girl?"

"Yes, certainly." The heat swept her face and she sneaked a glance at Will. He was listening to every word. Would everyone assume the worst? "Will was a . . . a complete gentleman."

It was true, in the strictest sense of the word, she realized. Even when he knew she responded to him, he hadn't pushed for more when she'd withdrawn.

Will turned to Sandy. "What's happening in the camp?"

"Not much more than you'd expect, Will. The men are sittin' around playin' cards. Some drinkin', lots of jokin'."

Sandy flicked his eyes toward Mattie, and Will knew they'd been the butt of the jokes. His mouth felt tight. The sooner he married her, the better he would feel. No one would dare make snide remarks about her then.

Will changed the subject. "The hunting parties get much?"

"Yep, sure did. A good sized buck and some rabbits."

Bram called up to Will. "I'll bring your horse on in, Will, if you and Miss Mattie want to get on back to camp."

"Thanks, Bram, we'll do that."

"Will, before we go, you should talk to Bram about the pass," said Sandy.

Will's head swiveled to look at Bram. "What do you know about it, Bram?"

"I know where it is, and how it leads into the back mountain."

"The devil you say!" Will studied Bram a long moment. The sun was warming with the morning, and the horse moved restlessly under him. "Do you know the hideout?"

"Not exactly know. I've heard tales of it." He paused, looking Will square in the eyes. "I've reason of my own to find it, Will. And I think if Miss Mattie and I pool our knowledge, we can get in there faster."

"How fast?"

"One more hard day."

Will looked with regret at his horse. "All right, we need to move fast, then." Pulling his saddle off, he swung it up to Sandy.

"Looks like you get a long rest, old friend," said Will, slapping the horse's rump. He looked about the slope where they stood. There was grass and water. He'd try to pick up the horse on the way back.

"Let's ride." Mounting again behind Mattie, he heeled Sensible into a trot.

Eleven

Smothered thuds, made by hooves wrapped in leather, and a faint creaking of saddles was all that could be heard when the large body of riders stopped near the top of the pass. Mattie and Will dismounted and eased around a boulder to view the valley that once had been her home. Others did the same.

The sudden magnifying of her old cabin, seen through Will's field glasses, gave her a jolt. Set apart up the slope from the others, it looked the same, but somehow different—old and small. The late afternoon sun softened the scene, making it appear peaceful.

It had no evidence of occupation. None at all.

She dropped the glasses and stared. Where was her ma?

"What is it, Mattie?" Will murmured.

She shook her head. Then taking a deep breath, she raised the glasses to her eyes once more. Mattie's hopes for finding and rescuing her mother from a life of hopelessness and cruelty felt tenuous at best. She fought to keep her hope alive. She swept slowly through the area with the glasses, while deep disappointment needled through her.

A sleeping dog lay curled up by the Sallinger cabin door. The big cabin belonging to Dorsey looked the same. Behind it, Mattie saw a man entering the main barn. She didn't recognize either of them. But why should she? Six years was a long time in the life of outlaws.

But Rosa's cabin had wash hanging close by—feminine wash. At least Rosa was still in the camp. Faint hope bloomed once more. Maybe Ma was living with Rosa now.

But Mattie knew the place was practically empty of men.

"They're gone," she announced and lowered the glasses.

"What do you mean?"

"I mean, there are only a few men there. Most of the Dorsey gang is gone."

"Them gol-dern skunks! They're prob'ly out robbin' us, again," said James. "Or drivin' my cattle down to Mexico."

"Well, what are we gonna do now?" asked Landon.

"I say we go down and burn out the rattler's nest anyway," said Smith. "Teach 'em they can't thieve from us and get away with it."

The sheriff moved up to look the place over with his glasses. "Miss Mattie's right. The men are probably out on a raid."

"We'll wait," said Will, a stubborn gleam in his gaze. "We've come too far to just put fire to the place and leave. They'd only find another hole to hide in and come back at us in revenge."

"Will's right," James said. "If we don't finish the job now, we'll have it to do again."

Mattie's emotions were in a turmoil as she listened to the talk. "Will, let me go down to visit Rosa. I can find out where the men are and have a chance to see if my mother is there."

"It's too risky, Mattie. You've said they put out guards."

"I'll go in after dark. And we should've run into a guard by now, so maybe there aren't any this time."

He hesitated, then said, "Only if I go with you."

Mattie regarded him in speculation. He wasn't going to let her go alone. "All right, then. But you have to follow my lead and let me do the talking. Rosa will clam up if you don't."

"Yes, ma'am."

The company of men moved out along the mountain trail with instructions for absolute quiet. If they were to be successful, this had to be handled with military exactness and obedience.

Hours crawled into darkness while Mattie watched the activity of the outlaw community. Her nerves grew tighter. She counted only six men throughout the afternoon, and they were too far away for her to recognize.

When night settled in, Mattie and Will moved down into the valley in silence, keeping to the shadows. She led the way around a dark corral and outbuildings to Rosa's small dwelling. With her back to the log wall, Mattie slid around the corner. She glanced furtively over her shoulder and knocked tentatively at the door.

"Who's there?" came from inside.

Mattie knocked again, this time a little stronger.

"Who comes to my door?"

"Rosa . . . it's Mattie Adams. Please, let me in."

The door opened a crack, letting out a stream of lantern light. Mattie felt herself and the door pushed from behind, with Will sweeping her through the opening and closing the door behind them, all in an instant.

"*Dios* . . . what is this? Little Mattie, it is you?"

"Yes, Rosa, it's me," she affirmed, swiftly glancing around the cabin. There was no sign of occupation by another woman. Mattie firmly reined in her disappointment.

"Who is this one with you?" A woman of about thirty-five, Rosa looked older, with wrinkles about her once-pretty eyes. Rosa tipped her head in Will's direction with a wide, sad gaze. Strangers were no novelty to her, but they were always to be questioned.

"He's my friend," Mattie said without looking at Will.

She walked to the one window and pulled the sacking Rosa used for curtains across the glass. "Rosa, where are the boys? Juan and Miguel?"

"What do you here?" Rosa ignored her question and nervously backed a few steps. "Why do you come?"

"We intend you no harm," Mattie stated in a firm voice while throwing Will a warning glance. He was keeping his bargain about letting her do the talking, but she could see he was spilling over with unasked questions. "May we sit?"

Not waiting for an answer, Mattie sat at the rude table. Rosa hesitantly slid into a chair opposite, while still throwing suspicious glances toward Will.

Wanting to reassure her, Mattie reached out and took the other woman's hand. "Rosa, I came for my mother. Do you have news of her?"

"No, I know nothing of her."

"But she is alive?" Mattie leaned forward, her eyes riveted to Rosa's while her mind hung in the space between them, waiting for the answer.

"*Si, si* . . . the last time I saw her."

It's true? Ma's alive? She'd survived that awful night?

She closed her eyes tightly, thankfulness overwhelming her. She drew a deep breath.

"When was that? Was she well? Oh, Rosa, please tell me all you know."

"I know but little. She left with her man about a year after you. She was recovered, but . . ." Rosa spread her hands in a wide shrug.

"You mean she was still weak? Oh, Lord," Mattie bit at her under lip to keep her emotions under control. "Where were they headed?"

"Some say *Californio*. The atmosphere is favorable for

business there. San Francisco has many gambling houses."

"San Francisco?"

The door latch rattled, and Will stepped back beside the opening with drawn gun. Mattie heard the hammer click and stood, swirling to meet the incoming person.

"Miguel?" She faced a small youth in early adolescence with the dark eyes and bronze skin of his Spanish heritage. He stared at her a moment.

"*Dios,* it's Mattie," he said and took two steps into the room before stopping. His face swiftly turned from joy to mixed rage and fear when he saw Will, crouched, ready to spring with his gun cocked for action.

"*Por favor, senor,*" Miguel backed away. His eyes shifted from Mattie's face to Will's. He trusted his old friend, but he didn't trust the man. Will shouted danger in every line of his body.

"Take it easy, kid. We're just here to talk, for now," Will said, and eased, dropping his Colt revolver to his side.

Mattie stepped forward, laying a hand on Miguel's shoulder. "I am so glad to see you, Miguel. I—that is . . . My friend and I, we need your help."

Miguel's uncertain glance rolled to his mother. "What goes on here? Why is Mattie here? She should be somewhere in the East . . ."

"Sit, my son. Mattie is come to inquire of her *madre.*"

Mattie licked her dry lips and took a deep breath. Steadily holding the other woman's gaze, she said, "Rosa, there's more. There's a large force of men camped at the head of the pass. They're ranchers and lawmen, and . . . well, you understand?"

Rosa's face paled as she whispered, "*Si,* I understand."

"You brought them here?" Miguel jumped to his feet in outrage. "You have become a traitor."

"Traitor? How so?" Mattie stared hard at him. "This way of life was never my choosing, or my ma's. We were brought here against our wishes, and lived here at the whim of the men who controlled the valley. There was never any choice about the matter." She turned to Rosa. "And what of you? Do you choose this life for your sons? Where is Juan?"

"He is out with Dorsey and the men," Miguel bragged.

Mattie couldn't hold back her distress. "Oh, Rosa, why? Why have you let him join the thieves? Juan is only fifteen. Would you see him start robbing and killing before he is even a man?"

"What have I to say to it? I argued against it. I even said I'd try to get Juan back to Mexico, but Jorge said it was time for him to earn his keep. I am helpless, Mattie."

"I, also, will go soon. I will be a fierce gunslinger," boasted Miguel.

"Oh, Miguel, no!" protested Mattie.

Will stepped forward. "Ma'am, we don't want to harm you or the boy, here. But my men and I are coming into this rattlesnake den and, one way or another, we'll wipe out these thieves. There's going to be a big battle, and your boys could get hurt. If you cooperate now, I promise we'll get you out and find work for you."

"What do you want of me?"

"Information."

"*Madre*, you cannot do this. *Por favor* . . ."

"Miguel, you do not understand. These are vigilantes. They will kill anyone who stands in the way of their purpose." Rosa turned back to Will. "You must protect my Juan. Tell your men, *senor*, they are not to shoot my Juan."

"We'll take all due precaution, ma'am. Give me a description of the boy to pass among my men."

"I will not be a traitor, *Madre*," Miguel rebelled.

"Miguel, would you betray your family?" Mattie laid a hand on his shoulder as she reasoned with him. "Remember when we were children, we often talked of moving away. You and Juan wanted to be *vaqueros* and go to *fandangos* in Mexico." She paused, chewing her lip. "Well, you are nearly a man, now, and very handsome. You don't really want to join those lawless men. To always be on the run, to fear going into each new town? To possibly get shot or hung before you have a chance to grow old? This is your chance to be on the side of the law, not the wrong side. Getting out to start a new, honest life is a good thing. Think of your mother. If you remain here, you have little chance to live to manhood at all."

Miguel stared at her a moment, his face a changing array of emotions. "All right, Mattie. For you, I have listened. I will be a man now, and help to take my *madre* from this danger."

Rosa made her final plea. "Will you get me and my sons to Mexico? I have family there."

"I'll do my best to see that you get home, ma'am."

"Very well. What do you want to know?"

"How many men are in residence here?"

"Sometimes twenty to twenty-five, sometimes less. Rarely more."

"Where are they now?"

"I do not know that, *senor*. I hear only they plan to rob a bank up north."

"How long have they been gone? When would they be coming back?"

Rosa spread her hands, shaking her head. "Who knows?"

"I think they come soon," said Miguel. "They have been very busy since the spring, and wish to rest a long while."

"Why do you say that?" Mattie asked.

"Because," he grinned, "I listen while the men play poker." He glanced at Will, shrugging. "I am a nothing to them, a flea to swat, a dog to kick. Someone to run errands. They talk . . . I listen."

Will placed his hand on the boy's shoulder. "Will you tell me what you've heard?"

Miguel studied Will's face for a long moment. Most of the men he knew would have hit him by now. Would it be true, then, that some men knew honor? His gaze shifted to Mattie. She would know, and she trusted this man. Miguel let go of all doubt.

"You wish to see a map, *senor?*"

"A map? What sort of map?"

"Senor Dorsey, he has a map. He makes plans with the map. He tells his men how many days to go, so." Miguel stabbed a finger in the air. "And how many men," he held up all fingers. "And last, how many days back. The men who are here now say the time is near for them to come."

"When? How soon?"

"Two, maybe three days."

"How many men are here now?"

"Seven, counting me."

"Ah, yes." Will moved a few paces around the cabin, thinking hard. He needed to get at least half of his men into the valley itself, to keep an element of surprise. But waiting for three days might stretch the men beyond his control. If he kept the troublesome ones under his eye, if he continued to stress their need for quiet and cooperation as a unit, it might work. "Miguel, do you know where Dorsey keeps the map?"

"*Si, senor.*"

"Good." Will turned to Rosa. "We will leave now.

Miguel will come with us."

"Oh, no . . . no, no." Rosa started to cry and wring her hands. "Please, *senor*."

"It's all right, Rosa. We mean Miguel no harm," Mattie reassured, then turned to Will. "I will stay with Rosa to assure her of Miguel's return."

"No." Will clamped his teeth shut on the word.

"It is the reasonable thing to do. Rosa won't fear for her son if I am with her."

"That is so, *senor*," Rosa added.

"No, Mattie." His voice was hard as he made one last plea.

"But how long can it be till you return? A couple of hours? I'll be safe here."

Will glanced around the room, assessing the soundness of the cabin, then swung back to regard her for a moment. "All right, you may stay here. But as soon as Miguel and I are out that door, you bar it and blow out the lamp. And talk in low tones. I don't want anyone to hear two feminine voices where there should be only one."

He turned his gaze on Rosa, and pursed his lips. "Let the men here think you have gone to bed. When you hear any signs of fighting," his eyes returned to Mattie as he reached out to clamp a hand on her shoulder, "if you hear gunfire, remain in this cabin. Do not acknowledge in any way that you are here, until I, James, or Sandy come for you. Understand?"

"Yes, sir, I understand." She gave him her best solemn word.

"Good." He turned to Miguel. "Okay, kid, are you ready?"

"*Si.*"

Will waited for Rosa to douse the light, then he and Miguel slipped out of the door.

Hours later, Mattie curled her arms about her drawn-up knees, hugging them to her chest. She and Rosa sat on the bed with their backs to the wall, waiting. They had talked in low tones and whispers for over two hours when they heard a commotion of a few shouts, running feet, and several gunshots. It was all over in a few moments, and now the two women waited.

A sudden sharp rapping on the door caused Mattie to jump, and then she heard James's voice. "Mattie girl, you in there?"

"One moment, Cousin James." She rushed to the door, swinging it wide. "Is everyone all right?"

"None of our fellas is hurt, but one of 'em from here took a bullet. The rest of 'em gave no resistance."

"Miguel?" Rosa questioned and broke into a flood of excited Spanish.

"Hold on, there, ma'am. The boy's all right. He'll be along d'rectly."

Rosa lit the lamp, and only moments later, Miguel came strutting in, his eyes bright with excitement and his own importance. Rosa hugged him to her ample bosom.

"Ho, *Madre*. Did you worry? No need, for I am *Senor* McCarthy's right-hand man." He smiled widely around the room, puffing out his chest. "Now I go again. *Senor* McCarthy wishes to see the map of which we spoke." He dashed out the door before his mother could object.

James stayed with the women, and Mattie turned to Rosa. "Do you have coffee, Rosa?"

"*Si*," Rosa murmured as she turned away from the empty doorway. "*Si*, coffee. And food."

Mattie busied herself helping Rosa over the hearth fire. Preparing food would help calm her nerves. She looked around in the corner where Rosa kept provisions. There wasn't a lot there. They hadn't had a hot meal since last night, and suddenly Mattie was hungry.

"Cousin James, Rosa and I'll cook some food, but we'll need some additional supplies. Have any of the pack mules come down yet?"

"Don't rightly know." He scratched his head. "Wait just a minute."

James stepped out the door while Mattie waited. She itched to go out and see for herself what was going on, but she had given her promise to stay in Rosa's cabin, so she contented herself with standing at the open door. Several horsemen trotted past toward Dorsey's cabin. That seemed to be where most of the activity was going on.

Now, where had James gone? He was nowhere to be seen.

Mattie inched around the door a little farther. She could see very little through the dark. Stepping away from the door altogether, she edged to the corner of the cabin and waited for her eyes to adjust. Gradually, she saw where guards had been posted, but she knew there were more she couldn't see. The night seemed quiet.

Except at Dorsey's cabin. Light shone freely from the windows and open door. Mattie saw shadows flitting, blotting the light momentarily. A number of horses stood tied to the hitching post.

Mattie turned again to look for James. All around Rosa's small cabin the night seemed as black as a cave. Muted sounds of Rosa's bustle from inside the cabin whispered out to her. She felt lonely, suddenly, and isolated. Everyone seemed to be at the big cabin. Edging up the road, she jumped across a ditch and stopped.

Something more than just a gathering was going on at Dorsey's cabin!

Setting her mouth, Mattie hurried up the slope. The ground beneath her feet felt familiar and she automatically dodged an old stump that her subconscious memory recalled. She slowed when she approached the porch, and eased up the step to stand in back of two men who blocked the entrance. A loud argument was taking place.

"No!" Will shouted. "We won't."

"Are ya gettin' chicken-hearted, Will?" a voice in the crowd asked.

A clamor of men's voices rose in heated debate and Mattie wedged through the congested doorway to stand in the press of bodies that packed the room. Stretched to her toes, she could see only part of Will's head facing away. She jockeyed and edged forward until she had a clear view of what was happening.

Five men, bound hand and foot, were pushed against the far wall. Three were bloodied and bruised, obviously having put up a fight. Will stood in the center of a small space. Facing him stood Smith and Landon in aggressive stances, hostility in plain view. They seemed to have a number of men backing them, bunched to show the size of their force. Glancing quickly around the crowd, Mattie spotted Sandy, Caleb, and Bram, loosely fanned out behind Will.

But it was Will who riveted her attention. He stood in cold authority, a badge shining on his chest and his hand resting near his heavy, low-slung Colt. His eyes, like chipped ice, shot slivers of warning into the crowd. His body was hair-triggered, ready for action.

Mattie gaped, her breath caught in her throat. She had never seen this side, this depth, in Will before.

This man was dangerous . . . possibly the most dangerous man she'd ever met.

"We'll keep these men for trial," Will stated. "Our purpose here isn't finished."

"But what's the good of keepin' these cow-thieves to worry with? They're gonna hang anyways," Landon argued.

"They'll have a proper trial in Wayside Station." Will was adamant.

"But thet's jes' extry work," complained old Skeeter.

"I say we string 'em up and be done with it," said Smith. His face was livid with hate and anger. "Sheriff Kimmel, here, will count for the law."

Mattie noticed the sheriff for the first time, leaning against a post. He seemed to be an observer like the rest of the men.

"Sorry, men. It's Will's show. His authority supercedes mine."

The room filled with curses.

Smith shot a seething look at the sheriff and turned back to Will. "The law can go to blazes," he stormed. "I'm not gonna stand by and see these thievin' varmints coddled. They played the game, now let 'em pay for it." He took a threatening step forward, with his hand on his gun.

"You try that, Smith, and you'll pay your own price." Will stood his ground. His hand hovered over his revolver.

Smith's face paled. He licked his lips and studied Will's face. Slowly, his hand moved away from his gun and he took a step backward. "Okay, McCarthy. You own the situation for now."

"Smith, if you can't hold your spite, I'll haul you back to Wayside Station in ropes along with these men, and lock you up for interfering with the law." Will's voice was hard and unyielding.

Glaring his animosity, Smith said nothing more. Turning, he shoved his way through the crowd, butting his

161

shoulder heavily against Mattie as he made his way to the door.

Mattie's head swiveled back to the front of the room, and her gaze collided with Will's. He looked fleetingly at her, but did not acknowledge her presence. Instead, he turned to Caleb, giving orders in a low tone pertaining to the imprisonment of the outlaws. The crowd started breaking up, milling out the door, and Mattie started to turn.

"Hold it, Mattie."

The command was sharp, and she stopped short, turning back. Will reached out to clamp a strong hand around her elbow, his grip tight and punishing. "Stay, until I can walk you back to Rosa's." Then raising his voice, he called, "Sandy." Mattie could feel the force of his reined anger, where it communicated through his long fingers around her arm.

She opened her mouth to protest, and then, looking into his crystal eyes, lost any desire to say a word. Holding his gaze, she nodded in silence.

Spurs clanked, and there was Sandy, with Bram a step behind. "Yeah, Will?"

"You set up the night guard rotation. And assign the men where to sleep." Will threw a significant glance toward the door where the Smith-Landon faction was leaving. "Bram, I want you to go back to the men we left in the pass, so they won't be getting itchy to come see what's going on down here. I'll need you to stay there . . . you know the signals we discussed."

"Right," Bram acknowledged, and left.

"You feeling a might uneasy about Fulton being left back?" asked Sandy.

"Yeah," Will grunted. "Frank has orders not to let Nick

out of his sight, but I'll feel easier when we know more than we suspect. If he makes one wrong move, if he tries to warn Dorsey, both Frank and Bram will be there to counterbalance it."

Mattie's mind was whirling. Nick Fulton was linked with Dorsey's gang? How could they know? Yet she was sure Will wouldn't accuse the man without certain knowledge. Then she thought of Sally . . . Oh, Lord, what that knowledge would do to Sally.

But it was obvious that Smith didn't know. Smith was ready to tear the culprits apart and hang them from the highest tree. The man would have apoplexy when he discovered his friend was a traitor.

She looked with awe into Will's face. He'd just faced Smith down, and yet had given away nothing of his suspicions about the man's son-in-law. How much more did Will keep wrapped up in the core of his being? How many sides of his personality were there yet to know?

Mattie, caught up with her tumbled thoughts, was startled when Will suddenly spoke to her.

"Let's go." He grasped her elbow and guided her firmly out the door, past the men still standing about, and down the slope toward Rosa's.

Reaching the open door, he glanced to see Rosa busy at the hearth. He pushed Mattie around the corner, into the dark shadows of the cabin.

"Now, Miss Mattie." His tone was hard. "I thought I told you to stay at Rosa's."

Mattie backed away from the harsh grate in his voice. "I did exactly as you asked," she defended with a huff. "I stayed until all the fighting was done, and James came to the door."

He leaned toward her, crowding her back against the log

wall, placing his arms against the structure on either side of her head. "So after that, you couldn't contain your curiosity, hmm?"

"Well, I started out to find some food supplies."

"Uh-huh," he drawled, the harshness seeping away. "Okay, I'll see that Bob comes your way soon. But meanwhile, I don't want you running around here loose. Especially in the dark."

"But Will, I know this place like the back of my hand. I'd like to visit my old cabin. Maybe Ma left a clue or something."

"After six years?"

"I know it's unreasonable . . . but still . . ."

"Not tonight. I'll take you first thing in the morning."

"I can go myself."

"No, you little rascal. You'll wait for me."

Suddenly, he swooped, capturing her mouth in a thorough, quick kiss. Her emotions tumbled as her mouth started to respond without her permission, and then he lifted his head. She was too stunned to speak.

"Come, it's late. You bed in with Rosa, so I know where you are." He once again took her arm, more gently this time, and guided her to the open door. "Good night, Mattie," he stated firmly. "I'll see you in the morning."

He turned without waiting for her response and strode away. The imprint of his mouth on hers lingered.

Twelve

Mattie stopped a few yards from her old home and stared. The logs sagged, making the small dwelling appear tilted and sunken on one side. The window was boarded over and grass had grown tall around the door. It obviously had been empty for some time. Someone, however, was still using the barn, for the corral fence was in good repair and fresh hay could be seen through the half-opened door.

"It looks smaller than I remember," she murmured, stepping over the doorsill. The air smelled musty and stale, and she pushed the creaking door wider to allow the morning sun to stream in.

Will silently followed her into the empty main room, watching as she poked her head through the door into the lean-to alcove. He glanced past her head. Nothing was there, not even a bed.

"Was this your room?"

"No, this was Ma and Larry's room. I had a bed near the fireplace out here."

Mattie led him to the side of the hearth where marks on the floor showed a piece of furniture had once stood in the spot. It was tiny.

"Right here. It was warm, mostly, during the winter. But I was getting too big for it and had to sleep either curled up or with my feet hanging over the end, that last year."

"Well, you have grown a mite, even since six years ago," he teased.

She nodded absently, and turned slowly around the

room, sadness filling her eyes. "There's nothing left of Ma . . . nothing at all."

"Oh, I wouldn't say that, Mattie." Will stood leaning against the stone fireplace and watched her face carefully. "You're a part of her. She's left you yourself."

Startled, Mattie turned to look at him. Sometimes he knew exactly how she was feeling and thinking.

"And since you're her child, she must be a beautiful woman," he added.

She gulped, fighting tears. "Thank you, Will. She is quite beautiful. But I look nothing like her at all. Aunt Elizabeth and Cousin Beatrice say I look just like my pa."

"But you are, too, you know. Quite beautiful." His voice dropped to a low pitch. Will had never told a woman such a thing before, but it seemed quite natural with Mattie. Her eyes looked soft as velvet in the dim light, and her red bandanna cast a red glow onto her cheeks. Her hair was tucked beneath her hat, but he imagined what it would look like brushed out smooth. "Yes, very beautiful."

Mattie's heart skipped a beat. She'd gone to sleep last night with the memory of how his mouth felt and the chaos it caused; he was a man who brooked no opposition to his purpose, a man of ultimate victory.

Standing now in the silent, still cabin, her spine tingled with the vibration of his husky voice. The words seemed to wrap around her like a blanket, warming and comforting. But beyond the seductive quality, she knew, was an implacable determination to make her his.

"Thank you, Will," she stuttered out, and fled through the door.

"Whoa!" Will muttered through clenched teeth. What had he said now? Why had she run away again?

That night on the mountainside, he'd made progress,

but now she'd retreated. Maybe it was this cursed place. He glanced about the ugly little room. Seeing where she and her mother had lived with cruelty and poverty made his stomach sour; it must have affected her worse.

Ducking his head through the door, he followed her outside. She leaned against a corral fence post, staring at the steep mountain walls that contained the valley. Strolling to where she was, he hung an elbow from a rail. He, too, stared at the mountains as he spoke in a calm voice.

"You were frightened again just now."

"Yes."

Good. She didn't deny it. "Can you tell me why?"

"It's just that . . . you're so determined . . . almost ruthless."

Will was silent for a moment, contemplating her words. He wanted to soften her view of him and soothe her fears, but he couldn't alter the truth.

"Mattie, I have to be determined, even hard. This country demands it for survival. But with you . . ." He stopped, not knowing what else to say. "I love you," he murmured, his voice husky with yearning. He let the words hang in the air and walked away. He didn't turn to see if she followed.

Mattie watched him go with mixed feelings. On the one hand, he was every bit as hard and ruthless as the country called for—as he needed to be for any situation. Hadn't he been hard as stone and just as unyielding last night?

But he wasn't applying those tactics to her, only to the "winning." On the contrary, he was hard toward her only where it concerned her safety. She remembered his tenderness after she'd been shot—she fingered her healing wound—and again when they'd been alone on the mountain. He could've forced himself on her then. Yet he hadn't.

Mattie returned to Rosa's cabin. The day wore heavily on, with periodic visits from Miguel enthusiastically reporting what was happening with the various men. James stuck close by the women, but Mattie saw little more of Will the rest of the day.

Nerves tightened with the waiting. Will kept as many men occupied as possible. Keeping tempers from fraying into open squabbles was more difficult. As twilight fell, he rode up into the pass to talk with the men assigned there for the night.

"How's it going, Frank?"

"Fine, boss. Everything's quiet."

"You didn't spend much time down below. Did you get some sleep?"

"Sure thing, Will. I like it better up here. And I ain't the only one."

"Oh?"

"Yeah, Fulton, there, ain't a bit int'rested in showin' his face below. He's been holed up in them rocks up yonder. Says he likes a high perch."

"Hmm. Where's Bram?"

"Bram makes hisself scarce too. He's . . ."

"Right here." Bram interrupted as he appeared beside them. "Saw you comin'."

"Got a good viewing place, have you?"

"Yep. I can see what I need to. Including Fulton."

"Anything interesting?"

"A bit. Fulton didn't seem too agitated early in the day. He even took a nap. But from about mid-afternoon, he started getting restless and looking through his glass often."

"Uh-huh," Will encouraged him. Bram usually had a point.

"Then, this last half-hour, he's settled down again.

Seems like he doesn't expect anything to happen after dark."

"S'pose he knows when the gang is comin' in?" asked Frank.

"Hmm," Will rubbed his jaw. "It sure appears that way. If Fulton expected the gang today, say, between three and sunset, and they didn't show, then it stands to reason they might come tomorrow at that time."

"Yep," said Bram. "Way I figured it."

"Good work, Bram." Will stood thinking a moment. "Did you see any sign of a mirror or such? I wonder how he plans to signal them?"

"No, I didn't see one, but that's not to say he doesn't have one."

"Well, keep your eyes peeled," Will advised. "Frank, have you got somebody you can station farther back on the trail who won't get caught?"

"Yeah, I can go myself."

"Okay. But stay out of trouble."

"Sure thing, boss."

Satisfied, Will returned to the valley. He advised key people of the latest information, coming to Rosa's cabin last.

"Evening, Mattie, James," he greeted as he stepped through the door. "Are those fresh tortillas I see?"

"*Si, Senor* Will. Do you wish to eat?" Rosa asked.

"I sure am hungry, ma'am, and would be real grateful to eat at your table."

Will sat down, extending his long legs before him, and glanced at Mattie from under his hat. She poured his coffee without once looking at him. Hiding a weary sigh, he answered James's questions while he ate.

"Have you seen my Miguel?" Rosa asked when James paused.

"He's coming right away, ma'am," Will said through a

mouthful of food. "I told him to hightail over here with the map."

"Ah. Thank you, *Senor*."

Moments later, Miguel burst through the door. "I have it, *Senor* Will, safe in my keeping as you requested."

"Very good, Miguel. Plop it down right here."

Will indicated the table, and Mattie hastened to assist Rosa in clearing the dishes. The men spread the map and huddled over it, talking of the known routes and trails.

Curious, she edged closer, leaning between Will and Miguel to see. The hand-drawn map had lots of details. Reaching out to trace a particular line with her finger, for balance she rested her forearm on Will's rounded back and bent shoulder. Seconds later, she became aware of her fingers brushing against his neck, the soft touch of his hair feathering against her skin. Startled, she turned to look straight into warm blue eyes, only inches from hers. There was a knowing look there, and seductive amusement. Heat flooded up her neck and into her cheeks. She jerked upright, snatching her hand away.

Trying to cover her embarrassment, she bustled about refilling coffee cups. How could she have allowed herself to do such a thing? He didn't need any encouragement for pursuit. She'd been totally unconscious of what she was doing, until she'd felt the tickle of his hair against her fingers. And the action had felt so intimate and comfortable, as though she had a right to lean against his body. Like that day by the river, when he had cuddled her against him after she'd been hurt.

It still embarrassed her to remember she'd been almost naked. But, she admitted, the embarrassment had begun after the other men were almost upon them.

That night they'd spent by themselves, in spite of her

fears, she'd felt such a longing and passion for him, there had been long moments . . .

Mattie retreated to the fire at that thought. It was time she was honest with herself. She liked touching Will. Sometimes she wanted—needed—to touch him. She wanted him to touch her, liked his stroking, needed his kisses.

Slowly Mattie turned to stare at Will. His attention riveted on the map, he was busily pointing out something to James. She gazed at him freely, taking in the tired lines fanning from his eyes and the lamp glow on the silky gilt of his hair. Deep in the pit of her stomach, a stirring began. Was this needing what he felt for her?

Even now she longed to stand near him again, to feel the strength of his shoulder muscles under her hand. She knew she wanted to brush more than the edge of his hair. She wanted to knock his hat off, as he'd done hers once, and run her hands against his temples and through the beautiful blond silk.

She swallowed, hard.

This morning, she'd told him he frightened her. But maybe the fright all came from her past . . . She had allowed past experiences to color her thinking about Will. Will was different from other men. Gentle and kind. At least, so far, with her.

"We'll be ready, then," James was saying. "An' I'll rest easier when this is all over."

"We all will, James." Will replied, rolling up the map. He started for the door, giving a soft, general goodnight while his eyes lingered on Mattie.

"Good night, Will." Mattie called after him. She wished he had taken her around the corner for a goodnight kiss as he had last night. She stood in the door and watched him disappear into the darkness.

Thirteen

The waiting came to an end the next day when a mirror flashed from a high pass in the early afternoon. The outlaws came earlier than the posse expected, and the men scrambled to find shelter, keeping hidden as much as possible. Dorsey's gang rode strung out down the trail. Posse nerves were high, and their guns were ready.

High on the inside wall of Rosa's cabin, Mattie watched through a peephole. She counted eighteen mounted men; she knew her view was limited. Climbing down from her precarious perch where her toes had clung between the logs, she moved to the window and glanced out.

James wasn't with them. He had gone to Dorsey's cabin to consult with Will. Mattie watched the oncoming men.

"*Por favor,* Mattie, stay out of sight," Rosa whispered and groaned. "Oh, where is that Miguel? *Dios* protect us, he will be killed."

"Now Rosa, Miguel's too smart to be in the middle of it," Mattie soothed, hoping she was right. "I'm sure he's in a safe place."

The first riders entered the village just as the reverberating sound of a rifle shot split the distant quiet, quickly followed by a second. Surprised silence lasted for only seconds before the gang scattered in all directions amid a cross-fire of flying bullets.

The fighting was hot and heavy for a time, and then dwindled down to sporadic exchanges. Mattie dared a peek to see what was happening. Someone was shouting, but she couldn't hear what was said. Heavy boots thudded close by in a run, and she twisted to see who it was. She saw a retreating back as a figure rounded the corner of Rosa's barn.

A revolver shot erupted close to the back of the cabin, and Mattie whirled to see Rosa anxiously watching through a chink of the rear wall. "Who is it? Where?"

"My Juan, he is there, in the barn."

Mattie rushed to the back wall and found a peephole of her own. She could see little but the sight of that hulking figure stalking the barn. A quick movement caught the corner of her eye, and her breath caught in her throat. A second man was circling. She recognized that beefy man. It was Landon. The other was Smith.

"Oh, Lord, oh, Lord, oh, Lord . . ." Old bark and mud crumbled beneath her hand where she clutched the wall. Smith and Landon. They would care nothing for Will's order to spare the boy. Their thirst for revenge wouldn't consider clemency.

Beside her, Rosa started to sob.

Rushing back to the front window, she surveyed the scene. Where was Will? Or Cousin James? No one was in sight, but gunfire sounded up the road in the valley.

Taking a deep breath, Mattie picked up her rifle, and cracked the door. A mounted figure dodged across the trail, melting into the trees.

She edged out the door and slipped around the corner of the cabin, stopping at the rear. She saw only Smith's shoulder where he crouched against the barn wall, but she had a full view of Landon's back. He was about to enter the barn, his gun at the ready.

Mattie crouched low and ran, dropping to her knees against a small corral post. Landon didn't turn.

"Back me to the left, I'm goin' in," he threw out of

the corner of his mouth.

She eased up behind him, the metal click sounding loud as she cocked her rifle. "You'll stand where you are, Landon," she commanded. "That boy in there is not to be harmed."

"You!" He started to turn. "I shoulda known. Protecting your outlaw chums, are you?"

"Hold it." She shoved the rifle against his back. She refused to answer his challenge. "Call Smith back around here."

Half-turned, a curse left his lips. "That kid's an outlaw, same as the others."

"Call Smith," she directed again in a hard voice.

He hesitated only a moment, angry sparks shooting from his gaze. Then he mumbled out, "Smith."

Silence reigned with the sporadic fighting sounding a background a short distance up the road. She raised the rifle to rest behind Landon's ear. She knew Landon felt the cold metal.

"I said call him," Mattie demanded.

"*Smith,*" he roared. Sweat rolled down his temple.

"Yeah, what is it?" Smith sounded fully irritated when he appeared around the corner. "I was about to . . ."

He stopped abruptly upon seeing the situation. Profanity erupted out of his mouth like a spitting snake.

"That's enough," Mattie commanded. "Shut up and be quiet. Move over here, closer to Landon."

"I don't believe you'll shoot," Smith took a step toward her, his face twisted with a snarl. "You'll have a lot to answer for."

"Do you want to try me?"

Smith stopped again. He didn't want to believe her. She waited for him to comply, almost too long. She raised her rifle barrel two inches.

"Smith," protested Landon.

Smith moved at last. Then holding the rifle steady, she backed closer to the barn and raised her voice.

"Juan, it's Mattie Adams. Come out and you'll be safe."

"Mattie?" came the young male voice from the darkened interior. She hardly recognized the adolescent Juan who cautiously looked out.

"My Mattie?" He glanced from her face to the men held at rifle point in front of her.

"Come here, Juan. You've been promised safety from the vigilantes, but you must come with me now." She risked a quick glance away from Smith and Landon to look at his face. "I promise. Understand?"

"*Si.*"

Mattie watched the expression on Juan's face. He didn't understand, but he trusted her. She blessed the times they dodged danger together as children.

She laid a hand on her old playmate's arm as soon as he came within range and pulled him to her back. They stepped away from the men. "All right, you side-winding skunks. We're going back to Rosa's cabin. Now git, or I'll tell the whole town you like your odds against kids and women."

"You'll pay for this," Smith warned. "You'll pay big."

"You talk to Will about it." She gestured with the barrel of her rifle and they turned, running back toward the sound of gunfire.

"Come," she directed Juan. Running swiftly, they dodged behind the shelter of the cabin, and along the side. When they reached the front corner, Mattie paused to search the area, and then stepped out.

"Juan," Miguel called from the barn opposite, on

the other side of the road.

Juan turned at the sound of his name. "Miguel?"

Mattie opened her mouth to call out a caution just as Miguel jumped out to run toward them. A gun snapped, and she watched in horror as Miguel stumbled and fell. From the doorway, Rosa screamed and reached for Juan.

Mattie's feet seemed to have wings of their own, for she was kneeling beside the young boy in a moment. Blood spurted from his thigh, and he groaned and called out the name of his brother.

"I'm here, Miguel." Juan knelt on the other side.

Glancing up, Mattie noticed Juan's face looked old, with his mouth set in a grim line. "We've got to get him to the cabin," she said.

"*Si*. I will take him." Miguel handed Mattie his long-barreled revolver. "You guard."

He bent, straining to lift the small body that was almost as big as his own.

Mattie rose and moved back, looking about her. They had to cross the nearby open road to get into Rosa's cabin. Lifting the heavy gun, she gave the signal to go, and stepped out of the shadow of the barn.

A snorting horse caused her to turn her head. Coming into view from behind the barn where he'd been partially hidden, a mounted man moved toward her. Only yards away, he stopped, yanking tight on the reins of the dancing, head-tossing animal. A huge, bearded, hawk-nosed man.

Nate Dorsey!

Frozen, Mattie stood still while he slowly broke into a toothy grin, his dark eyes covering her body from head to toe. Her stomach clenched and rolled in revulsion and fear. Instant memories of his ruthless assault on her six years earlier wiped away her confidence. She felt the old helplessness wave over her.

"Well, well. Miss Mattie Adams, all growed up. Come back to me, did ya?"

"Mattie." Juan whispered from the corner of the barn where he was out of Dorsey's sight.

Without turning around, Mattie knew Juan was struggling to hold his brother. They couldn't delay; they had to get Miguel back to the cabin. Shakily, she raised the revolver and aimed it directly at Nate.

"Don't come near me," she ordered Nate.

"Ya owe me, good, girl. I paid hard cash for ya, did you know that? Five, six years ago." He nodded. "Yep, I paid your pa—"

"Not my pa." The words of denial wouldn't be stopped.

"Your step pa, then." He moved the horse forward. "An' ya stole my best horse an' all."

Mattie retreated a step. "I'm warning you, the posse is all over the place. Leave me be."

"The little lady is right, Dorsey, and you're under arrest," Sheriff Kimmel said as he stepped out from behind Juan with his gun in hand.

Nate snarled, his face twisted with malice, and raised his gun. He called her an ugly name. "You brought them. You—"

Without warning, he dug his spurs into the horse's flanks, causing it to rear and spin.

Mattie whirled and ducked back behind the sheltering barn. The sheriff stepped forward, his gun blazing. The deafening noise of the roaring firearms matched the thunder of her heartbeats. Over her gasping breath, she heard the thuds of a retreating horse.

"Quick." Mattie waved Juan into motion. They ran, holding Miguel between them, toward Rosa's cabin. She looked back over her shoulder as she reached the door where Rosa waited. The sheriff lay crumpled on the ground.

A groan from Miguel jerked Mattie's attention back to him, and she glanced worriedly down at his face. As soon as she and Juan laid the boy on the bed, Rosa, immediately calm, sprang into action, apparently knowing just what to do for such a wound.

"Mattie, help me, *por favor*."

Mattie jumped to follow Rosa's crisp directions. Juan stood guard. She only faintly registered the information when Juan announced the posse was winning the fight.

Finally she sat on the floor by the foot of the bed. Miguel lay quiet, barely conscious, but the intense look of anguish was gone from Rosa's face. Without asking, Mattie knew Miguel would survive.

Harsh knocking brought her head up just as Juan pulled his gun in line with the door.

"Mattie, it's me, James. Let me in, girl."

"It's okay, Juan, it's my kinsman," she reassured him. She rushed to the door and swung it wide.

"Most of the fightin's over, and I . . ." he stumbled to a stop and gaped as he took in the two boys and the bloody pan of water sitting by the bed. "What in tarnation's been goin' on here?"

"Everything's okay now, Cousin James. This's Rosa's other son, Juan, and we've had some trouble." Mattie brushed a hand against the stray lock of hair. "I think the sheriff may be bad hurt, up by Dorsey's barn."

"Yeah, I know 'bout Tom. He's dead, Mattie."

"Oh, no . . ."

The jangle of spurs and a swift intake of breath brought Mattie's eyes back to the open door. Will filled it, looking tall, strong, and forceful. She had an enormous urge to run into his arms, and she fought a stinging of tears as she held onto her shaky breath. Thank God, Will was unhurt.

"What's happened here?" Will's eyes darted to grasp the situation. "Mattie?"

"I'm not hurt, Will. But Miguel, here . . ."

Long strides carried him to Miguel's side instantly. "Is the boy badly hurt?"

"*Si*, he has lost much blood. But he will live," Rosa said. "If God wills."

Nodding, Will swung to place a hand on Mattie's shoulder. "All right, I want to hear it all, but I haven't time right now. I'll be back as soon as I can." He strode to the door. "Stay with them, James."

Hours later, Will, James, and Sandy sat and stood around Rosa's small cabin and exchanged stories of what had happened to them during the day. The fighting had been fierce in some instances. Eight men had died, three from the posse, including Tom Kimmel. The prisoners they'd taken were being held in Dorsey's barn under heavy guard.

"It was Fulton's shot that jumped the gun?" James asked.

"Yep. But he waited so late to give warning, it didn't help his cohorts much. As for the posse, guess he thought he could talk it away like it was an accident," said Will. "But Bram was watching him, and he knew it wasn't. He was losing the game all the way 'round."

"What'll happen to him now?" asked Mattie.

"He'll stand trial like the rest of them. There's several of the gang willing to testify to Fulton's part in their raids."

"How're we going to get them all back?" queried James.

"We'll get them there, don't worry. There's a shorter way in, as we suspected, so it won't take but two-three days going out, if we push. I plan to push it." Will paused, and looked at Mattie. "Now it's your turn, Miss Mattie."

She nodded and took a deep breath. Glancing at Will, she sucked her bottom lip. He'd probably yell at her for putting herself at risk, but she'd tell it all anyway. Punctuated with details from Juan, she narrated her rescuing of Juan and then the wounding of Miguel and their run-in with Dorsey.

"When we got back here, and I looked to see what was happening, the sheriff was on the ground, and Dorsey was nowhere in sight," she finished.

"Yeah, poor Tom got it right through the heart," said James. "It's better this way. He died a hero's death rather than a falling-down drunk who'd lost his office through his own carelessness."

A moment of silence, then Sandy spoke. "You always did have courage, Miss Mattie."

Flushing, she lifted her lashes, staring at Will's face. He hadn't said anything, but now she noted speculation and concern dwelling deep in the blue eyes.

"Yes, Mattie. I'm sure Juan and Miguel appreciate your bravery." He'd been standing with one foot against the hearth, drinking coffee as he listened. But now he stood straight and moved a step toward her chair.

"And I saw some of it, but I was too far away to help. I was working my way down to you when Tom appeared. By the time I could get to the scene, you were back in the cabin. And Tom was dead."

He touched her cheek, and Mattie's heart thumped. She stared at him with eyes wide.

"You've done as well as any man on the posse today, Mattie." He turned and paced back to the fireplace. "But, God, I wished we'd gotten Dorsey."

She felt the blood drain from her face. Her hands tightened into fists. They didn't get Dorsey? "What do you mean?"

"He got away. Clean away. No one has seen him since Tom was killed."

"No one?" She felt sick with unusual dread. They'd have it all to do again. Turning her head, she stared out into the night. Dorsey was out there.

"Do ya think he got outta the valley?" questioned James. "I thought no one could get past the guards."

"He didn't try that way, or Bram would've seen him. But he's not been taken prisoner either. Nobody's seen him."

"But his power's broke," observed James. "I'm thinkin' he'll take out and leave the country."

"Yes, he's probably long gone," Mattie said to reassure herself.

"Maybe. But I want everyone to keep their eyes open. I can't spare but a few men to stay behind; I'll need all the rest to take the prisoners out."

"We'll keep the guards posted, Will," Sandy said. "The noose is too close for him to try anything except to save his own neck."

"Yeah, that's so." Will let out a long gusty breath. "Okay, men. We'll leave as soon as possible in the morning."

Will and Sandy left with brief goodnights. James spread out his bedroll by the fireplace. Juan rolled into his blanket next to his brother's bed and instantly slept.

"Rosa, I'll help with Miguel through the night," Mattie offered. It would help her nerves to be busy.

"*Gracias,* Mattie. You have been a good friend."

"You saved my mother's life," she replied simply. "But I'm sorry you'll be without your man."

"That one," Rosa spat out. "I am glad to be rid of him. He is not good, not like your Will. I will be better off without him . . . an' maybe my sons will have a chance to live to old age."

Her Will? Mattie hugged the thought tight.

"Sandy," Will called, and jerked his chin to indicate he needed to talk. His spurs clanked loudly as he paced the main room of the Dorsey cabin. Keeping his hands from becoming fists took a concentrated effort, while his jaw ached from clenching it so tight.

"What is it, Will?"

"Where's Caleb?"

"Out in the barn."

"Well, get him in here."

Moments later, Caleb joined them. "Yeah, Will, what's the problem?"

"We've got one helluva problem." He stopped, rubbing his palm against his jaw. "Smith, Landon, and that bunch are in the Sallinger cabin, dead drunk."

"That's not surprisin'. Smith is feelin' the shame, what with Nick turnin' out to be in cahoots with Dorsey an' all," replied Sandy.

"I guess you're right, but I wish he'd waited till after we'd gotten back to Wayside Station."

"You figure this will delay us?" asked Caleb.

"It'll sure change our plans. We've lost three men, counting Tom," Will enumerated. "Two others are so badly wounded they can't ride. Fulton's a prisoner, and now five of our men are so drunk they're no good to us." He renewed his pacing.

"Shucks, Will, we still outnumber the prisoners," said Sandy. "What's worryin' you?"

"We have to leave five or six men behind with the wounded, and Dorsey's still free."

"You think he'll try something?" Caleb queried.

"He might. And we can't be sure we got 'em all. Juan says there were some stragglers following up the trail. Whether they hightailed it back down, or are hanging out to ambush us, we don't know."

"You still plan on leavin' in the morning?"

Will stopped pacing. "Yeah, I still think it's best to get these prisoners back to jail pronto."

"What about Smith and them?"

Will's voice became hard as nails. "They'll ride tomorrow, even if they have to be hog-tied to their saddles. I'll not leave 'em behind to fight with the men who stay. Or to end up hanging that kid Juan."

"I'll stay behind, Will," Caleb offered.

"Thanks, Caleb—I was planning on you. But you know the risks. If Dorsey comes back, you might find a bigger fight on your hands after we leave."

Caleb laughed. "Just leave me Bram. He's worth five men."

"Done."

Fourteen

Early the next morning, Mattie gave Rosa a hug, her eyes misty. "Thank you, Rosa. For your care of my ma, and shelter now. I can't say enough—that is, you've been more than a friend. Thank you."

She bent to place a kiss on Miguel's cheek, and left the cabin. James stood waiting with the saddled horses.

"The boy doin' all right?" he asked.

"I think so, Cousin James. Rosa's a good nurse."

They mounted their horses and rode up the rough village road to where the trail began at the top of the pass. Others were already there. Pulling to a halt, Mattie shifted in her saddle to look back. The outlaw village would remain empty now, and eventually time would destroy it.

She hid her shudder. Thank God, she'd never return.

The Smith faction straggled to join them. Landon could barely sit and looked bruised about the face. Old Skeeter hung over his pommel; Mattie saw where he was tied on with his bandanna. Smith, looking pasty and grim, refused to look anyone in the eye. For the moment, he had lost his bravado.

Will rode up and down the column, checking everything one last time. He posted a heavy guard both front and rear and then gave the signal to leave.

With Will's hard push, the long day felt like a punishment. Night was upon them before Will called a halt, and Mattie slid, exhausted, from her saddle.

The camp, focused around guarding the prisoners, was

strictly no-nonsense as the posse went soberly about their chores. Gone was the feeling of high adventure and righteousness, the quick exchanges and jokes. Those not assigned to immediate guard duty rolled into their blankets as soon as their cold supper was finished.

Mattie, like the others, fell asleep instantly. She'd given up her tent altogether and placed her bedding beside Will's. Sometime in the night, she woke to hear a long sigh of exhaustion. She could see little in the darkness, but knew Will was finally settling himself for sleep. Wishing to give him comfort, she silently reached out to touch his hand, wrapping her fingers into his palm. In silence, he clasped her hand, taking it to his mouth to press his lips there. Then, holding her hand between them, he became still. Mattie, feeling comforted herself, returned to sleep.

For the next day, Will pushed. But the going was slow because of the wounded and the need to keep careful guard on the prisoners. But they'd had no real trouble. Smith brooded to himself, while Landon was unusually cooperative.

Will felt uneasy. However successful the expedition, he couldn't get over the feeling there was more to come. Maybe he was just tired. The long, difficult task of command was draining. He should feel better, he told himself, after tomorrow. Another hard day would take them to Wayside Station. The prisoners could be turned over to Judge Titus and the lawmen he would appoint.

Walking the rounds that night while the camp settled in, he observed the equally exhausted men. Some of them had been chasing this bunch of thieves and rustlers for years; it had almost become a sport. A grim sport, he reminded himself.

Well, he for one would be glad to retire from the game

and concentrate on his own business, his own needs. Mattie. The thought of her made him turn toward where she sat next to Bob's cooking fire, sipping her coffee.

"Can I have a cup of that?" he asked Bob. Sinking to his haunches beside her, he accepted the hot brew and a plate of beans gratefully. He ate rapidly, thinking about the trail they'd take the next day. When the corner of his eye caught the movement of her hand as she placed another biscuit, made fresh tonight, on his plate, he turned to her with a smile. The one lock of hair that was constantly astray curled against her cheek, and he reached to brush it back. "We'll be home tomorrow, and you can sleep in a bed again."

"Yes, and I'll be ready to eat something besides beans for a while."

He chuckled. "Yeah. I've a yearning for a piece of Ma's berry pie just about now."

"Will," she hesitated. "How soon will these men go to trial?"

"Soon, if Judge Titus has arrived. I sent word just before we left Wayside Station." He set his plate down and rubbed his forehead. "Lordy, but I hope he's there."

"Am I going to be needed to testify?"

"Don't rightly know, but there's enough evidence that you shouldn't have to, if you'd rather not. Especially since we didn't get Dorsey."

"No, I don't really want to. And I'll probably be gone by then."

"Gone?"

"Yes, to San Francisco." She looked puzzled for a moment. "That's where Rosa said Ma was headed when she left the valley."

"But Rosa didn't know that, she was just guessing."

"Well, it makes sense to me. After all, Larry earned his

living as a gambler when Ma met him, and San Francisco has a lot of gambling houses."

"By heavens, Mattie." Will's voice reflected his tired irritation. "You can't go haring off on only a rumor."

"Oh, no?" her voice rose in equal vexation. "I came West on just such a rumor."

He was in no mood to argue with her. "Mattie, be sensible."

She jumped to her feet. "Sensible. Sensible. It seems to me you expect me to be mighty 'sensible' when it suits your purpose. Well, let me inform you, Mr. McCarthy, your brand of being sensible doesn't always suit mine. I'm not going to jump just because you say so—it doesn't mean a thing to me."

She spun on her heel and marched to her bedroll.

Now, what? Will rose when she did and watched her stomp away, half tempted to go after her. Then he realized he was the focus of several pairs of eyes.

"Ahh . . ." he exploded under his breath. He knew they had to finish this, but now was not the time. She was tired, he was tired . . . They'd discuss it after they got home and had rested.

He once again made the rounds of men, prisoners, and horses.

Lord in heaven, would he be glad when this was over and done. Then he was going to make Mattie his wife, lock her up, and throw away the key. He'd find the biggest bed he could for their bedroom, keep her there for a year, and let Luke run the ranch without him.

The thought of Mattie in his bed softened his irritation, and he slowed his heavy pacing to lean against a tree near the horses. Remembering the way her lips tasted set up a longing need, and he sucked in his breath. Waiting was gol-dern awful. But wait he would, until this was done and they could be married. And tomorrow they'd be home. They'd get this idea of going to San Francisco straightened out then.

Low murmuring voices drifted in from the far side of the sleeping camp, and Will turned toward the sound. The prisoners were that way. Automatically, he stepped cautiously and approached the voices in silence. In a small clearing away from the main body, he found two men.

"You hadta know I didn't get that money outta the air," Nick Fulton was saying to Smith. "You squandered the money you got when I bought in as your partner, and didn't ask where it came from when you wanted more."

Will edged closer to the two figures. Fulton, his hands and feet tied behind him and pulled up to his knees by Smith's ham-fisted grip at the front of his shirt, showed disdain. His face was a white blur. Smith's menacing figure swayed slightly while he brandished his revolver about.

"Ya shamed me good, ya low down snake," Smith's drunken voice whined. "The town'll think me a blind fool. An' I oughta kill ya outright for what yer bringin' on my little Sally."

"Sally got what she wanted." Fulton laughed low in his throat as though at a dirty joke. "She wanted me, an' I was happy to oblige."

A thud, followed by a grunt of pain caused Will to move forward. At the same time, he was aware of Frank and Sandy, then James, moving to stand beside him.

"Ya—" Smith repeated his cursing with another thud. "Yer a low-down thief in the worst way, a traitor."

"Now hold on, there, Smith . . . umph . . . I married her, didn't I?" Fulton sneered. "I coulda had her without marriage." Another thumping, as Smith let his temper run.

"Stop it, you crazy old man . . . *umph* . . . you didn't complain none when I bought Sally them fancy clothes an' that new buggy she wanted to show off with around town."

Will moved swiftly and folded his hand into the back of Smith's collar. He jerked mightily to haul Smith off Fulton. Smith came stumbling away with fists flailing, his gun waving about. Will reached and yanked it from his hand.

"That's enough, Smith. I know you have cause for bad feelings toward Fulton, but I can't let you beat on a bound man who can't defend himself."

"I gotta right, McCarthy." His glare was red and spiteful.

"Well, some would agree with you on that, but Fulton will have a trial." Will spoke almost regretfully. "You can testify then about how you were betrayed, including where all that money you spent fixing up your place came from."

"I didn't know it was tainted money."

"As Fulton pointed out, Smith," James said, "did ya ever ask him where it was comin' from?"

"Damn you, McCarthy . . . you planned this. Give me back my gun. I'll show you . . . I'll show the whole town." Smith staggered where he stood. "Ya wanted me to be shamed. You an' that dirty outlaw girl."

A loud crack split the air as Will's fist made contact with Smith's jaw. He stepped back, shaking his hand from the impact. He watched the man fall unconscious at his feet without one feeling of regret.

"Glad ya did that, Will," James said, standing at his shoulder. "Smith had it comin'." He shook his head. "He's right about one thing. The town's gonna think he's a fool."

"Buster," Will barked toward the small cluster of men that had gathered on the opposite side of the clearing. "Get Smith to bed and see he doesn't find any more whiskey."

While Buster hauled Smith away, Will ordered a passing man to take Fulton back to the other prisoners. Then he assigned an extra guard to the bunch.

"I'll be almighty glad when this thing is over," James remarked as the men trooped back to bed. The men were either prisoners or guards at this point, and the balance was tenuous.

"Amen to that," agreed Will.

"Mattie," James called to her the next day at the noon break. "We're goin' to split off here, with Frank an' Bob, an' head more d'rectly home with the pack mules. It'll cut the time back-tracking for us, an' we'll be home for supper."

"Fine, Cousin James." She flashed a grateful glance toward Will. They wouldn't have to go into Wayside Station at all. She felt relieved. "I'm looking forward to a hot bath."

A glint entered his blue eyes, and suddenly Mattie felt her face flush. She turned away to hide her embarrassment.

James walked away to consult with Frank, and Will moved to stand beside her, handing her his canteen. She raised it to her lips and swallowed, all the while aware of his nearness.

"It'll be late by the time I'm through in town, Mattie, but I'll come by as soon as I can tomorrow. We have lots to talk about."

"Yes, Will, that'll be fine. I'll be looking for you." Talk . . . if only Will was ready to listen, she could persuade him of her need to go to San Francisco. Once she settled this matter about her mother . . .

Oh, Ma . . . if it is only true you're there . . . alive.

Excitement welled up and she looked at him hopefully.

His expression was warm and inviting, and she got the idea he wanted to kiss her. Unconsciously, she ran her tongue into the dry corner of her lips.

"Mattie," he growled low in his throat. "Don't tempt me."

"Will," called Sandy. "You ready to move out?"

"Sure thing." He replied in a raised voice without removing his gaze from Mattie's face. Dropping his tone once more, he promised, "Tomorrow," and swung away.

Mattie watched the men mount and move out in double file, then pick up their pace to a steady trot. Will wasn't wasting any time.

Quiet descended slowly and Mattie turned back to James. He and Frank were examining the hooves of one of the mules, while Bob was busily packing up the remains of the meager noon meal. She idly picked up a piece of jerky, chewing steadily, thinking of the morrow.

"Hate to leave a good mule behind," Frank grumbled. "Hope Bram remembers to pick up the boss's horse when he comes through that mountain."

"Yep," James agreed. "Will sets store by his horses. But that black he picked up in the valley is one of the best pieces of horseflesh I ever seen. Makes ya wonder where in tarnation them outlaws find all the best stock."

"Dam balky critter," muttered Frank. "Might as well make yourself comfortable for a bit, Miss Mattie. We'll have to shift a load on this here mule."

Sighing, Mattie followed Frank's directive. It might be later before she got her bath. She leaned against a tree and allowed her droopy eyes to close.

A low laugh rumbled into her sleepy consciousness, which caused her heavy lids to lift. A frisson of alarm ran up the back of her neck. Suddenly, a mule plunged and bucked, making a high piercing scream.

"What the . . ." Frank never finished, for he fell in a heap with the first sound of whistling bullets.

Leaping to her feet, Mattie ran to her mount and tugged her rifle free of the sling while her eyes frantically searched the area. James, behind a boulder, was returning fire toward three mounted men coming at them through the trees. From the corner of her eye, she saw Bob raise his gun and fire. She whirled toward the attackers just as Bob fell.

"Mattie girl, make a run for it," yelled James.

Ignoring him, she jumped behind a large rock and positioned her rifle, pulling the trigger almost instantly.

"Mattie," his voice begged.

"No, Cousin James. I'll not leave you." Several minutes of roaring exchange caused the little copse of trees to be heavy with smoke. The remaining mules broke and ran. And then Mattie realized she was the only one firing.

Cautiously, she listened as her heart beat with terror. There was no sound from Cousin James. She clenched her teeth in sudden grief as understanding hit her.

Oh, God! James . . . Were any of them alive? She edged out, but saw nothing.

Mattie stood, turned, and went rigid. Dorsey stood only yards from her, bold as you please.

"Now the odds are back in my favor." Nate Dorsey laughed, and the low, exultant sound reminded her of coiled snakes; terrible fear and dread slithered up her body.

Mattie stepped back a pace, her eyes darting to the men lying on the ground. All that showed of James were his boots from behind the boulder. They didn't move. Frank and Bob lay sprawled where they'd fallen. Blood flowed everywhere.

Her stomach wrenched as though a giant hand squeezed

her middle, and then heaved. She covered her mouth against sudden sickness. Dragging her gaze away, she forced herself to look back at Nate.

"That's right, Mattie. They're dead. And now you pay your debts." The smile faded from his lips and cruel triumph entered his face like a January blizzard. He threw an order over his shoulder. "Horn, check 'em."

A smallish man with a black scruffy beard spoke in a sour tone. "They ain't gonna bother us no more." He spat a stream of tobacco juice out of the corner of his mouth. "Neither is Jake, there, gonna be no more help."

"Jake got it?" Nate kept his eyes glued to Mattie. "Fair enough. I got what I came after." In two strides he reached her, flicking her rifle from her in the blink of an eye.

Mattie fought, but Dorsey yanked her toward her horse, all the while kicking and screaming. "Mount up, slut."

Wrenching her arm cruelly, he picked her up and threw her into the saddle, quickly tying her hands to the pommel. He turned to his own mount, and Mattie twisted to look over her shoulder as her sobs broke. She stretched to see once more where James lay behind the boulder, but tears blinded her. Dorsey jerked her reins into a tight hold, which brutally pulled Sensible around. Mattie reeled as she battled to retain her balance.

They rode fast, heading due south for some hours, never stopping. Mattie, her tears drying, froze into solid ice inside. She knew what Dorsey intended for her, knew he was quite capable of rape and horrible brutality. A resolve gradually built to solid substance in her soul.

She would survive this. By God's grace, she would live through it; others had. She dreaded the thought—but sooner or later, she'd have to kill this man in exchange for her life.

★ ★ ★ ★ ★

Darkness lifted slowly. It felt, to James, as if he fought toward consciousness through a giant web of thick cotton. But the growing sense of alarming urgency knifed through the cloudy thickness and cleared his mind.

Mattie. He had to help Mattie.

Pushing hard against the sluggishness, he rolled over with a groan. His head hurt horribly. Reaching up, he felt the stickiness of blood against his cheek. As he pulled himself to stand, he felt the heavy rock boulder burn underneath his hand. Subconsciously, he realized it must still be afternoon, for the stone held the sun's heat.

A light breeze covered the stillness of the area as he looked around the devastation. A faint dust cloud on the southern horizon told him which direction they'd gone. The enemy had left, but they'd taken Mattie. Stumbling toward Frank and Bob, he confirmed what he was already sure of; he could do nothing for them.

Galvanized into action, James caught his horse, raking his spurs across the horse's flanks the instant he was in the saddle. The horse leaped forward, and James kept him at a flat-out run. He had to get to Will.

Someone toward the back of the posse yelled. Will turned, instantly alert, and wheeled his mount to the rear. A rider was approaching at a dead run.

James? Wearily, he wondered—what is it now?

Spurring his horse, he wheeled to meet him.

Several men reached out as the lathered horse came to a stop, spreading his legs to blow heavily. James reeled in the saddle and Will stretched to catch him. Dismounting, he helped the older man do the same and eased him to the ground.

"Will. Dorsey got Mattie."

A second of stunned acceptance, then, "Where?"

"At the stop. Soon as you was out of earshot. We fought, but . . . They headed due south from there."

"Frank and Bob?"

James merely shook his head.

Will was mute for a moment, sorrow for the loss of his old friends cutting through him like a knife. Then fear for Mattie took precedence.

"How long ago?" asked Sandy.

"The attack came less'n an hour after you left. Don't know how long I was out," James answered.

"How many men?" Will asked. The thought of Mattie in the hands of Dorsey shot lightning bolts of agony through him, leaving him hot, then cold.

"Only Dorsey an' one other, now. We got one of 'em."

Will rose and stood frozen for a full minute, thinking hard, then started firing out commands in rapid demand.

"Sandy, you, Thomas, and Blane, come with me. Jackson and Williams, you get James home." He stalked to where Smith and Landon sat on their horses while the remainder of the posse guarded the prisoners.

"You, gentlemen . . ." his voice was hard and caustic while he held their eyes with steely command, "are going to see that these men make it to the Wayside Station jail. If you lose one man I will personally come after you and nail your hides to the jailhouse wall. Got that?"

"McCarthy, we . . ."

"Get." Will roared, his Colt leveling in line with Smith's chest. He allowed himself only five seconds to watch them move away. Then, whirling, he leaped into his saddle.

An hour later when he viewed the ugly scene of death, he silently cursed, and touched the faces of his fallen men with deep sorrow. Both Frank and Bob had been with him since the early days. Grimly, he assigned Thomas and Blane to take the bodies on to the ranch and, resolutely turning his back, headed south.

Dorsey chose a dip in the land near a stream to camp for the night. It was a natural spot with trees offering additional shelter.

"Ain't we stoppin' awful quick?" asked the little man.

Dorsey was contemptuous. "Aw, that posse is all the way into town by now. We'll be long gone before they figure out somethin' is wrong an' come lookin'." He stepped down from his saddle. "Start camp."

Mattie watched him move toward her with a coldness she'd never before experienced. Inside, she cringed when he laid a hand on her thigh while he helped her dismount. Outwardly she showed a stony face, rubbing her wrists where the rope had burned. The skin was raw.

"Now, you little slut, you can start by cookin' supper. Then I'll show you what it's all about."

He laughed hatefully, and she turned her back. She was safe for an hour or so, if she could draw out the task of making supper.

"Can I go and wash?" she asked woodenly.

"Yeah, but stay in plain sight. I won't hesitate to use a switch on ya if I have to," he threatened.

Mattie moved to the stream, kneeling close by the edge to plunge her painful wrists into the cool water. She gritted her teeth until they nearly cracked and swallowed down a groan. He would not see her weaknesses.

"Hurry up, Mattie." He lounged back against a log that he was using for a backrest. "I'm a powerful hungry man." He laughed uproariously.

"I'm a mite woman hungry, myself," Horn said, giving her a sly look from where he was building a fire.

"The devil you are." Dorsey sat up and glared. "I ain't sharin' this one."

Horn spat, and a dribble of the tobacco juice ran down his chin. "Ain't sharin', huh?"

"Nope."

"What about the money you got stashed down in Mexico?" Horn watched the big man carefully.

"You'll get your share of that when we get there." Dorsey returned Horn's stare suspiciously until, apparently accepting the answer, Horn turned away.

Mexico! They were taking her to Mexico?

"Get to it, woman," Dorsey barked.

Jumping in spite of herself, Mattie turned to pull out supplies from the saddlebags. Horn stared at her, and an idea was born. She dragged out the making of supper until Nate hollered at her slowness again.

"It takes time to cook." She gave him a stolid reply without looking at him. Keeping her back to him, she tipped her head slightly to wink at Horn.

"Well, I ain't gonna wait all night," Dorsey said in a milder tone.

Horn didn't respond by so much as a twitch of an eyebrow, but Mattie felt hopeful just the same. If she could play one against the other, she might provoke enough suspicion so that Dorsey wouldn't dare divert his attention from Horn. Dorsey couldn't rape her if he had to watch Horn.

When the meal was ready, she served Dorsey first. He cursed when she handed him the tin plate. "Careful, woman. That plate is hot."

Saying nothing, she carried a second plate of food to Horn, allowing her fingers to brush his as she handed it to him. Raising her lashes, she looked him in the eye and slyly dropped them again. At the same time, she pursed her lips slightly, silently imitating a kiss.

"Get back over here, woman," Dorsey barked from across the fire. "Now eat."

"There isn't an extra plate," she commented in an even tone and rejoiced at an added delay. She sat by the fire and stirred the coals.

"You can use mine when I'm done."

The thought revolted her. However, Mattie waited in silence until she heard the clatter of the tin plate as Dorsey threw it down beside her. Sneaking a look to see what he was doing, she realized he had walked to a tree to relieve himself.

Holding her nerves together with the glue of desperation, she casually sidled over to Horn. She softened her voice and shamelessly fluttered her lashes. "I'll take your plate now."

Mattie held steady as Horn licked his lips and reached out a hand to touch her.

"Mattie," Dorsey warned. He sounded as though he still had his back turned.

She waited, gripping the plate so tightly her knuckles showed white. Dorsey said nothing more, so, giving Horn one last flutter, Mattie slowly pivoted and walked back to the fire, swinging her hips the way Coralee had.

"I want my share." Horn abruptly stood.

Dorsey took a couple of steps back toward the center of camp, his face distorted with menace. "I told you . . ."

Mattie swallowed and edged away.

"The girl. I want my share of the girl . . . now." A heavy long-barreled revolver sprang into Horn's hand, aimed across the fire at the bigger man.

Mattie dove behind the log and flattened herself hard against the ground.

Dorsey cursed as he threw his body to the side. He fired his own gun from the hip.

The loud report was followed by Horn's gun, and Mattie waited with her face pressed against the hard earth. Harsh breathing sounded close, and she was jerked up and shoved to sit on the log. Beyond the fire, she caught a glimpse of Horn's body sprawled with out-flung arms.

Dorsey's heavy hand snaked out to strike her hard across the face. She fell backward, tumbling to the ground with her legs caught on the rough bark of the log. Giving her no quarter, he jerked her up again, mercilessly pinching her cheeks between his hard, sausage-like fingers.

"Don't you ever so much as look cross-eyed at another man again," he snarled into her face. "Got that?"

Mattie stared at him through a painful haze. If he hit her again . . .

If? He'd end up beating her to death.

"Now I'm through being patient." He circled her neck with his hand, stretching it, as he pulled up her chin. Squeezing, he cut off her air as he clamped his mouth to hers.

Frantically she pried at his fingers against her throat, while her stomach roiled and heaved. She couldn't breathe and was fighting the blackness that threatened to engulf her. She was near to fainting.

Instinctively, she lashed out, scratching his face and pulling his hair. Then, almost by accident, her thumb gouged his eye.

"You bitch," he screamed and threw her down as he clapped a hand to his eye.

She sobbed for breath as her lungs screamed for air.

Crawling a few paces out of reach, she stumbled to her feet. She had to get Horn's gun.

"Oh, no you don't." He laid hold of her shoulder and twirled her around to face him.

Mattie wavered and ducked, eluding his clutch only to stumble over a large stone. She fell, hitting the ground on her bottom. Like a flash, she rolled away from his reach, coming to a halt against a jagged boulder near Horn's outstretched hand. Instantly, she snatched at the gun lying only inches away.

A heavy boot came down on her hand and pinned her to the ground. Dorsey's fisted hand raised, but never descended.

"Dorsey." Will's voice shafted the air like a steel lance.

Fifteen

Mattie twisted her face toward the sound. Will stood in the fringe of the firelight with a gun in each hand, and both were trained directly on Dorsey. Will's tall figure looked like an avenging angel in a ten-gallon hat.

"Thank God," she breathed. "My Will."

"Move away from her."

The hulking figure turned, his face carved into an ugly grimace.

"Step away easy, and raise your hands," Will ordered in a deadly tone. "Or I'll let you have both barrels at once."

Slowly, Dorsey complied. "You McCarthy by any chance?"

"That's right," Will agreed through his teeth. "Mattie, come here."

She started toward him, circling wide of Dorsey.

"Heard about you." Dorsey halted, talking in an even tone. "You're the one's been on my tail?"

"Right again."

"This girl lead you into my hideout?" He tipped his head and squinted into the distance, as though he were reflecting on life.

"Yep."

"Figures." The word and his gun were out together, and he fired while flinging himself to the ground.

Will's guns blazed in return, while he hit the ground and rolled, then raised and fired again. At the same time, Sandy's gun blasted from the trees, and Will heard a smothered groan as Dorsey took a hit. He twisted to see where Mattie was, and was satisfied when he saw her behind a boulder.

The spurt of a bullet furrowed the ground next to him, as he ran, crouching, to join Mattie. He reached the rock, heard the ping of a bullet hitting the stone, and spun to face Dorsey.

The man stood upright while blood spurted from his shoulder. Will watched in fascination as Dorsey's gun came up, aiming right at him. Without hesitation, Will fired.

Dorsey swayed, and then crashed to the ground like a giant tree.

Slowly, Will rose from his crouch and walked over to the bandit. Will looked down at the big body. Dorsey didn't move.

"Will? Oh, Will . . ." Mattie bounded to him, leaning against him while she tried to hold back the shuddering.

His arm went around her and hugged her tightly to his side. "You're safe now, sweetheart."

Nodding her understanding, Mattie slid her arms around his middle and leaned her forehead against his chest. Her hands clutched his back, solid and hard. The trembling eased and the tears of release began to flow.

"It's okay now, darlin'. It's all over." He looked at the bruises beginning to form on her face while he soothed and wrapped his other arm about her. She'd have a doozy of a bruise. She sobbed, and he swayed and rocked her closer. After a moment, the tears subsided, and he brushed the stray lock of hair back against her temple. "Are you all right?"

"You're here, you're here." Pushing her face into the open collar of his shirt, she gratefully breathed in the smell of him. "Will," she hiccupped out, "I prayed you'd come."

"I did a little praying, myself," he whispered against her ear. "God, Mattie, you couldn't have been more frightened than I was."

He gently kissed her neck, and then regretfully let her go. "Come on in now, Sandy."

"Everything okay?" Sandy stepped out of the trees.

"Yes. Let's get this vermin out of sight."

Mattie turned her back while they carried the two bodies into the trees, and sank to the ground beside the fire. Needing to be busy, she fed it until it was a roaring blaze. She wanted warmth and light against the night. Later, she would make coffee.

An hour later, she curled up next to Will, sharing his blankets as she put her head confidently on his shoulder. She didn't care a fig what Sandy might think from where he lay on the other side of the fire. In low voices, she and Will shared their separate stories of what had happened. She cried anew, when she learned James was alive

"Oh, I'm so very glad . . . I couldn't have looked Cousin Beatrice in the face if . . ."

"Go to sleep now, sweetheart." He kissed her lightly. "We'll be home in a day or two and can get this business behind us. Then we can be married before the month is out."

Mattie lay very quiet as she listened. His voice was gentle and deep with love.

"I built a house, you know, just for us," his voice low. "It has a huge stone fireplace in the great parlor and lots of room for guests. There's a long porch on the front and side that'll catch the summer breezes. But we'll have to find a bed for our room. I want a big one, one that'll see you through the birth of our children, and maybe their children. I want to sleep in it with you by my side, sweetheart . . . Sweetheart?"

She didn't answer and his voice stilled. A moment later, she knew he slept. He'd thought this out, she realized. Made plans. Plans that included her.

The long ride into Wayside Station the next day with the two bodies in tow was exhausting. The last hour, Mattie rode by sheer, concentrated willpower, determined to stay in the saddle. They didn't arrive until dark.

"McCarthy's come in," a voice suddenly shouted from in front of a saloon. "And he's got the girl with him."

"McCarthy's in," echoed another, and then another.

People started filling the street.

"You got 'em, huh? Dorsey?" buzzed the questions.

"Somebody find the judge," said another.

"Will, Mattie . . . thank God you're safe," Josie called to them. Her husband Ben followed her as she rushed to the edge of the wooden sidewalk. "We've been worried sick."

Will guided the small party to the rail in front of the mercantile and halted, helping Mattie to dismount. He gave her a reassuring squeeze and turned to his sister. "Josie, take care of Mattie for a while. I'll be back when I can."

"Sure thing, Will." Josie moved to receive Mattie in her arms. "Let's go inside. Ben, put some water on the stove for Mattie's bath. My stars, Mattie, how'd your face get so bruised?"

Mattie didn't answer. Instead, she watched Will and Sandy move away down the street, dismounting at the jail. At last she turned gratefully to Josie.

"How's Cousin James?"

"He's all right, recovering at home. But his head is going to have a scar. He's been fretting about you. An' so's the rest of your kinfolk."

Josie guided Mattie to the stairs, which led to her and Ben's apartment above the store. "Ma's been worried near out of her mind. Reckon we ought to find someone to ride out an' let everybody know you an' Will are safe."

"Yes, please do that, Josie." Mattie sank down on the sofa.

"Well, at least it's all over. With those thieves cleaned out, maybe the county can get back to honest living and some peace. This town's been like a sideshow these last weeks, strangers coming in asking about the posse an' such. An' then you being kidnapped by Dorsey, why . . ." Josie stopped to draw breath.

"Oh, Mattie, I'm sorry I'm chattering so, but . . ." Sudden tears stood out in her eyes. "Ma's not the only one been worried," she confessed. "Your kinfolks, me, Luke . . . anyway, we're all glad it's over."

"It's all right, Josie. D'you suppose the bath water is hot yet?"

"I'll go check on it, and send Ben out to the ranch with the news you're home. Then I'll make you some real English tea. An' something to eat . . ." Her voice trailed behind her from the kitchen.

Mattie put her head back and closed her eyes. She was limp with exhaustion. She as yet had to go through everything with Josie, to tell the tale. She'd want to know it all in detail. The idea was daunting.

Josie thought everything was over. Will seemed to think so too, and was planning the future. He had it all mapped out, even a house. Will had built it for her, Mattie, and she longed to see it. The thought of living with Will, being his wife and bearing his children, filled her with a yearning so deep, it started in the pit of her stomach and overflowed her mind.

"Oh, Will," she murmured. "I do want to live with you, I want to be your wife . . . I'm not afraid anymore. I love you.

I love you so much it hurts."

Her tired mind whirled and cried out as she struggled with the decision she'd already made. Because, for her, it wasn't over. Not until she found her mother, if she was still alive, however long that would take. She had to go to San Francisco.

Three mornings later, Will rode into the J-B ranch yard, just before noon. Dressed in a brand new shirt, fresh jeans, and with a wedding ring in his pocket, his hopes were high. This was the last time he'd need to propose. A smile insisted on spreading across his face, and he felt like a newborn calf just discovering the world. He could hardly wait to see Mattie.

They'd both been so worn out, they scarcely talked when he delivered her to the Cramer ranch the morning after they returned. He'd claimed a quick kiss when he helped her dismount and told her he'd call on her in a day or so.

Will was impatient with the demanding legalities of the expedition, but he did everything he needed to satisfy Judge Titus. The number of people that wanted to congratulate him on the success of the posse, slowing the process, staggered and fretted him. Gratefully, he accepted Luke's taking over the funerals for Bob and Frank. Dealing with his sadness over their loss was, at best, difficult.

As far as he was concerned, most of it was finished. Now he planned to spend the next fifty years and longer concentrating on Mattie. His grin spread wider as he knocked on the Cramers' door.

"Come in, son, I been expecting you," James called. He laid down his spectacles and the paper he was reading. He wore only a patch of cloth on his head wound.

"Oh, yes, Will, do come in." Beatrice spoke, nervously

twisting a dishtowel as she dried her hands.

"Morning, ma'am. Good to see you recovering so well, James." His smile flashed to each of them. "I've come calling on Mattie."

The Cramers exchanged a glance. His smile faltered a little. What was wrong? The place was too quiet. "Where is she?"

"Will, uh . . . I'm sorry, boy. Mattie's gone."

The smile faded into soberness. Instantly, he knew James didn't mean Mattie'd just taken a trip to town. The twin emotions of keen disappointment and anger kindled in the pit of his belly. But as he listened to both James and Beatrice stumble through explanations, the disappointment waned as the anger flamed into a raging fury; she'd left without talking with him.

". . . and she left you this letter." Beatrice ended her telling and handed him the folded white paper like a peace offering.

"Thank you," he murmured. He turned away to stand by the open window, and read the letter in silence. The stillness was so full of waiting, Beatrice's prized mantel clock tick sounded loud.

The letter said little more than what Beatrice and James had already told him. Despite his anger, he almost laughed at the formality of the note.

Will,

I am sorry to upset your plans . . . and feel deeply your disappointment. However, I must go to San Francisco to search for my mother. Aunt Elizabeth will accompany me, so please do not concern yourself with my welfare. If, when my task is complete, you still wish it, I will be honored to be your wife.

Thank you for your devotion and care during the recent danger we faced together. May God bless you.

Mattie

He refolded the letter as he stood staring out the window down the ranch yard to the outbuildings. The summer sun was high, and the old barn looked hazy in the heat waves. Idly, he rubbed his thumb against the smooth, white paper.

There was a spot that rippled under his touch, and his fingers automatically sought the place again and again, setting a rhythm as his thoughts tumbled and swirled. A ripple in the smooth.

He looked down at it. It was a dried water spot, about the size of his thumbnail. Or . . . a teardrop? Once again, this time tenderly, he ran a thumb across it.

Abruptly, he turned to look at the two older people that had become like his second parents. He felt his face set.

"You goin' after her?" James's face was hopeful.

"Yep." As suddenly as his spirits had plummeted, they rose again. He wasn't too ready to let go of his anger, but a grin worked its way out of him in spite of himself.

"Oh, that's lovely, Will. That's fine," said Beatrice. Her smile spread across her face like the sunrise.

"Well, ya better hurry, son. Mattie an' Elizabeth has a two-day start on ya," James drawled.

"Yes, sir." He shook hands with James and kissed Beatrice's cheek, and mounted his horse in one leap.

It took an agonizingly slow two days for Will to settle family matters with Luke and finalize legal ones with Judge Titus. Luke was eager to try his hand at running the ranch. Judge Titus asked endless questions. But finally, he was ready to leave. Luke and Sandy saw him off.

"Don't take no wooden nickels," advised Sandy.

"An' don't get shanghaied on no ship," added Luke.

"Beware of them big city slickers," Sandy continued.

"An' stay away from . . ." Luke began again.

"Enough, you galoots." Will chuckled. "I'm dry behind the ears."

"Okay," said Luke. He cocked his head. "But Will . . . one last thing. Don't come home without her."

"I don't aim to, Luke." He slapped his brother on the back and climbed into the Wells Fargo coach. He'd never been out of his territory, and the thought of visiting San Francisco excited him. He didn't look back.

Will stood outside the train station and gaped. San Francisco was a marvel: tall buildings, bustling traffic, fancy hotels, restaurants, and saloons. And more people than he'd ever seen in his life. For the first time, he truly understood the difference of the life he led in comparative isolation with that of a city dweller who had all the finery one could ask for.

When he saw the ocean, the endless body of water staggered his imagination. He ate dinner that night from a wharf-side stand, tasting fish he never knew existed, and watched the sun sink into the ocean.

But none of it daunted him. He couldn't let it. He found a rooming house and paid a week's lodging in advance. He'd find Mattie if he had to stay all summer, Will determined. Then if they had to hire a dozen detectives to find her mother, they'd do it.

Deciding that a systematic approach was the best, he started making the rounds of the prominent hotels. He inquired for both Mattie and her aunt by name from the desk clerks, talked to bell-boys, and, along with a big tip, left descriptions of both of them. When he could, he left messages for them. At night, he searched the saloons on Montgomery Street for a gambler named Larry Potter.

Three days later, Will returned to his rooming house tired and a bit lonely. He'd had little sleep, what with staying out to the early morning hours each night and searching each day. He'd checked with all the main hotels in the downtown area and, that day, extended his search to the outer districts.

Now he climbed the stairs to his third-floor room feeling discouraged. And then, as he swung open his door, he stepped on a folded white paper. His heart thumped hard against his ribs as he opened it.

"*Yahoooo!*" He let out a cowboy yell that caused a couple of doors to open down the hall.

It was a message from Elizabeth, telling him at which hotel she and Mattie were staying, and inviting him to dine with them that evening. He grinned at the other curious roomers. "I've just come into good fortune," he told them. Closing his door, he gathered clean clothes to have a bath in the fancy bathroom down the hall.

Later in the evening, Mattie paced the parlor of the suite of rooms she shared with Aunt Elizabeth, marking the perimeter one more time. She'd been in a fidget all afternoon, ever since she and her aunt had returned from a shopping trip to find Will's message. Her first thought was that he'd be angry with her, and at the way she'd left without talking to him. Mattie bit the inside of her mouth. She'd hoped by the time she returned to Wayside Station, he would be over his anger. But to have followed her all the way to San Francisco . . . he must be white hot with rage.

Nervously Mattie stopped in front of a mirror and smoothed a hand down the cream silk dinner dress she wore. It showed her neck and shoulders, with deep lacy flounces over the full sleeves. It was a true evening dress. She hoped Will would like it.

She turned and retraced her steps. She didn't know why she'd been surprised to find him in San Francisco. From the first time she'd met him, Will had been like this, going after or holding onto something like a bulldog, demanding and cajoling to get his own way. And he'd certainly been making his claim on her obvious. He wanted her.

Mattie stopped to fiddle with the cut-glass lamp on the small table beside the sofa.

"Maybe he didn't get the message." She glanced up at her aunt, who sat serenely plying her needle in a piece of cloth.

"I'm sure he'll come soon, Mattie. It's still early," Elizabeth soothed. She turned as a firm knock sounded against the door. "There, my dear, you needn't have fretted."

Mattie's heart stopped, and then started again in double-time. On trembling legs, she walked to the door and opened it wide. She looked up into Will's deep blue eyes as he stood, legs slightly apart as though braced for a high wind, with his hat in his hand. The hall lamps edged his hair with gilt and cast shadows into the hollows of his face. His expression was sober. Mattie's heart kicked into triple-time.

"Evening, Mattie," Will said in a calm, even tone.

"Will, please come in." She stopped to lick her dry lips. "I'm so glad you're here . . . I mean . . . that you could join us for dinner."

He stepped into the room and glanced around. It was richly furnished and carpeted in shades of red, with gold-framed mirrors and pictures on the walls. It was a far cry from his sparse place at the rooming house. Or anything he had at home. Letting his gaze roam through a partially opened door, he saw a bedroom decorated in blue. The bed looked huge.

"Good evening, Will." Elizabeth held out her hand.

Will brought his gaze back to the two women and took Elizabeth's hand.

"Evening, Miss Adams," he returned her greeting with quiet assessment. He didn't know yet if she was on his side, or if he was going to have to do his courting against her wishes. Elizabeth held his gaze, apparently making her own assessment. After a moment she seemed to have come to a favorable decision, for she smiled.

"Please sit down." Elizabeth directed him to a chair. "We have only a few moments before dinner. We have a seating arranged for us in the downstairs dining room in about thirty minutes."

"Thank you, ma'am." He sat down gingerly. He wasn't used to the refinements of this life; his frontier existence hadn't prepared him for such graciousness. He glanced tentatively at Mattie. She sat on the edge of the sofa while her lashes fanned her cheeks.

Will stared at her creamy shoulders sloping from a long throat. Her hair was piled high on her head in burnished curls, but one stray lock cascaded down her back. In her ears and nestled against the curve of her neck, were pearls.

"When did you arrive in San Francisco?" Elizabeth asked. She sat next to Mattie.

"Almost a week ago, ma'am." He didn't miss Mattie's flutter of lashes, and thought he might just as well come out with it. "I followed you out as soon as I could."

"You followed?" Elizabeth looked puzzled and then cast a sidelong glance at Mattie.

"Yes, ma'am. Mattie and I have, ah . . . uh . . . an understanding." One side of his mouth dimpled in an effort to contain his sudden amusement.

"Oh?"

He watched her lashes lift a fraction. His amusement fled. "Yes, ma'am. She is going to marry me and I am going to help her find her ma." He watched in satisfaction as Mattie's eyes flew open to meet his gaze. Her mouth formed a circle.

"Oh, Will." She jumped up, her voice full of gladness. "I thought you'd be so furious, I was . . . just . . ." Her voice trailed away as she stared into his eyes.

A faint knock sounded on the outer door and her aunt rose to answer it.

"I was, Mattie, and I still am." Will held her gaze with a hard one of his own, allowing her to see the anger in his eyes. He watched the pink flush that crept up her cheeks, and then her chin came up in defiance.

"Yes, I see you are." She pulled her back into a straighter line and propped a hand on her hip while she glared at him. "But if there is to be a marriage . . ."

"Not *if*, Mattie, *when*—" he interrupted, his voice firm as he rose. Facing her squarely, he continued in a lazy drawl, "*When* we marry, we will make all big decisions together. You won't be going off by yourself, again." A smile crept into his voice as his expression softened. "And I think it must be soon now, or I might end up embarrassing you in front of your Aunt Elizabeth."

Mattie's pink face flushed into rose as she returned his unyielding gaze and her voice went a notch higher. "Oh, you are much too sure of yourself, Mr. McCarthy. Just too high-handed, indeed."

He allowed his gaze to roam lazily down her features, coming to rest for a moment on the curve of her mouth. He couldn't keep the smile from curving into place as he thought of her response the last time he had kissed her. "I have reason to be, Miss Mattie. Or have you forgotten?"

Mattie felt the heat travel down her body. Looking into the deep blue eyes, she became entangled in the depths of his gaze. She lost all sense of surroundings and her pique dissolved as she felt wrapped in the hot desire she saw lurking there beyond his amusement. Her mouth softened and she wanted very badly at that moment to be kissed.

"We are ready to dine now, children." Mattie heard Elizabeth speak from somewhere outside their enclosed circle. She felt pulled back from the brink of falling down a deep well, and went scarlet once more. A bit dazed, she turned to her aunt.

"You can discuss this over dinner," Elizabeth said.

Will turned toward Mattie's aunt, feeling he could have gladly thrown the woman out of the room on her head at that moment. If they'd been alone, Mattie would have melted into his arms. He struggled to curb his impatience and, fed by the image of Elizabeth bouncing on her head in the hall and the scandal it would create, allowed his amusement to surface once more.

"Yes, ma'am," he murmured politely. Turning to Mattie, he saw she had stiffened again.

Moments later they were seated in the hotel dining room and Will did his best to act the perfect escort. He kept his face bland and his voice politely neutral as Elizabeth talked about the city. He set himself to woo Mattie, throwing her glances of love and secret smiles. Watching carefully, he was aware when her body relaxed and she began to enjoy the food. A break in Elizabeth's dialogue allowed him to catch Mattie's direct attention with a question.

"What have you done toward finding your ma?" he asked quietly.

"We've engaged the Pinkerton Agency, but so far they haven't found her, or Larry either." Mattie laid down her fork. "I was wondering, Will, now that you're here . . ." She hesitated to say what she had in mind, for she knew he'd explode in protest. "If you and I visited some of the saloons, then I might spot Larry."

"Absolutely not."

"Mattie!" Elizabeth gasped.

"But, don't you see, I'm the only one who knows what Larry looks like. I suspect he's changed his name. We hadn't a picture to give the Pinkertons, only a description, and the only one I have of Ma is when she was sixteen."

"Mattie dear, you can't go into the saloons," protested her aunt.

"But Aunt Elizabeth, if Will escorts me I won't be in any danger. I realize I can't go alone to those places at night." She laid a hand on Will's arm and turned beseeching eyes directly on him. "Please, Will. I can't sit around doing nothing any longer."

"Mattie, do you realize how rough those saloons can get?"

"Yes, but some of them are very high class, catering to the best of society," she persisted. "And Larry was very elegant when Ma first met him."

Will felt his resolve slipping away as he looked into her pleading face. She wanted to find her mother so badly, she would go to any lengths.

"You'll be with me," she added in a soft voice.

His heart thumped a little harder and he knew he hadn't a chance. Covering her hand, he curled his fingers around it in a firm clasp. "All right, Mattie, but you'll follow my orders, and if I feel we need to leave a place, then we'll have no argument. If I don't like it altogether, we won't go in.

You'll hang onto me like you're growing out of my side."

Will gave Mattie one of his no-nonsense stares. They had been through this process before. The now-familiar demand for promises to obey him felt like a pattern he was doomed to follow. He was in for more trouble, he was sure. Gritting his teeth, he said, "Understand?"

"Yes, sir," she flipped back instantly. A slow smile spread across her face. Will was doing this just for her, because of his love for her.

"Well, I don't approve, but you must do what you must," said Elizabeth. "Under the circumstances, I suppose you'll be safe with Will."

Safe with Will? The idea so startled Mattie that she turned to stare at her aunt.

"There's never been a man I've been more safe with, Aunt Elizabeth," she murmured, and held her breath. Something drained away from her mind at that moment, and Mattie felt the last dregs of bitter distrust of men, distrust of love, dissolve into nothing. Suddenly she knew she'd always be safe with Will. His love was a warm shelter from past hurts and wounds, as well as the growing excitement of desire yet to be fulfilled.

Mattie turned to gaze again into his eyes. "I've always trusted Will with my life," she stated simply. "And now I trust him with my heart."

Will sat in stunned silence for a moment. He almost felt unmanned, for he wanted to cry and shout at the same time. This was the first time she'd come close to admitting her love for him.

He'd won. At last he'd won her.

He stared into the amber-brown pools where her soul shone through, and he knew she was ready to face her need of him and their marriage bed. The promise shone from her eyes more brilliant than the stars.

"Mattie." He stopped and swallowed, then glanced at Elizabeth. "May we get the bill now, ma'am? The sooner we get started on this search, the sooner I'll have a bride."

"Very well, children." Elizabeth couldn't suppress her smile.

Sixteen

Will accompanied the two women back to their rooms and waited for Mattie to get a cloak against the evening chill. He and Mattie said goodnight to Elizabeth and set out.

"Cabby," Will called to a passing carriage. The driver was a small man of color who sported a bright red vest. "Do you know of a . . . ah, genteel place that I might take a lady gaming?"

"Surely do, sir, surely do. They's the Golden Nugget that 'lows ladies in, and the Hill Palace." He looked Will over carefully. "They might not let a cowboy in, though. Begging yo' pardon, sir, but ain't you got no proper evening clothes?"

Will looked down at his old town suit and chuckled. It did look a little worn. Buying new clothes for himself hadn't entered his head. "Reckon I don't, at that."

"Oh, Will," Mattie pleaded. "We can shop for evening dress tomorrow. But let's not let that stop us tonight."

"Okay, Mattie. We'll go where we can tonight, and get on with our search." Turning back to the cabby, he asked, "What's your name?"

"Gabriel, sir."

"Do you know this city well?"

"Surely do, sir. I've been driving a cab here for ten years."

"Well, Gabriel, I have a proposition for you. This lady and I are searching for someone, a gambler. And also, a woman. We'd be much obliged if you could direct us around a bit, you know, to the gaming houses and saloons, but steer us clear of the real low-life places."

"It's a mighty big city, sir," Gabriel responded, shaking his head. "Might take some time."

"I realize that, Gabriel, but it's important. I'll pay you double your usual fee for as long as we're searching. Is it a deal?"

"Yes, sir, it surely is. Climb up, Missus."

Will helped Mattie into the buggy and settled himself beside her. When they pulled up in front of the first establishment, he leaned down to her ear. "Stay close."

"Yes, I will." True to her word, Mattie clung to his arm throughout the evening as they went from one gambling spot to the next.

"It's after two, Mattie," Will murmured as they climbed into the carriage once more after a disappointing inspection of the fifth place. He gave her hand an encouraging squeeze. "I think we should get some sleep and try again tomorrow night."

"All right. I suppose that's best." She leaned her head against his shoulder and let her eyelids droop. "I am tired." She yawned and nestled closer. "But I feel so much better doing something myself."

"Yeah, sweetheart, I know what you mean." Will slid his arm around her and sat content for the few minutes it took to return to her hotel. "Just a minute, Gabe," he directed when the cab stopped. Gathering Mattie into his arms, he kissed her with gentle, undemanding pressure. Now, he knew, was not the time to initiate passion. He escorted her to her door and returned to the cab.

Ten minutes later, he climbed down in front of his own quiet rooming house. "Well, Gabriel, I'm much obliged for your help." He reached up with a handful of bills.

"Thank you, sir. An' I'll be in front of the lady's hotel at nine o'clock sharp tomorrow night, jus' like I promised."

The next day, Will found a tailor and ordered a set of evening clothes. He also bought a new suit, shirts, shoes, and everything he could think of to make him appear a gentleman. Cowboys weren't plentiful among the gambling crowd, though he'd spotted a few. He didn't want to be among them, easily spotted because of his dress.

Early in the afternoon he called on Mattie and Elizabeth. Begging Mattie's help to pick out presents for his mother and sister, they went shopping. He carefully observed Mattie's own taste in jewelry. Tomorrow, he would come back and make a purchase for her.

That night, Mattie opened the door to Will with a welcoming smile. "Oh, my stars, Will, you do look the town beau," she teased, pulling him through the door. "Aunt Elizabeth, come and see how handsome Will is in his new brown suit."

Mattie walked around Will, running her eyes up and down his tall figure. "I think I'll have to hold your arm especially tight from now on, or some of those saloon girls might . . . I do declare, Will, you're blushing."

"Yes indeed, Will, you do look mighty handsome," agreed Elizabeth. "Now, get along with you. I sincerely hope you have better luck tonight."

"Yes, so do I, Aunt Elizabeth." Mattie swung her cloak over an arm. "Goodnight, dear. Don't wait up."

"You little tease," Will growled in her ear as soon as they climbed into Gabriel's cab. "You're asking for trouble."

"Oh? What kind of trouble?" She fluttered her lashes.

"The kind you know perfectly well I'm not in a position to give you right now."

"Why, Will. Whatever do you mean?" Mattie caught her

bottom lip between her teeth to keep from laughing.

"You'll find out fast enough, my darlin', as soon as my ring is on your finger." Will lifted her left hand to his mouth and gently nipped at the tip of her ring finger.

A streak of pure ecstasy bolted straight to her belly. "Will," she gasped. "Stop that."

"Mmm. There'll come a day, Mattie. Or maybe I should say, there'll come a night," he promised.

"Here we is, sir, *this*'s the Gateway Club," Gabriel called out. "They's a show in the front, an' gamin' in the back."

"Thanks, Gabe," Will said. Helping Mattie down, he noticed this was a much finer place than the ones they'd visited last night. He escorted Mattie proudly through the door. She looked very beautiful in a deep red gown, and the fact that she turned heads didn't escape his notice. After an hour, they left to continue their search.

Toward midnight, Will helped her out of the carriage once again. The evening seemed a repeat of the night before and he could see Mattie's weary discouragement.

"This is the fourth place tonight," Mattie said with a sigh.

"Now *this*'s the Fool's Delight Saloon," announced Gabriel. "Mr. Will, sir, are you sure you wants to take Miss Mattie in *there?*"

Will half turned to look up at the old driver. "Is it too rough, Gabe?"

"Well, sir, on second thought, it ain't too nice, even though some society gentlemen goes there."

Mattie was watching two men as they approached the entrance of the club. As customers, they looked like well-dressed gentlemen. Glancing at the modest club front, she didn't see any reason not to go in. She was about to say so to Will, but then one of the men tipped his head in conversation with his companion.

The light flooding out from the saloon window highlighted the man's features. Cold chills ran up her arms. Immediate revulsion made her recoil, and she turned into Will's shoulder, hiding her face as Larry Potter strolled past and entered the doors.

"Oh, Lord, it's him. Will, that was Larry."

"Are you sure? Did you see him that well?"

"Will, I'm absolutely sure. How could I not know someone who—" she gulped, "—made my mother and me so miserable?"

"All right, sweetheart, all right." Will squeezed her hand and turned to Gabriel. "Did you get a good look at those two men, Gabe?"

"Yes, sir, I did. I don't know which one of 'em you're in'trested in, but the tall one is Mr. Horace Brown, an' the shorter man is Mr. Lawrence Watson. They owns this establishment, sir."

"Own it?" Mattie was amazed and confused. "How? I mean, when did Potter . . . that is, Watson . . . come here? Do you know?"

Gabriel lifted his hat and scratched at his bald head. "Reckon 'bout three or four years back, I guess."

"Gabriel, by any chance do you know where he lives? Does he have a wife?" Mattie asked.

"Don't rightly know, Miss Mattie. But I tells you what. My cousin Suellen works for a saloon gal from here. I reckon she'd be willin' to bring you any information you want, as a favor to me."

"That's an excellent notion, Gabe," said Will. "Mattie, I think we'd better return to the hotel for now, and wait until we see Gabe's cousin."

"But, Will—"

"No buts, Mattie. Remember? Now that we know where Larry will be, we can question him any time. I think it would be better done in the daytime."

She stared at him for a long moment in open agitation. But she'd given her promise, and finally she nodded her agreement. Will assisted her back into the carriage.

"Can your cousin come by the hotel first thing in the morning?" Mattie asked when she alighted at her hotel.

"Jus' soon's ever she can, Miss Mattie."

Nodding, she turned and walked through the carved doors.

Will bent his head to kiss her goodnight at the door of her room, but she responded in an absentminded way. Puzzled, he tipped her chin up to scan her face. Her eyes held a longing that struck a recognizable chord.

"Oh, Will. I wish you didn't have to leave. I wish we were married now, so we could sleep together."

The long days had taken their toll. He adopted a lighthearted tone. "Why Miss Mattie," he said in a mock scandalized tone. "Is that an indecent thought wrapped up in a marriage proposal?"

"No, indeed." She backed away a little and leaned against the door. "You very well know what I mean. Will, when we were out on the trail, I . . . I . . . liked lying in your arms at night. I liked going to sleep together."

A low chuckle rumbled up as he leaned his forearms against the door frame, surrounding her head and shoulders. He bent to trail kisses along her cheekbones and ended with a thorough tasting of her mouth. He heard her draw a deep sigh as he pulled away.

"Darlin', you're going to like a lot more than just lying in my arms by the time I'm through loving you. And that's a promise."

★ ★ ★ ★ ★

Mattie slapped the folded newspaper down on the chair arm and drummed her fingers against it. Where was that girl? Suellen, Gabriel called her. Here it was almost noon and Mattie thought she would have been here by midmorning. She rose to pace.

"Mattie dear, please try to relax. You're wearing out your nerves faster than you're wearing out the carpet," Elizabeth cautioned.

"I know, Aunt Elizabeth, but I just can't stand this waiting. We know where Larry is, and I want to march right over to the Fool's Delight and confront him. And here I am waiting on this girl who might know something."

She stopped to stare out of the window, idly fingering the lace curtains. "Maybe Gabriel couldn't find her, or maybe she's sick. Or maybe she doesn't know anything and won't want to come."

"Will is due to arrive any moment now, Mattie," her aunt soothed. "He'll probably bring her with him."

"Oh, do you think so? Yes, that would follow." The tightness along Mattie's shoulders relaxed a little and she let go of the curtain. It fell back to the floor with its now-crumpled middle.

The moments dragged until the knock sounded, and Mattie rushed to the door, flinging it open with breathless anticipation. "Will, I'm so glad to see you. Where is Suellen? Didn't you bring her?"

"Slow down, Mattie." He slid an arm about her waist. "Yes, in fact I did bring her, but she's coming up with Gabriel. They'll be here shortly."

Five minutes later, Will opened the door to Gabriel and a small woman of color with snapping black eyes.

"Here we is, sir. This's my cousin, Suellen Washington."

"Sit down, Miss Washington," Will directed. He noticed Suellen's eyes round and then shift to Elizabeth.

Gabriel shuffled his feet and cleared his throat. "Ah, sir, ah . . ."

"That's quite all right, Gabriel." Elizabeth spoke in a friendly but businesslike way. "Please be seated, both of you. We've invited you here to ask favors. We'd be . . . um . . . obliged if you'd be seated. You'll be well compensated."

"Oh yes, Suellen, please sit down," Mattie added, seeing the uncertainty behind the dark eyes. "We need your help."

"Thank you, ma'am," Suellen said in a well-modulated voice. Nervously, she sat on the edge of a chair.

"Now then. I understand from Mr. McCarthy that you work for a woman employed by the Fool's Delight?" asked Elizabeth.

"Yes, ma'am. I work for Miss Dee Dee Littlejohn."

"How long have you worked for Miss Littlejohn?"

" 'Bout four years, now."

Mattie impatiently interrupted. "Suellen, what I . . . we really need to know is about the man Larry Watson. Could you please tell us everything you know about him?"

Mattie watched as Suellen assessed her a second before answering. "Well, Mr. Watson, he an' Mr. Brown, owns the Fool's Delight. He appeared about, um, three years back, I think. Don't know where he come from, but grapevine say he won lotsa money gambling an' that's how he bought in at Fool's Delight. My mistress, she a gambling lady, an' she say he never won it fair, 'cause he don't allow no even shakes." Uneasiness crossed her face and she leaned forward to beg of Mattie, "You won't tell nobody I say this, will you?"

"No, of course not, Suellen. Tell me more. I need to know it all."

"Well, Miss Littlejohn say trouble brewing. She say she think Mr. Watson maybe cheating on Mr. Brown."

"Why does she say that?"

"Mr. Brown, he sweet on Miss Littlejohn. He tells her things. An' he's suspicious. He don' like the way Mr. Watson been running things. He ask her to keep her eyes open."

Mattie took in the information. Licking dry lips, she asked, "Is Mr. Watson married?"

"No'm, not that I knows of. He has a woman, though."

Mattie's heart knocked against her ribs. "Tell me about the woman, please."

"She tall an' dark, part Mex. Name . . ." Suellen stopped as Mattie jumped up and turned away.

Mattie fought the tears, squeezing her hands into tight fists at her side. She had so hoped . . . Feeling Will's arm slide around her shoulders and tighten, she looked up at him and tried to smile.

"I reckon we'll go talk to Larry after all," said Will. He wasn't too sorry. Before he left the city, he'd planned to look up the man who had attempted to sell Mattie—like a horse or cattle or something to trade.

"Thank you, Miss Washington." Elizabeth was handing the woman a large bill when Mattie turned back to add her thanks.

Suellen looked at the bill in surprise. "Wish I could've helped you more, ma'am," she said. "I hopes you find the lady you's looking for."

She walked to the door with Gabriel a step behind, and then turned. "Ma'am, I has some friends working 'round town. If you like to give me a description of her, I be glad to pass it along."

"Oh, would you?" Mattie leaped at the new hope. She touched Suellen's hand. "She's small and blond, and is thirty-six years old. Soft-spoken. Her name is Marianne Potter . . . or she might be using the name Adams." Mattie glanced from Suellen to Gabriel. "I need your caution."

"Yes'm, I understand."

Gabriel nodded. "You has my word, Miss Mattie. We'll be careful with the information you's giving us."

Mattie licked her dry lips again. "I'm looking for my mother, you see. She used to be married to the man you call Watson, only his name was Potter then. Six years ago, she was very ill, and I . . . I thought she'd died. Now I've learned she recovered, but . . . I'm not sure . . ."

She remembered to breathe, and started in a stronger voice.

"But I do know they . . . she and Larry . . . headed here to San Francisco over four years ago. And last night . . ." she turned to Gabriel, "that was him going into Fool's Delight."

"Yes, ma'am, I hears you." Gabriel nodded in compassion.

"Thank you, Gabe," Will reached out to shake the old man's hand. "Please wait for me downstairs. I'll be along shortly."

Will closed the door behind them and turned to Mattie and her aunt. "Ladies, I have business to attend to this afternoon, but I'd be obliged if you'd take supper with me this evening."

"Thank you, Will, we would be most happy to do so," Elizabeth answered.

Mattie frowned at him suspiciously. "Where are you going, Will?"

"I have to pick up my new clothes, Mattie," Will told her smoothly. "And I need to make a draw on my funds at the bank."

"Oh." Mattie felt sheepish. She had suspected he was planning a visit to Fool's Delight without her.

"Now don't go fretting this afternoon," Will said, and took her hand as he walked to the door. "I have an idea that Gabriel and Suellen's grapevine might turn up more than your Pinkertons."

He kissed the tip of her nose and left.

When he reached the street, Will looked for Gabriel. The cab was parked a few spaces down the street. He watched Suellen bid goodbye and walk away as he approached. That was just as well, for he had to talk to Gabriel about something he'd just as soon not share with the women.

"Where to, Mr. Will?"

"I have several stops to make, Gabe." Will leaned against the cab and, pulling two cigars from his pocket, handed one to the cabby. He seldom smoked, but thought this called for it. "But before we start, I wonder if you could help me out."

"Thank you, sir." Gabriel grinned. "Yes, sir, if I can."

"Well, this is the deal." Will accepted the light Gabriel offered, and puffed. "I'm used to traveling with my outfit, you know, partners I can trust to back my play." He watched as Gabriel nodded his understanding. "But I'm a loner here in this town, and I might be in need of a couple of . . . ah . . . friends to watch my back if, or when, I have to face down Potter. And while I'm here, I might need them to keep watch on what he's doing."

"Uh-huh. Well, sir, I'm mighty relieved you're nobody's

fool. You see, sir, since last night, I done a little more asking around about Mr. Watson an' Mr. Brown. Seems both have a reputation for rough dealing. I hear Mr. Brown once killed a man for cheating 'im outta two dollahs." Gabe shook his head. "Reckon I c'n find you a couple of friends by tonight, if you'd be willing to make an extry stop this afternoon."

"In that case, let's go." Will flipped his partially smoked cigar in the gutter and climbed into the carriage.

On the surface, Mattie enjoyed the evening. Will was very considerate of both her and Elizabeth. After dinner, they attended a theater that devoted its show to music. But she felt as though she was marching in place. When at last Will escorted them back to their hotel sitting room, she felt exhausted with nerves.

"I'll leave you to say good night, my dears. Thank you for a lovely evening, Will." Elizabeth left them.

The minute she walked out of the room, Will pulled Mattie into his arms. "Sweetheart, I've been wanting to kiss you all evening," he groaned.

He led her to the sofa, then lowering his head, he sought her mouth.

Mattie slid her arms around his neck and stood on tiptoe to return his kiss. Fire raced through her, and she was suddenly restless, needing to push herself closer. She stroked the side of his face with her palm, running her thumb against the corner of his mouth where their lips clung together, then brushing it down the soft hair of his mustache. Pulling away, she leaned her forehead against his chin while she gulped for air.

"Mattie, darlin', I love you," Will murmured against her ear. "You're so beautiful," he whispered. She shivered and pressed closer. Lifting his head, he tipped her chin up to meet his gaze. Her eyes held a sleepy sensuality, which surprised him a little, but the realization that she'd been welcoming his advances excited him. The urge to hear her say it, to say she wanted him, swept through his mind and he asked, "Does that frighten you anymore, Mattie?"

Her voice was reduced to a husky purr. "No, I don't feel scared of anything with you, Will. I . . . I think I'll like being your wife."

Speaking of such things made her revert to shyness, but she wanted to reassure him. "I know there's lots more to making love than this, and I . . . like what you make me feel. Your mouth . . . oh, Will, it feels so good. When you kiss me, I sometimes think I'm drowning while at the same time I'm dying of thirst. And Will," she reached up to cradle his face between her palms, "I love you more than I can tell. It fills me up so . . . I sometimes can't think how much, it's so big."

"Sweetheart, you don't know how long I've waited to hear you say it. I was beginning to think you never would or maybe you couldn't."

"Oh, darling Will," she punctuated her speech with kisses, placing them on his nose and eyes, "I want you, too. It's hard to wait . . . but . . . we must. It wouldn't do to insult the Lord by disobeying one of His laws. Especially not after His kindness. Besides, Aunt Elizabeth is in the next room and she always checks on me at bedtime."

Then she kissed him with all the fervor she'd been saving for him. Reluctantly she pulled away, once more cradling his face in her hands.

"Will, I'll love you till the end of the earth and I'm dying to let you teach me everything about loving, but if you . . . we . . . don't stop this right now . . . Aunt Elizabeth will be too shocked for words. For if you kiss me one more time like that, I won't be responsible for what may happen next."

Mattie felt Will's chest heave as laughter rumbled up and rolled out of his mouth. He laid his head back against the sofa and shouted with it.

"Darlin'," he pulled her to rest against his shoulder. "I don't think I'll have to teach you anything. You seem to have a natural talent, once the barriers are down. But you're right, we don't want to abuse Aunt Elizabeth's sensibilities or the Lord's righteousness. We want to do this right."

He rose in one swift motion and set Mattie on her feet. "But I'm going to collect on all the promises you've been making."

"Promises?"

"Yes . . . the ones you've said, and the ones you've made with . . . in other ways." Putting his arm around her shoulders, he started for the door.

"You've made promises, too."

"Yes, ma'am, and I intend to keep every one of them." Bending, he kissed the tip of her nose.

"Is that the way you'll always give me a goodbye kiss?"

"Complaining already?" He grinned. "Look, sweetheart," he stepped away from her and folded his arms behind his back. "If I touch you once more tonight, we really will shock Aunt Elizabeth. So be a good girl and help me say good night. God knows, I don't want to leave."

Folding her hands, she gave an exaggerated sigh. "All right, then. Good night, Will." Leaning far out, she closed her eyes and pursed her lips. With the fleetest of kisses, Will brushed her lips, and then before she opened her eyes again, he was gone.

Seventeen

Afternoon sunlight shafted through the window, showing Mattie the dust motes dancing in the air as she paced. She hadn't seen or heard from Will all day, and she was beginning to fume.

She'd promised Will not to see Larry on her own, but she itched to face her stepfather—despite the deep-seated fear. Now that she knew where Larry actually was, this delay agitated her intensely held anger against him. She hadn't realized how strongly she felt until the possibility of facing him was realized. When she left the outlaw stronghold, she'd felt only fear. Anger and humiliation and shame—that's what she felt now, but she was no longer afraid. He was an unscrupulous, no-good son of Cain whose duplicity had caused her and her mother great harm and grief. She wouldn't hesitate to extract the information she wanted from him at gunpoint. He'd have to tell her about her mother then.

A soft knock on the door brought her quickly to attention. It wasn't Will's strong knock, so it must be the tea she'd ordered. "Aunt Elizabeth, the tea has arrived," she called through the open door to her aunt's bedroom.

A moment later, she opened the door to see Suellen.

"Suellen. Oh, does this mean . . ." Mattie's heartbeat quickened. "Please come in."

"Yes, ma'am, I might have good news for you." Suellen walked into the room and stood waiting for further directions.

Aunt Elizabeth walked forward. "It's good of you to come, Suellen."

Mattie couldn't contain her eagerness. "Yes, yes, it certainly is. Very good. Now please tell me your news." She gestured the woman into a chair.

Suellen sat down and shifted her gaze from one eager face to the other. "They's a woman works in a mission off Montgomery Street." She held her breath, enjoying the drama. "She might be your ma."

"Why do you think so? Does she look like the lady I described?"

Suellen slowly nodded. "Yes, ma'am."

"By any chance . . . did your informant know her name?"

"She say it's Annie Adams."

"Annie Adams." Mattie's hand flew to cover her quivering mouth and then she turned to her aunt. "Oh, praise God, it's her! Aunt Elizabeth, it must be my ma. My mother is really . . . alive. When I was a child and she played with me, sometimes we pretended her name was Annie."

Her voice broke. She took a moment, then reaching to lay a hand on Suellen's arm, Mattie begged, "You must take us there immediately. Please?"

Suellen backed away a little on her chair. "Oh, no, ma'am, I got to get back to work. I can't be late, or I'll be fired."

"I'll make it well worth your time, Suellen," Elizabeth spoke up. "And if such a thing should occur, I'll see you have other employment."

Suellen studied the two women. "All right, ma'am. But we got to hurry, 'cause supper hour'll be comin' on us right quick. I'll be needed soon after."

"Oh, thank you, thank you." Mattie ran into her bedroom to gather her purse while calling over her shoulder. "Aunt Elizabeth, I'll just write a note to leave at the desk for Will."

"I'll go on ahead and have the doorman get us a cab," said Elizabeth.

Only moments later, Mattie climbed into the cab beside her aunt. She chafed at the delay when Suellen took her time giving directions to the driver. Plucking at the strings of her purse, she looked out of the window. Were those horses a hundred years old? Their rate of speed felt like it.

They traveled down Montgomery Street for a few blocks and Mattie recognized when they passed Fool's Delight. She craned her neck as they went by, but saw nothing unusual. Two blocks away, the carriage turned a corner and continued on for about a mile. When it pulled to a stop, Mattie gripped the door handle in unbearable excitement.

Climbing out, she stood looking at the large rundown house while waiting for her aunt to follow. She pulled harder at her purse strings in nervous anticipation. Small children played on the porch while a woman attended them. But there was no sign this was a mission or anything like an institution. Was this the right place?

Mattie turned to look at Suellen for confirmation. "Yes, ma'am, this is the one my friend say." Suellen nodded.

"Suellen, you stay with the carriage. I don't want to have to hunt for a cab later," instructed Elizabeth.

Mattie walked slowly up the walk, with Elizabeth taking her arm, and they stepped up to the porch. Her gaze was all over the place.

"Excuse me, please." Elizabeth called to the care-worn woman bent over a child. "We're here to see Mrs. Adams."

"Annie? She's likely in the kitchen at this hour," the

woman replied. "Go on in, I 'spect Mrs. Jackson'll be there to help you."

Mattie's heart raced. Her ma was here!

Her aunt thanked the woman, and Mattie opened the door and stepped through into the dark hall. The house smelled of harsh soap and cooking, but it appeared clean. She could hear a baby crying from the floor above.

"I am Mrs. Jackson. May I help you?"

Mattie turned to the tall, plainly dressed, middle-aged woman who came out of the door to the right.

"Yes, if you would, please," Mattie said over a lump in her throat. "I understand you have a woman named Annie Adams here. I . . . we'd like to see her."

"I see." The woman looked them over in an assessing manner. "May I inquire what business you have with Mrs. Adams? She is busy with her work at the moment."

"It's personal," Elizabeth snapped.

Mrs. Jackson pinched in her mouth. "Very well. Please be seated in the parlor while I fetch her."

The woman turned away, leaving them in the hall, as she walked through a door in the back, closing it with an angry snap.

"Come, Mattie," said Elizabeth as she opened a door. "I believe this is the parlor."

Mattie followed her aunt into a sparsely furnished room. Elizabeth sat on a straight chair, but Mattie stood so she could face the door.

They waited. She could hear muted sounds of the children outside, and the baby above stairs stopped crying. Ten minutes dragged by. Elizabeth looked at her timepiece and tapped her foot.

"Aunt Elizabeth," Mattie came to a sudden conclusion, "I don't think Mrs. Jackson intends to help us. Stay here."

"Now Mattie, don't—" Her aunt's voice trailed behind her as Mattie headed out into the hall and opened the door in the back through which Mrs. Jackson had gone.

The door opened into another hall that joined another, making a T. Mattie was undecided which way to try first. But the odor of onions wafted strong to the left, and she turned that way, passing two doors that were locked. Finally opening the last one, she found the kitchen.

It was large and, unlike other sections of the house, apparently well equipped. A heavy, big-boned girl looked up from washing vegetables in a bucket on a table. Mattie's eyes traveled to the other side of the room and halted.

Her heart beating in her throat, Mattie stood very still.

A small, blond woman stood with her back turned while she stirred something on the stove. Her elbow moved vigorously as she worked, vibrating her whole body, just the way Mattie remembered. A humming, lilting melody filled the air and Mattie recognized the old dance tune that was her mother's favorite.

"Ma." It was a whisper. The woman hadn't heard her. "Ma."

Through tear-blurred eyes, Mattie watched her turn, a big wooden spoon in her hand. Her face was full of inquiry. "Yes?"

When the spoon clattered to the floor, Mattie laughed. Her voice, nearly strangled with emotion, cracked when she said, "Ma, it's me, Mattie."

Stunned, her mother stood staring with unbelieving eyes.

"Mattie? My Mattie? Oh—" A sob broke from her mouth. "Oh, it is . . . my little Mattie." Marianne rushed to meet her daughter in the center of the room. "Oh, heaven be praised, it's you!"

Mattie wrapped her arms about the small frame and

could say nothing for a long moment. Emotions shook them both, and Mattie wasn't sure her mother's sobs were any more or less than her own. "Oh, Ma. For so long I thought you were dead."

"I know, dear, I know." Marianne whispered, gulped, then pulled back and looked up. "But I thought it better that you believed such, at first. Oh, my darling girl, I was so frightened for you. Lord only knows how scared. But I knew you were safe when Maxwell reported seeing you in Wayside Station. Then I knew you went on to St. Louis and Elizabeth."

Mattie saw the sorrow in her mother's eyes. "Well, I am safe. And everything worked out just as you planned so long ago." Mattie bent and kissed her mother's wet cheek. "Aunt Elizabeth is waiting in the front room. She's wanted to find you as much as I have."

"Oh, my, she has?" Marianne still felt dazed. "Daniel's sister," she murmured, looking down at her soiled apron.

"Ma, Aunt Elizabeth won't worry about what you look like," reassured Mattie. She searched her purse for a handkerchief. "And we've been here for more than twenty minutes. That Mrs. Jackson was supposed to be fetching you."

"Really? Wonder what happened to her? Well, never mind. She's a bit peculiar at times." Marianne turned to her helper. "Hilda, you'll have to finish getting supper ready by yourself."

She returned her gaze to Mattie as she untied her apron. "My stars, Mattie. You're so tall. And such a beauty. I knew you were turning into one."

"Oh, Ma," Mattie smiled. She wiped her eyes with the small linen square and offered it to her mother. "I'm so glad to find you. I've missed you so much."

"I missed you too, Mattie, dreadfully so."

Arm in arm, they walked back to the parlor talking at a furious pace, to where Elizabeth sat waiting. Then Mattie stepped back to watch her mother and aunt greet each other. She knew her mother had met Elizabeth only once. Happiness caused her to smile at the loving embrace her aunt gave her mother.

"Dear Marianne, how glad I am we've found you at last."

"I'm so sorry. I didn't know you were looking for me."

"No, I realize that . . ." Elizabeth broke off.

Mattie turned as they heard the front door slam against the wall, followed by two pairs of footsteps. Someone was making a lot of noise. The door to the parlor swung wide.

Smirking, Mrs. Jackson gawked at them from where she stood beyond the shoulder of the man. Mattie heard her mother gasp as she recognized who filled the doorway.

It was Larry.

"That'll be all, Mrs. Jackson," he said and handed her a coin. Larry Potter sauntered into the room as though he owned it, including the women there. Money jingled, as he slid his hands in his pockets and rocked back on his heels. His lip curled as he ran his eyes over the three of them. "So. It's little Mattie, come to see her ma."

Marianne stepped forward. "What are you doing here, Larry? What do you want?"

"A man can see his wife any time he chooses."

"I haven't lived as your wife for years, so I see no reason to see you. We agreed to go our separate ways when we arrived in San Francisco and you agreed to leave me alone. I've been content here at the mission. And you've another woman."

"I've left you alone, but I always know what you're up to," he laughed in a nasty taunt. "And my woman is young and good-looking; she draws the men into my place like flies to honey."

"So? You have what you want. Why do you bother me now?"

"I wanted to see what my little stepdaughter has become. When Mrs. Jackson described your visitor, I knew exactly who I'd find." His mouth curved in a serpentine smile, and his eyes roved over Mattie, even though he spoke to Marianne. "Perhaps I'll take you back. I can use you and Mattie can act as a hostess in my club. The men will flock in, and with a little training, she can—"

"No, you can't do such a thing." Marianne blanched. "I won't let you. I won't go back to you."

"You dirty snake. I wouldn't go with you if my life depended on it," said Mattie.

"I have the law on my side, I'll have you back if I choose. You're legally my stepdaughter, I can command you to do anything I want." He turned to Marianne, his voice harsh and ugly. "As your husband, I'm her legal guardian until she's twenty-one."

"Now see here, you have no rights—" Elizabeth raised her shocked protest.

Mattie stepped in again. "You no-good slimy skunk, I wouldn't let you near my mother again no matter what the law says. She's coming with me and we're leaving right now."

Larry clamped his hand around Mattie's arm, his fingers tightening. Mattie stepped back, but he held on. "Sass, always sass. Well, I'll knock that out of you soon enough. Shouldn't have let you run so wild as a kid."

"Stop that. You can't." Marianne started to cry. Rushing at him, she began beating against his shoulder.

With one backhand, Larry sent Marianne flying into the corner.

Incensed, Mattie jerked her arm away, spinning from his reach. He followed in a giant step with a raised fist. She heard her aunt scream. Lifting her arm to protect her head, she ducked. His heavy blow glanced off her forearm, but she was knocked off-balance and fell onto the sofa.

A loud crash brought her head up. It was the parlor door banging hard against the wall.

"Get away from her, you dirty lowlife," Will roared from the doorway.

"Will, thank God," Elizabeth welcomed. "This man's gone totally mad."

Potter looked around, eyeing his new opponent.

Joyfully, thankfully, Mattie watched Will enter the room. Shakily, she rose. "I'm glad to see you, Will," she said, an understatement if ever there was one. Keeping a wary eye on Larry, she edged out of his reach and went to help her mother.

"I'm glad I'm here, too, sweetheart," he calmly spoke back while watching Larry. Will stood, feet slightly apart, and silently cursed the fact that, in compliance with the city's rules, he'd left his guns in his room.

Larry whirled and took a stance with his back to the fireplace. Wary assessment showed for an instant in the snarling face, and then, except for his eyes, his features dropped into a bland set. Curling his thumb in his vest pocket, he stood in a nonchalant manner. But his other hand rested on the lapel of his coat, near a slight bulge in his coat. Angry resentment glittered in his eyes. "Who are you, mister?"

Will's arm shot out like lightning as he took a choking hold on Larry's shirt front. He hauled him up to where Larry's toes were barely touching the floor. "Potter, I'm Will McCarthy, and you look at me good and hard, because

I'm itching for an excuse to hang you for the low-down, woman-beating, cattle thief you are. I buried your one-time partner, Nate Dorsey, and if I weren't out of my territory, I'd hang you from the nearest tree. Now, you touch my wife again and I'll shoot you without giving you time to draw breath."

"Wife?" Larry squeaked out.

"Yes, my wife, Mattie." Will twisted the cloth about Larry's neck a little tighter. "And if you ever so much as bat an eyelash at her ma again, you'll find yourself running with the steers instead of the bulls. Got that?"

"Yeah, sure, cowboy." Larry wriggled, trying to loosen Will's hold on his shirt. "Ease up there."

Mattie watched in fascination. The man who had bullied and frightened her so as a child looked small and ineffectual in Will's grasp. But suddenly, she saw his hand ease under his coat.

"Will, he's trying for his gun," she cried out.

"You sidewinder," Will jerked hard on the shirtfront and, yanking aside the jacket opening, he pulled a small handgun from its holster. "That does it," he said as he handed it to Mattie. He let his fist fly. It landed with satisfactory thud against Larry's chin.

Larry's head snapped backward and he fell hard against a chair. Quickly recovering his balance, he ducked and crouched as he scrambled to get out of Will's reach.

Will went after him. "Besides threatening my wife and her ma . . ." Grabbing hold of his shoulder, Will jerked Larry upright and let his rage go as he slugged him again.

"You'd fire off your little toy . . ." he barely waited for Larry to fall, before once more pulling him up, ". . . right here in the house with all those youngsters out in the hall." Will threw his fist one final time.

Larry went down with a heavy thump.

Will stood over him, feeling both triumph and dissatisfaction. He'd feel better if the bastard was dead or in jail, but he had no evidence of the man's thievery to take to the authorities in this city. And he couldn't simply call Potter out, as he'd have done at home. Good thing Gabe's friends had kept him informed about the skunk's activities.

Frustrated, Will gave one final warning. "Now, then. One more time, mister. If you ever come near my family again, I'll kill you."

Will heaved Larry into the hall and pushed him hard toward the front door. Several large-eyed children scrambled out of their way and crowded up the stairs. Two of the children, peeking from outside around the open front door, squealed and ran as Will propelled Larry out and down the steps.

Mattie, jubilant, followed in their wake, feeling as wide-eyed as the children. Marianne and Elizabeth were right behind her. The children, along with the woman caring for them, brought up the rear.

"Oh, dear me," said the woman. "What a shock. Oh, my, my, my. Who are all these men?"

"You won't get away with this, McCarthy." Larry turned, still weaving from the blows. He spat out a string of curses as he wiped blood from his mouth with the back of his hand. "That woman's my wife," he said and pointed at Marianne. "No judge or jury will allow you to stand in the way of a husband claiming his legal wife."

Will snapped his fingers, and Mattie noticed two tall, burly men for the first time. They'd been lounging against the porch posts, and now stepped forward at Will's signal. Immediately, they flanked him.

Never removing his eyes from Larry, he spoke to the two

young giants. "Sam and Jeremiah, this snake is Larry Potter. If you ever see him near my womenfolk, here," he indicated the three women standing on the porch, ". . . you are to feed him to the fish or drop him down a deep well. Got that?"

"We gotcha, boss."

"With pleasure, boss."

"McCarthy, you can't be watching your back all the time. But I will be."

"Oh, that reminds me, Potter. About watching your back. I met your partner, Horace Brown, yesterday. Interesting man. I hear he once killed a man for cheating him of just two dollars. Yep, we had a nice long talk. And you know, he was very interested in why I was looking for you. Seems he's been a bit suspicious of your actions recently. He said he was going to do some checking into the management of your club. I believe he's there right now. He made some mention of wanting explanations for all that money you got stashed away that he didn't know about."

The angry red in Larry's face drained to a pasty white. He threw Will a murderous look as a vile curse erupted from his twisted mouth. "You'll pay . . ."

Will took a step toward him, but Larry spun on his heel and fled.

"Sam, keep an eye on him will you?" Will directed. "And stay in contact with your man inside the club. Let me know if you think Potter's trying anything ugly."

"Sure thing, boss." The young man took off after Larry.

For a moment Will watched Larry disappear with the hulking Sam trailing behind, and then turned to the women and crowd of children standing on the porch. "You ladies all right?"

Mattie rushed down the porch steps to melt against his

side as he slid an arm around her and drew her close.

"Yes, yes. We're all right. Oh, darling Will, how did you know we were here? And you know I've found Ma. Oh . . ." She turned to beckon to Marianne, "I want you to meet her."

Mattie drew her mother to join them. "Ma, this is Will," she introduced in a soft voice.

Her eyes misted once more as she watched Will reach out and take her mother's hand.

"Mrs. Adams, I'm right pleased to make your acquaintance." Will used his gentlest tone. "I've been looking forward to meeting you for a good long while."

"Well, I'm afraid I didn't know about you," Marianne responded with a tentative smile. "So you're my Mattie's husband?"

Mattie blushed and Will cleared his throat. "Uh, well, the truth is . . ." started Will.

"The truth is, Marianne," Elizabeth spoke through a broad smile and stepped forward, "they're engaged and plan to marry very soon, now they've found you."

"Oh, you've been waiting to find me?"

"That's one of the reasons, Mrs. Adams. But now there's no reason left at all."

"Oh, Will. We can talk about this later." Mattie turned to her mother. "Ma, come back to the hotel with us now. We've so much to catch up with, so much to say. Now that I've found you . . . oh, Ma . . . please come."

"Yes, Mattie, of course. Let me get some things."

Elizabeth sent Suellen on her way in the waiting cab and fifteen minutes later, they all climbed into Gabriel's carriage. Will was pleased when Mattie scooted to sit close by his side, and he automatically placed his arm around her. It meant she felt she belonged there.

"Tell me then, dear, when do you plan to be married?" Marianne addressed Mattie while her eyes flew from face to face.

"Immediately," Will answered.

"Today?" Marianne's voice showed her surprise.

"Yes."

"Not today," said Mattie.

"Tomorrow, then," said Will, looking into her glowing brown eyes. He began to smile.

"By the end of the week, probably," said Mattie, her smile igniting from his.

"Promise?" he said, and his smile flashed brighter. His hand, resting against the curve of her waist, gave her an ever-so-slight caress.

Blushing furiously, Mattie compromised. "All right then, two days." She watched his eyes flare in pleased triumph. Laughing outright, she turned to her mother and aunt. "Ma, Aunt Elizabeth . . . will you help me?"

Eighteen

Supper was a bit frantic. Elizabeth ordered it served in the privacy of the hotel suite to ensure their freedom for easy speech. Will sat back and watched the three women talk as they tried to catch up with years of separation. Mattie seemed to be the bridge between her mother and aunt, trying to fill awkward gaps. He noticed she was too excited to eat much, as was Marianne.

He'd never seen Mattie so lively or talkative. When she was relating something frightening, she frequently patted her mother's hand in reassurance. But under the table, her other hand clasped his tightly.

When a rapid, urgent pounding sounded on the door, Mattie abruptly lost her voice. Her head swung to the intruding noise.

"Allow me, ladies." Will rose and strode across to the door. Seconds later, he opened it to Sam, the man he'd assigned to watch Larry. Standing just inside the door, they talked in low tones.

Will came back to the table, and Mattie's stomach clutched as she saw his frown. More trouble. Oh, when was it going to end?

"What is it?"

"Don't know for sure. I'll have to go see. But Sam says there's been a shooting at Fool's Delight between Potter and his partner. You women stay here. I'll get back as soon as I can."

"Oh, love, please be careful." Mattie felt her body tense

as she followed him to the door.

"Yes, I will Mattie, don't worry. I'll have Sam and Jeremiah with me."

He kissed her quickly and left.

Time dragged. Mattie tried to occupy her own mind and to help her mother's waiting by talking of the things she'd studied in school, her trip to New York with Elizabeth, and her love for Will.

Marianne, in turn, asked questions of Mattie. And she answered Elizabeth's questions about that long-ago time with her long-lost Daniel.

Finally, Will returned. After a brief knock, he walked in to stand and stare at them a moment. Placing himself beside the sofa where Mattie sat, he reached for her hand. He spoke to Marianne.

"Ma'am, I'd hoped not to shock you anymore this day, but you must know. Potter is dead."

"Dead? How?" Mattie asked.

Marianne was silent, and Will continued. "It seems his partner Horace Brown found he'd been cheating him. According to the men who saw it, Potter tried to bluff it out, and Brown called his bluff. Potter then pulled a gun from a desk drawer, but Brown was ready for him and shot him through the heart."

Marianne stared at her folded hands and shook her head. "Indeed, Will, that news no longer has any power to shock or upset me. Actually, I've been waiting for it. I've known this would happen eventually."

She looked up, misery in her expression. "He lied and cheated too many people not to get caught at last."

"Ma, do you know what this means?" Mattie spoke in elation as she reached and took her mother's hand. "You're free. You're free of all the meanness and abuse, and . . .

Ma, you can breathe easy for the rest of your life."

A tentative smile edged across her mother's face. "That's so, isn't it? I'm completely free."

"Oh, Ma . . . Will. We're all free of it." Mattie laughed. Rising, she entwined her arms around Will's middle, and looked up at him. "It's really over. We can go home, now."

Will smiled down into her brown eyes, and then flicked his glance to her mother and aunt. "That's so, sweetheart. But Mrs. Adams, there'll be questions you'll need to answer tomorrow for the authorities. His partner didn't know Potter had a wife. I'm afraid you'll have to furnish proof of your marriage."

"It's all right, Will, I'll do what's necessary." She turned to Mattie. "It shouldn't take much time. I want nothing of his. But no matter what, I don't want any of this to delay your wedding another day."

Mattie flashed a smile up at Will. "All right, Ma. We'll be married on time, just as we planned it this afternoon."

Mattie was the last to step out of Gabriel's cab in front of the small white church in which she and Will were to be married. It was late afternoon, and she hadn't seen Will all day. Brushing her hand down the skirt of her leaf-green silk dress, she nervously looked around for him.

"There's Reverend Thomas," nodded Marianne, directing Mattie's attention to the church door.

Mattie, her mother on one side and her aunt on the other, walked up the path, just as Will opened the door from the inside. He cradled a great bunch of white roses in his arm. Their fragrance filled the church vestibule. Silently, he offered them to her.

Reaching out to accept them, Mattie was lost for a moment in the deep blue of his eyes. For that moment, there was a faint questioning, and a hungering, as though deeply held emotions were being kept at bay. Her mouth softened into a smile. She watched in fascination as the uncertainty faded and a shining adoration took its place.

"Thank you, Will." She felt her love for him ooze from her very pores. Could he see in her eyes what she saw in his? Shyly, she touched the petals of a rose. "They're beautiful."

Her murmur sounded soft in his ear as he took her hand. "So are you. More lovely than I know how to tell. But I'll spend all the rest of my life trying. Are you ready?"

"Yes."

And she was. Joy overflowed her as she exchanged promises with the tall, golden-haired man who made her feel so loved. In addition to the spoken one, Mattie made a silent vow. Never again would she run away from her own deep love and need for Will. As she smiled up into his eyes, she knew, like he, it might take the rest of her life to share.

It no longer frightened her.

That night, long after the wedding supper, Will closed the door to the private suite Elizabeth had reserved for him and Mattie. He turned the key in the lock of the carved wooden door and leaned back against it. Mattie swung about to look at him and smiled.

"Wasn't it a lovely dinner?" She glowed. Feeling so full of love, she'd been too excited to eat much.

"Yes, it was right good. Never tasted some of that stuff your aunt ordered though." Will smiled back and watched her flit about the small sitting room as she looked at the furniture and pictures. He knew the bedroom was larger, for he'd moved his things in that afternoon, before leaving for the church.

He moved away from the door and loosened his tie. His

new suit was comfortable enough, but he was still getting used to town clothes. Stopping in the middle of the room, he watched Mattie examine a vase of flowers.

"Look, Will. These roses are such an unusual shade of pink. They smell heavenly."

"Uh-huh. There's more roses in the bedroom."

"Oh."

"Wouldn't you like to see them?"

"They couldn't be any prettier than these." Mattie giggled a little and looked at Will from beneath her lashes. She shouldn't tease him, she knew. Like he, she'd been waiting all evening to lie in his arms. With melting eyes and secret caresses, he'd implied he could hardly wait. Now he seemed almost hesitant.

Will strolled to where she stood with one rose pressed to her nose. He wasn't sure, now that it had come to the wedding night, how well Mattie would really take his passion. She'd been so responsive the last time he really kissed her. But that was several nights ago, and since then, so much had happened, they'd scarce had time for other than quick pecks.

With one long finger, he tipped her chin up to meet his gaze. "Sweetheart, do you need any help getting undressed?"

The giggles fled as Mattie looked into sapphire eyes that made no effort to hide the banked fires. She shook her head.

"No, I can manage. I'll . . . not take very long."

Mattie paused in the bedroom doorway and glanced at him over her shoulder. As he'd done so many times, he stood watching her, but this time she didn't miss the smoldering desire in his face.

Returning his look for only a second, she closed the door.

The creamy silk nightdress slid easily over her head and

she sat down at the dressing table to remove the hairpins from her hair. She let her long dark hair fall, and brushed out the tangles. It felt silky to her own touch, thanks to her mother's loving care that morning. After Mattie washed it, her mother had brushed it while they talked.

Now laying the brush down, Mattie stood and looked at her reflection in the mirror. Her cheeks wore the soft flush of anticipation, and her skin was a pearly cream that contrasted with her dark hair. The soft lace yoke at the top of her gown dipped almost to the peaks of her breasts, and fell low on her shoulders. Its gathered length ended in more lace near her feet.

Pushing her hair to stream down her back, Mattie took a deep breath and opened the door. The sitting room was dark except for one dim lamp.

"Will?"

Will stood leaning against the hearth with a glass in his hand. As her soft call reached him, he looked up and saw her standing in the stream of subdued light from the bedroom, outlining her silhouette. Setting the glass down on a nearby table as he went, he held her gaze as he slowly crossed the room.

Mattie watched him come and backed up a step or two as he approached. He'd undressed down to his trousers, and she was fascinated by his bare chest. She'd never seen Will without a shirt before, and her eyes followed over the bulge of his upper arms and shoulders. Somehow, their breadth surprised her. Evidence of his outdoor existence showed in his deeply tanned face and neck, as compared with his lightly tanned torso.

"Lord, Mattie, but you're so lovely," he murmured. He put out a tentative hand and stroked her shoulder. She was his wife.

Mattie felt a desire to be kissed. Shyly, she stood on tiptoe to seek his mouth.

Will was more than ready to help her find it. His mouth covered hers as his arms gathered her close.

"Oh, Mattie, darlin' . . ." He kissed her cheekbone, then slid his mouth once more to hers.

Straining to stand taller against him, she stroked the back of his neck and jaw, then moved to feel the shape of his ear. He smelled of the piney soap he'd used for shaving. "Will . . . I love you so."

"Mattie, I want you . . . You're not afraid anymore?"

"No, never again. It's all right, Will." She kissed him, then looked earnestly into his face. "Ma and I talked a long while this morning. You were right, you know."

He bent and nuzzled her neck, pressing his lips against her collarbone. "About what?"

"She said that loving . . . mmm . . . with my pa . . ." she gave a little gasp as his tongue flickered out against her skin, ". . . was glorious."

Kissing and stroking was returned with kissing and stroking, making him wild with need. "Sweetheart . . ."

Later, she lay close in his arms for long moments while the room slowed its spinning. Her nose brushed against his cheek and his fragrance filled her nostrils. Gradually, her heart returned to its normal beat and she could think.

Will thought he must be crushing Mattie. Had he hurt her? Slowly, he started to lift himself.

"Don't go," she murmured. "Not just yet." She caressed his back with the palms of her hands.

He began to laugh.

"What's funny?"

"Those nights we lay close together on the trail. I wanted you so much, only the Lord knows how I kept my control. I dreamed of you often, the years you were away. I had nightmares that you were being courted by those Eastern dudes."

It was Mattie's turn to laugh. "None of those Eastern men could hold a candle to you. Besides . . ." She nuzzled into the curve of his neck.

Will's hand stroked down her arm where she lay pressed against his chest. "Besides?"

Mattie hesitated while she searched for the right words. "Those men treated me with respect and politeness. Some even courted me, knowing of Aunt Elizabeth's wealth. But for most of them, I was just a pretty girl from a good family, which made me acceptable."

She rubbed her palm along his jaw, taking in the texture of stubble as it excited her skin. "When I was young, most of the men I met wanted a woman only for her body. For them, I was just a thing to be used. And for some of the ranchers and such, it was the same. I was the outlaw's brat . . . not worth much. To be thrown away when they were done with me."

Mattie raised herself to rest against his chest as she looked down into his face. The one low lamp gave just enough light for her to watch his expression as she tried to share the depth of her love.

She held hard against the tears, this time tears of joy, but one slipped down her cheek anyway.

"But you . . . you gave me value then . . . and now, you make me feel . . . more precious than rubies and pearls. You see me as valuable. You honor me as God intended. Will, I could never see any man but you as my love."

Speechless, Will reached up and brushed her hair away from her face. Moisture slid under his thumb as he ran his fingers against her cheek and into her hair. Then he curved his hand around the base of her head to bring her mouth up to his. The kiss was long and tender, holding and giving mute promises for the long loving of their future.

And Mattie knew in the moments that followed that all Will's loving would be glorious.

Epilogue

The buckboard rolled around the half-mile curve that led from the McCarthy ranch house to the stone and timber structure that Will had built. Mattie sat eagerly forward and strained to see her new home in the distance. "Will, it looks just the way you described. Oh, hurry."

Will chuckled at his bride's impatience, but he silently admitted he was mighty glad himself, to be home at last. He'd been gone so long that summer was fast fading into fall, and there was much work to be done. Besides which, with over a week of travel in which abstinence was the only choice if he didn't want to embarrass Mattie, he was anxious to make love to his wife again.

"Well, it doesn't have much for comfort yet. But with a nice fire in the hearth, we can make do for the night with blankets spread over some piney branches. But we'll have no trouble looking for food. I 'spect Ma and your cousin Beatrice filled the kitchen, knowing them."

"Mmm. I'm sure you're right. They were all whispering during dessert, something about stocking my cupboard with enough dried apples. Will?"

"Hmm?"

"I hope you'll be patient . . . you know . . . about me learning to cook."

"That's okay, darlin'," he chuckled. "You're good at other things. And you're fast at learning."

"Oh, you . . ." She turned away to hide her flushed cheeks. "Anyway, it was sure sweet of your ma to have supper ready when we arrived. I noticed how nice she treated my ma, too."

"They've had nearly a month to get acquainted, you know. But your Aunt Elizabeth's been gone a long time from her home. Do you think she'll be content to stay longer, so you and your ma can visit?"

"Yes, I think so. When they left us in San Francisco for our honeymoon, it was with the idea that Ma and she would stay here for a long visit. I don't know how Ma'll like living in St. Louis, though. Even though Missouri was her girlhood home, she may eventually want to live back here with us."

"We'll cross that bridge when it comes. You know she's welcome here." He reined the team to a stop and hopped down to lift Mattie out. Placing a quick kiss on her nose, he murmured, "Besides, we may need her to help with the children."

"Yes," she answered. But she hadn't really heard him, for she was inspecting the long front porch that ran the length of the house and the two wide windows that flanked the huge front door. Her eyes flicked to the twin stone chimneys, one at either end, that framed the house like bookends.

"Like it?"

Mattie nodded. "It's so much bigger than I pictured."

"Room to grow. Well, someone's been here. There's smoke coming from the south chimney. Come on, let's see."

Will opened the door and Mattie was all eyes as she looked around the huge room that was to be their parlor. Its polished beams showed but dimly in the fading twilight, but Mattie was impressed with the height of the ceiling. The large stone fireplace at the end of the room took up most of the wall, with a door on either side. Mattie could see through the hearth to another room. The kitchen, most likely.

"Oh my, Will. It's going to be lovely when we have our furnishings."

Pleased, Will directed her to one of the doors in the wall beside the fireplace. "This way's the kitchen. It's the only room I've outfitted."

She followed him through the wide door to find a room twice the size of Cousin Beatrice's kitchen. Sure enough, the parlor fireplace doubled to serve this room as well. It was equipped with a modern stove, with four cooking plates, a large oven, and a warming oven topping it. Against the back wall, a work counter sat underneath shelves where several iron pots and pans hung. A heavy square table with benches completed the room.

"We'll be able to feed an army around that table." Mattie laughed. "Do you plan on raising one?"

Will flashed his teeth at her in a teasing smile. "I plan on trying hard."

"Oh? Well, why don't you show me the room you'll do most of your hard work in?" she teased back. Flirtatiously, she cocked a brow at him.

"This way, ma'am."

Walking back through the parlor, Will curled an arm around her waist and, leading the way down a short hall, opened the door at the end. Mattie held his gaze with a smile, her moist lips parting in invitation. He smiled back and bent to kiss her before turning into the room. Mattie caught a fleeting glance into the room and held her breath as Will took two steps in and abruptly halted.

"Who . . . where . . . that's the . . . biggest bed I've ever seen."

Mattie started to laugh at Will's utter shock. He usually wasn't so lost for words. She looked around in pleased wonder at the way the mammoth four-poster sat against the wall, with the matching tall chest and wardrobe also in place. "I'm so glad the boys got everything put together."

"The boys? Luke and Sandy, you mean? And what do you know about this?"

"Well, yes, I . . . um . . . actually, Will, I bought it in San Francisco. It's my wedding gift to you."

"You bought it?" He was puzzled. "It's beautiful, Mattie." He bent to kiss her, then drawing her with him, he moved to run a hand along the gleaming dark wood. "It's a marriage bed to last our lifetime. But darlin', when did you have time to buy it? Since we married, you've not been out of my sight."

"Well, the truth is, I had it shipped before we were married."

"Before?"

"Yes. Remember that night on the trail when you talked about wanting the biggest bed you could find? One to hold a lifetime of loving and one to birth our children in?"

"I thought you hadn't heard me."

"I heard every word. And one day in San Francisco, I saw this bed while out shopping with Aunt Elizabeth. And I knew this was the one."

Will was still a little dazed. He knew she'd inherited a little money from her father. She must have spent it all on such a beautiful set. "Sweetheart, I'll treasure this for the rest of our life, but don't go spending any more of your money. You might need it sometime. Or save what you have left for the youngsters we'll be having."

"I can do that easily enough, Will. But I've a lot left."

"A lot? What do you mean by a lot?"

She named a round figure and watched her husband's mouth drop with shock. "Actually, half of it can now go to Ma. By rights, even though my grandfather wouldn't recognize it, she is legally my father's widow."

"Whew, thank God for that." Will began to laugh. "I wouldn't want to deal with a wife that's richer than I am." He gathered her into a bear hug and swung her around. "Since it's almost dark, and the boys were kind enough to build us a fire, and everything . . ." He bent to kiss her long and hungrily, then raised his head. "I'll go take care of the animals and bring in the grips. It won't take me long."

"I'll be waiting," Mattie laughingly called after his retreating back. Turning back into the room, she saw a bathtub had been drawn up close to the fire. Water steamed from a large kettle on the hearth. "The boys must have gotten out of sight by the skin of their teeth," she mused out loud.

Swiftly, she started to peel away her travel-soiled clothing, tossing them on the bed. Then she noticed the quilt. Even in the dim light, she recognized the pattern. Needing to look closer, she turned to light the oil lamp on the night table, and held the light high.

Mattie caught her breath. It was a wedding ring quilt. The multitude of bright-colored pieces and tiny stitches represented hours of loving labor. Tenderly, she traced the patterns of the double rings, recognizing pieces of cloth from her cousin's scrap basket. Some were from the red gingham and blue calico of her own dresses of long ago. Some, she recognized from Josie's and Will's ma.

She could hear Will's distant whistling command to the horses, and realized he must be putting them in the corral she'd noticed off to the side of the house. He'd be in soon. Turning again to the bath, she hurriedly stepped into the warm water and began washing. Lathering her cloth with the sweet verbena soap she found nearby, Mattie raised one long shapely leg above the tub and scrubbed down its length.

"Lord, Mattie, but you're a beautiful woman." Will stood just inside the door. This was the first time he'd seen Mattie in her bath, and the sight took his breath away. Just looking at her made him hard and ready.

"Will, close the door. You're letting in a draft."

He swallowed. "Sorry, sweetheart." He closed the door and walked over to the side of the tub. Without warning, he bent and hauled her up against him, planting his mouth against hers in a searing demand.

Mattie was the one who groaned when he finally pulled away. She put her forehead against his chin to catch her breath, then rising to her toes, she lightly kissed his jaw. "Darling, I'm making you all wet." She kissed his cheek. "Get out of those clothes and have your bath." Then, returning her mouth to his, she ran her tongue against the sensitive corner. "And please hurry," she whispered.

"You little tease." He stepped back and chuckled as he started throwing off his clothes. "You get in that bed, because before you have a chance to say 'Jack be nimble' I'll be there."

Laughing at him over her shoulder, Mattie climbed onto the high mattress and pulled down the quilt to reveal finely woven cotton sheets. She leaned back against the headboard to watch him hurry through his bath. "Don't you mean 'Will be nimble'?"

Splashing noisily, Will gave her a meaningful look. "Will is nimble, all right, but Will will try not to be too quick where it counts." He watched in glee as the color flooded into her face.

"Oh, you scallywag." She ducked her head as she snuggled down. Moments later, he slid in next to her and immediately drew her into a stunning kiss.

The first loving, due to the necessary abstinence of traveling home, was greedily consumed; the second was long and savored. Afterward, Mattie drew a long breath and let it out with deep satisfaction. She was almost asleep. But she wanted to know one more thing.

"Will, did you notice the quilt on our bed?"

"Mmm."

"It's the wedding ring pattern. Cousin Beatrice must have worked hard to get it ready, and your ma and Josie, too."

"It's been ready for more than a year."

"It has? But how . . ."

"Darlin', everybody but you knew I was hog-tied and ready for branding by you, since you were that courageous, rag-tailed little loner." Will stroked her shoulder, pushing back the long strands of her hair to give his hand access to her skin. He loved the feel of the back of her neck. "You don't know how hard it was for me to let you go East when you were fourteen, to give you time. If you hadn't come home this summer, I'd have gone to fetch you."

"You would have?" She lifted herself on one elbow to look into his face.

"Yep. Without a second thought. You said I made you feel more valuable than rubies and pearls. That's because you're my greatest treasure. A man is only half alive without the treasure of his heart."

"Sweet William." She laid her lips tenderly on his. And Mattie knew she'd be treasured for all her life.

About the Author

Ruth Scofield was first published in 1993, by Harper-Monogram. Her first western, *Sweet Amity's Fire* went to the RITA finals. She wrote four westerns for Harper-Monogram, under Lee Scofield, before the line closed. Then Steeple Hill's Love Inspired imprint was born, and under her second name Ruth Scofield, she has written ten books for them. Her first, *In God's Own Time*, won the HOLT Medallion. Also, she has finaled twice in this contest. Ruth lives with her own hero, Charles, in western Missouri.